The Past That Kills

JEFFREY HAMMERHEAD PHILIPS

For Kitty

Thanks for suggesting we move to the mountains.
More adventures continue…

Prologue
Twelve Years Ago

Jennie Lee hid in the shadows. The wooden loading platform was devoid of people, luggage, and cargo. Even Old Man Johnson, the security guy, wasn't milling around the hundred-year-old-plus depot. He must've been inside sleeping.

Too strange.

Her heart raced. In the glow of the station's lights, a single, silver passenger car with a vista dome was hooked to a maroon-colored engine and it called to her. What was strange was what the train was doing here at one in the morning.

She knew the times and the route. The Tennessee Central ran here once a month. It left Nashville in the morning, stopped at Del Monaco Winery for a lunch, then Monterey for an excursion to Bee Rock, with dinner and an overnight stay at the Imperial Hotel, then back to the big city.

Another oddity was that this line ran with eleven cars packed with riders. She shivered.

But nevertheless, this was it, her ride out of town. A town she considered a dead end, with nothing but losers and old people living in it. Where a big night was hanging out at Jake's bar on Friday nights--except they wouldn't allow her to enter the joint. Had to be eighteen to step inside—two long years away. The place, like the town, was Dullsville.

This world had exciting places to visit. She'd seen photos of New York City, Rome, Paris. Yes, Paris, the epicenter of music, arts, and love. What it must feel like to experience men from diverse cultures. It was time for her to become a woman in a glamourous city.

A wooden sign hanging over the entrance creaked in the wind. The noise seemed to travel forever in the clear air. Would it awaken Johnson?

Damn sign, it's going to give me away.

She stared at it as if her gaze could stop it from swinging. The rough-cut, brown lettering on the sign which read, "Established in 1905," didn't seem to care that she needed it to stop.

Hurrying to the gap between the locomotive and the other car, she jumped onto the iron coupler. The pounding of her heart continued as she looked out over the top of the ticket office to the summer sky filled with stars. In the constellations, she spotted Delphinus, the swimming dolphin, Cygnus, the flying swan, and Hercules, pointing the way. The heavens spoke; her adventure lay before her.

She slid the door open and stepped into the passenger car. The overhead dome lights, running on both sides of the ceiling, were on. Their rays of light didn't reach the floor. They were more like white moon glows in photos she had seen of resort hotels at night.

"What are you doing here, missy?" a man asked.

"Looking."

The room was too dim to see the man, but he sounded like he was on the other side of the room.

"You need to leave."

"Can I catch a ride?"

"Private party tonight." The man leaned against a dark-stained door.

A month before, she had been in this car. After the customers had disembarked for their hike, she had snuck on board. Now, she walked to the center and stood under an overhead observation bubble. The car was divided into two main sections: the front half a lounge and eating area, the back, a hallway on one side and a private bedroom on the other side.

Inside was the biggest bed she had ever seen. Off to the side was a humongous bathroom.

"I don't see anyone boarding," she said.

The man stood in front of the door which led to the bedroom. He clicked on a lamp with a red shade and fringe.

Again, the light did little to brighten the room, although she could see his features. An old man, same age as her dad, but not as old as her grandpa. He wore a white shirt, thin tie, slacks, and work boots.

"How old are you?" he asked.

"Twenty-one."

He looked at her with a knowing grin.

"Eighteen," she said.

"Here's what I see. Your skin is smooth and tanned from spending the days at a lake. Too much blue eye shadow, which you think goes with your blonde hair. The band tying your ponytail is too flashy for an adult. I'd guess fifteen or sixteen. And a runaway with no luggage."

The man sure knew how to size up a teenager. Too creepy for her. And she preferred to think of her lack of belongings as no baggage. As she saw it, she was making a clean break. She'd left everything her parents had bought her behind. She had her favorite green blouse on, the tight blue jeans she liked, and a pair of sturdy walking shoes.

"Let's get you outside," he said.

She flipped her hair. "I need a lift out of town."

"Go catch a ride from a trucker."

"I have cash."

"Tennessee Central pays me well."

Hooves clip-clopping outside on the packed gravel caught the man's attention. He looked out of a rectangular window.

She went over to his side.

Two men, wearing muddied drover coats and grimy, worn Stetsons pulled low over their eyes rode on mules.

Mules meant one thing in this town: the men had travelled

from a certain holler which contained a mine. Rumors filled the town about what was taken out of it. Her daddy said nothing good. It was a rough area filled with ruffians, a place no God-fearing person would venture near.

Both men slid off their mounts. One headed in the direction of the engine, the other, walked straight to the passenger car. His duster parted. A machete in its sheaf hung from his belt. Slung under his armpit was a revolver.

"You want a ride, you'll need to pay the toll."

"I figured as much," she said.

The man nodded toward the door he had leaned against. "In there. Stay in the lavatory and keep quiet or he'll pitch you off and fry my ass."

She did. The bathroom was gigantic compared to the one where she lived. This one had a huge tub, a shower she could turn around in, two sinks, and a little room for the crapper. The room had an aroma of a pine forest. No rotten egg smells like at home.

She heard footsteps entering the lounge area.

"You're late." It was the man who'd told her to hide.

"You will address me as *sir* or *Mr. Roberson.*"

She cupped her right ear, wanting to hear better. Roberson didn't speak like she would expect. Her daddy would have said their words were crude and littered with blasphemies. Even with proper English, the weapons on him told her he wasn't an upright citizen.

"Open the safe," Roberson said.

She hadn't seen a safe, but it didn't surprise her; the room was too dark.

The closing of a heavy metal door sounded.

"My colleague will be with the engineer. I'll stay stationed at the back stoop. Our stop is an hour away. Kill anyone who tries to board."

She could hear both men walking through the passageway, then the back door being locked. A minute later, the front one. A jolt knocked her into the sinks as the train moved forward and gather speed down the tracks.

After what seemed like fifteen minutes, the lavatory door opened and the man she had met earlier said, "You can come out." He switched on a bedside light, then removed his shirt, revealing a chest of black hair.

"How much is the toll?" she asked.

"Disrobe."

The thought of having sex with this hairy ape disgusted her. "For an hour ride, seems like an expensive toll. I'll give you a hand job."

"Nope."

She hadn't really thought he'd agree to it, but it'd been worth a shot. Lucky for her, she knew what the football team liked—he'd go for it also. "I'll take my top off. You can fondle me while I give you the best B. J. you ever had."

He rubbed his crotch, then his eyes shifted as if an idea came to him.

"Come here and look at this." He opened a metal case, similar to her dad's gun safe. He removed something from the purple velvet lining and held his palm under the light.

Two diamonds sparkled in his hand. Not like ones she had seen on TV. These flashed green, blue, and silver.

"They're called Tarpon Diamonds. This accidental find at the mine could be worth a million each."

She gasped. Two million. No one in her family would ever earn that much. And none of her friends' households would ever see that huge amount of money. Images of those cities she wanted to see flashed through her mind.

"Let's get in bed. Afterward, you can play with them."

"I want to hold them first."

"Sex first."

"Where am I going to go?" She cocked her head. "You can manhandle me since I don't have a choice in paying the toll, so, please let me hold them before we start. I promise you'll go to heaven—twice."

He sneered as he pulled her to the dresser and mirror and

stood behind her. "Hold them up to your ears. Imagine what they'll look like when they're polished."

She did--and gasped. Oh, they looked good on her. Just like the photos of what the ladies wore with their long gowns at those fabulous balls.

The man ran one hand across her ass before placing both hands on her hips. "You like?" he said. His hands moved up to cup her breasts.

No, she didn't like—and she whipped her elbow into his nose.

He stepped back, a hand to his face, blood seeping through his fingers.

She grabbed the metal diamond case and crashed it into his head.

He fell to the ground.

The passenger car wobbled, the train braking before it started the steep decline off the mountain.

She tucked the diamonds into her pocket. Walking to the front door, she unlatched it, then stepped outside onto the coupler.

The stars were bright before her, as was the world. When the train started into the bend, she leaped into the darkness.

One
Current Day

Today, Sheriff Mary Beth Coupland's eyes worked.

Which wasn't every day.

She'd had experimental surgery--testing new technology. *Second Sight* it was called—microscopic cameras inserted into the corner of her eyes, with electrodes connected to microchips implanted in her retinas.

Fantastic most days, but there were glitches at times. Harsh light or total blackness sometimes left her blind, and, for some reason unknown to her or the doctors, the color blue dominated all other colors. Thus, she wore blue uniform shirts and customized her boots with blue inlays which since the surgery, for some reason, had become her favorite color. Besides, the sheriff's outfit needed a touch of femininity.

She didn't tell anyone she'd gone under the knife—afraid it would cost her her job. Officers of the law were expected to have perfect eyesight.

She stood on the bald, limestone bluff at the end of Bee Rock Lane, testing her sight. It was one place she could admire the Tennessee mountainous terrain. The dark green dense forest of hickory and oak trees stood in a wonderful contrast to the deep blue sky. A red shouldered hawk dove onto an unsuspecting prey.

"Public disturbance on Meadow Creek Road," came across her car radio.

Reaching inside the vehicle, she grabbed the black mic and squeezed the transmitter button. "What's the address, Helen?"

"One-four-five-zero-nine, Coup."

She smiled. *Coup*, the nickname her dad had given her. She liked it, but not everyone in Monterey called her by it. "Ms. Whitmore's place, right?"

"Roger dodger."

Coup slid into her black Dodge Durango squad car. The car rode rough, but the engine ran smooth and fast. The gold lettering on the side—*Responsive to all, second to none, every time*—was bold and impressive. The motto made her proud to be a third-generation sheriff.

After five years as head cop, she wondered how it was, in a town with a population of around three thousand, the majority of the calls came from a few people. Public disturbance… how was that possible? Ms. Whitmore's nearest neighbor lived two miles way.

Coup remembered other calls Ms. Whitmore had made— someone stole corn cobs off her autumn display. It was the squirrels. There was a fungus growing on Main Street. The county had sprayed a slurry on the road before the pending snowstorm. Ms. Whitmore was always pleasant, but Coup suspected her morning bourbon affected her logic.

Coup slammed the gas pedal hard enough to spin the tires on the dirt road, sending plumes of dust into the air. The fastest way to the scene meant going through the town. She slowed for the two traffic lights, then screamed her engine onto Route 62, one of the four state roads entering and leaving Monterey.

Twelve minutes later, she turned onto Meadow Creek, a two-lane, asphalt road which followed the rocky stream. After another three miles, she pulled into Whitmore's gravel driveway and parked in front of a white, two-story wooden house with a widow's walk and wraparound porch. A fifth-generation home. She'd heard Crockett had once stayed here.

Coup slid out of her car and looked around. No one else seemed to be in the area. "Where's the disturbance?"

"Follow me, Sheriff," Ms. Whitmore said.

She trailed the elderly lady to the backyard.

The woman had to be pushing ninety, and, from her dark, wrinkled skin, she had never missed a day of being in the sun. Ms. Whitmore wore a long-sleeved, pink shirt, frayed blue jeans, and hiking boots, which had seen more trail dirt than hers. Ms. Whitmore's yellow, wide-brim hat showed her face.

Even in Coup's summer uniform—a short-sleeved, pale-blue shirt and no undershirt—the mid-morning heat had made her dewy. Her damp shirt clung to her like the morning fog on rhododendron leaves. They'd had twelve days in a row of ninety-degree temperatures, the longest heat wave on record for middle Tennessee.

"I don't have time to hike around your yard, Ms. Whitmore. I don't see any evidence of a disturbance."

"Right here, Sheriff. Look for yourself." Whitmore pointed to a patch of ground.

The tall grass surrounding the house was clumped as if someone had started a garden in an area about the size of an SUV.

Coup stooped and ran her hand over the wet soil with some corn, acorns, and bird seed someone had scattered over the area. The churned dirt smelled musty, like decomposing black mud. She wanted to cover her nose but backed a few feet away instead. "Looks like wild hogs to me."

"Of course it is."

"This is not a public disturbance." Whitmore had called her out on another nonsense call. She wished she could lock up the old lady for a day or two. Maybe she'd stop wasting the city's money.

"It was this morning when the damn beast chased me into the house."

"Were you standing here when it happened?"

"Yes. Spreading food for the fawns and birds."

"This is prime hog food." Coup sighed. "This is a matter for the Tennessee Wildlife Resources Agency."

"They don't consider one hog a nuisance. Told me to handle it myself."

"Don't you own a gun?"

"You betcha. A double barrel." Mrs. Whitmore beamed. "It will cut down a tree."

"Then use it on this hog."

"I pay taxes. This is your job."

Coup shook her head.

The house had a buffer of grass about forty feet around it. Up against the lawn was a thicket of underbrush and a hardwood forest—a good place for hogs to roam, eat, and breed. Those animals wouldn't give up a free meal.

"Get ready," Ms. Whitmore said. "I'm gonna show you what happens."

"Don't entice wild animals."

Ms. Whitmore reached into a fifty-pound bag of assorted wildlife feed and started to broadcast it around them. "This is what I do every morning. If a woman can't enjoy nature, then why bother living?"

Coup smelled the feral stench of wet hair. Her gut told her that, from somewhere inside the tree line, she was being watched.

"You'll need a thirty-ought-six," said Ms. Whitmore, "to tame that monster."

Coup placed her hand on the butt of her Remington 1911 semi-automatic pistol holstered to her hip and almost drew it. It seemed to her that most female officers preferred a nine-millimeter because it was lighter. She liked the heaviness of her automatic. It had a seven-shot capacity, and a good kick.

Though, it wasn't much of a kick for her one-hundred-sixty pounds. Conceivable a tad more, but her five-foot-eight-inch frame carried it well. And, being in her forties, she had a figure to be proud of. At least, it's what she told herself. With this model, whoever she fired at would stay down.

Still, she knew that, even with a forty-four magnum, if the bullet hit the hog's shoulders or ribs, it would not stop the thing. With her gun, she'd need to punch the eye to drop him.

The head of the hog appeared first, sticking out of the underbrush, its snout sniffing the air. Three-inch tusks protruded from the jaw. If the tusks didn't gouge her, the jaws were strong enough to break her arm in half.

"Stay calm and be still," Coup said.

The hog stepped onto the lawn and eyed the scattered corn. The animal had a bulk of about four-hundred-fifty pounds. The largest one she had ever seen.

"Run for it," Ms. Whitmore said.

"No. Stay behind me."

Ms. Whitmore turned and dashed to her porch.

The hog charged. Coup drew her auto, aimed between the eyes, and fired.

A red mist blew from the animal's forehead, but it continued to run toward her.

"Holy hell," she said.

The beast barreled toward her, closing the gap.

Stand firm. Stand firm. Don't miss.

She fired again.

This time, an eye socket blew out.

But the hog didn't waver.

She wanted to wipe her brow because her eyes stung from sweat. The gun bucked in her hand as she fired the third round, again into the forehead.

Blood poured down the animal's face.

The animal stopped. He snapped his head back and forth, pounding the ground. With its one good eye, it seemed to lock onto her.

She swore a demon glow came from it.

The hog came at her with barreling speed.

Coup continued to fire.

Blood and gore erupted from the beast's head.

But it came on like a dump truck.

She pulled the trigger non-stop, until the slide locked in the open position, all the rounds spend.

The animal kept coming—then tumbled forward and landed at Coup's feet.

After breathing heavily six times, she kicked the beast once. Satisfied it was dead, she holstered her weapon.

Brain matter coated her blue cowboy boots. "Sweet Momma's tea. These are only a week old." She shouted at Ms. Whitmore. "Call TWRA to come get it!" Then she inhaled deep, twice, to calm her breathing.

The radio in her car squawked.

Now what? She headed back to her vehicle to answer the call.

"Urgent! Urgent! Coup, you hear me?" Helen's voice was high pitched and shaky. "There's a missing boy at Devil's Cave."

God. She hoped the kid hadn't entered the abyss.

Two

Coup parked her squad car at the trail head of the foot path to Devil's Cave, an hour's walk down a rocky, twisty track. Boys had gone missing before along the creek at the bottom. A few had been found at one of the secluded coves with their girlfriends. She wasn't worried unless he had entered the cave.

Standing on the north side of the dirt lot was Simmons Miller, an excommunicated Mennonite. His posture was stiff, giving the elusion his thin, five-foot-seven-inch frame looked over six feet. His hair was as black as the bark on sugar maples.

Coup walked toward him. Her daddy had said Miller's eyes were cold like those of convicts, and not to be trusted. But, to her, they were the eyes of someone with an unfathomable loss.

She often thought they hid a sadness in his life. His wife had left him years ago, and the church had shut its doors on him. The leaders said a man who couldn't control his home didn't belong.

"Have you found the boy?" she asked.

"Don't know. Ms. Warren sent me up here to contact the police and wait."

She tied shoestrings at the bottom of her pants, then snugged them tight. She didn't need any chiggers dining on her calves. It was hard enough to keep her legs lady-like; the red bite marks showing when she wore her skirt were just ugly.

Pointing to the wooden sign describing the trail, she said, "Let's go."

"I know a quicker route."

The Mennonite trotted off into the thicket. She had to run in spots to keep up. His thick boots found sure footing on the deer trace, while she stumbled from time to time. Miller was as fast as a runaway toddler, even though his age wasn't much beyond thirty. Although she was about ten years older than Miller, she felt like his grandmother as she slogged through the hardwoods.

His tan trousers and red shirt seemed to repel the briars and tree snags. For her, everything reached out and grabbed at her clothing.

At a small outcropping, Miller stopped.

She caught up with him and puffed a few times to catch her breath.

He handed her a rope. "Wrap this around you. I'll lower you down."

Peeking over the edge, she saw the trail resumed fifty feet below her.

She looped the line around her like she'd been taught by her father. Her first repel had been at the age of eight. To pass her mountain training, she'd had to fly down a two-hundred-foot bluff. If it wasn't for having to find a missing person, she'd find leaping over the edge fun.

With the rope secured, she jumped backward into the open space. The side of the mountain cut away, and she stared into a large cavern. Walls white like stark bones surrounded deep blackness. She let herself swing sideways, then kicked off the mountainside again. After another kick, her feet touched the earth.

By the time she had freed herself of the rope, Miller thumped beside her.

"Another four or five minutes," he said and once again, headed off at his quick pace.

Coup checked her watch when they reached a group of six children and one adult. Miller had cut forty minutes off the usual time.

Debbie Warren, the principal of Monterey's elementary school, was seated on a rock, crying. "Sorry, Coup," Debbie said. "I was distracted for only a minute and A.J. was gone. He might have had another fainting spell and that's why he hasn't responded when we yelled his name."

"We'll find him." Coup nodded. Why would the principal bring the pre-teens down to this creek? Off the plateau, in the valley, there were several scenic waterways within an easy walk. The woman wasn't dressed for this rugged terrain. She was wearing shoes, instead of boots, shorts, not pants, and a flowered, loose blouse rather than a work shirt. The principal had lived here all of her fifty-plus years, and she still didn't know the wilderness?

"Miller," Coup said, "do a head count. Anyone else missing?"

"Nickee-Dee."

Before Coup could respond, a young girl's voice yelled out from down the trail.

Coup ran to a boulder in front of Devil's Cave and found Nikee-Dee kneeling on it.

The pre-teen wore pink shorts, pink top, and matching pink shoes, plus, a dab of pink eye shadow above and below her eyes. The foolish girl must have thought they were going to the mall in Nashville.

"There." The girl pointed to a hole the size of a car door.

The opening descended downward at a sharp angle into the cave's darkness.

"A.J.!" Coup cupped her mouth and yelled into the black. "Can you hear me?"

"Yes," he replied with terror in his voice

"Are you hurt? Can you climb out?"

"No. The devil's got me. He's dragging me to hell."

The air flowing out of the blackness became colder. The smell of something rotten—decaying and sulfuric like spoiled eggs—rode with it.

"A.J.!"

He didn't answer.

Damn, she didn't want to enter the darkness.

She inhaled deeply. No choice. She rubbed her eyes and hoped the microchips in her retinas didn't malfunction.

"He's going to die." Nikee-Dee burst into tears. "I just know it."

Coup turned to Miller. "Set your radio to channel six. Keep the kids calm."

"Should I start back?"

"No. Wait until I can assess the situation."

Nikee-Dee let out another wail.

Miller pulled her into his arms.

Coup tugged her LED tactical flashlight from her utility belt, then stuck her head into the cave's opening. "Stay calm, A.J. I'm coming."

A mustiness tainted the air.

Coup slid into a prone position and eased inside the rocky entrance. The limestone edges tore her shirt and cut into her arms. The thousand-lumen beam from the flashlight did little to cut the darkness. Or maybe it was her eyes refusing to work in the extreme low levels. God, would the technology stop and leave her blind? The diameter of the hole decreased. Hell. Her breath came rapidly. She wanted to back out. Horrid images flashed in front of her. All she needed was to get stuck. Could Miller pull her out by her ankles if she did? *Don't get wedged!* shrieked her brain.

A howling bayed in the distance and goosebumps popped onto her outstretched arms.

She hated caves—bad experience from her college days when, for her sorority pledge, she'd been taken into one and left there. It'd been blackout dark, and guano from the bats had dripped down on her. She'd tried to wipe the stench off, but, instead, had smeared it over her hair and shoulders. Remembering their high-pitched squeaks sent chills through her. To escape, she'd crawled to one side, then let the wet, rough wall guide her out. Damn those rich bitches and their pranks. A few days after the abandonment, she'd snuck into their dorms, poured neon purple dye into their styled hairdos, then dropped out of their snobbish group.

She closed her eyes and slowed her breathing. *Fight the urge to leave.*

She removed her utility belt and scooted it in front of her. She pulled her body forward again and again. It was faster than crawling. At times, she could dig her boots into the pebbles and push to gain a few feet at a time.

A.J. continued to sob. Terrified, but alive.

"Please don't kill me." His voice sounded weaker.

What could have grabbed him? A list of animals clicked through her mind. Cougars? Coyotes? Snakes? Both timber rattlers and copperheads slithered in these rocky terrains. And bears. A large population of black bears inhabited the plateau. If she could crawl through this, so could a six-hundred-pound predator. She racked her mind for her *Ursus* knowledge. There were many known cases of bears swiping their victims to debilitate them and dragging them off.

She struggled forward. The steep decline helped her advance, but the tunnel narrowed and squeezed her. The edges no longer scraped her, but bit at her flesh. Her heart banged against her chest. She couldn't raise her head to see. The space between the ceiling and floor meant her body had to stay in an even plane.

Whispery shadows danced in the beam of her light. Her breath quickened. How much farther?

The rocks tightened around her torso. Voices echoed around her. Some muffled and far away.

"A.J.?"

No reply, but a moan vibrated along the ground.

"A.J.!" she yelled.

A coolness swept past her. The mustiness of the cave filled her lungs. Wet dust coated her tongue. She tried to spit.

Nothing.

The silence brought images of death. Even with the dampness, beads of sweat formed.

She pushed forward. The floor changed to a sliminess. Her blouse was wet with the mixture of sweat, mud, and scat.

The slope became almost vertical, and she slid downward. She dug her toes into the loose gravel but was unable to slow her descent. She flared her elbows into the cave's slick sides. Pain shot through her arms.

Then she tumbled several feet into a room.

At first, she was dazed. One shoulder was sore from hitting the ground first. Her hands felt scuffed, but she couldn't focus on them. God, had the tumble knocked out her eye microprocessor?

No. No. No.

She squeezed her eyes tight, counted to ten, then opened them a little bit at a time. Blackness surrounded her.

Then she saw the white beam of her flashlight.

Thank God.

After clearing her vision, she panned her light. The distance between the walls were about the width of a dozen jail cells. The ceiling was low but allowed her to stand with a slight stoop. The floor was of river rocks washed smoothed like some mythological monster's eggs. She looked for creatures. And for creepy spiders and copperheads.

In front of her lay A.J., unmoving.

She crab-walked to his side and felt for a pulse and breathing. Both normal.

She passed the light over his body.

The hand of a human skeleton clutched his ankle.

She unfolded the bony fingers, then started a head-to-toe check.

Airway, breathing normal, maybe shallow. Felt his head and neck. No deformities, blood, or other body moistures. No fluid coming from his eyes or ears.

She sighed. No neck or head injuries.

Next was the check on his shoulder blades, shoulders, and collar bones, applying slight compression. Again, no irregularities.

She slid her hand down the length of both of A.J.'s arms, hands, and fingers. All good.

Ribs, abdomen, and spine were next. The spine check was tricky. She had to feel for swelling or deformity without moving the body. The terrain battered her knuckles and the back of her hands.

Lastly, pelvis compression and examining his legs and ankles.

No broken bones, no internal bleeding. She was satisfied with his condition.

The boy appeared stable, so she pulled him several feet from the bones.

Tapping the boy's face, she said, "A.J.? A.J., it's me, Sheriff Coup."

A.J.'s face was pale and covered in mud. Blood seeped from a gash in his head. His eyes opened. "Am I dead?"

"Let's get you out of here."

"I passed out, didn't I?" A.J. said. "It happens when something scares me. My teacher knows, but not my buddies. Please don't tell the other kids. They'll laugh at me."

"Your secret is safe with me." She pulled him in close for a hug.

A scraping noise sounded, then huffing. A.J. shivered.

"Be quiet," she said.

The boy's eyes rolled to the back of his head.

"Oh, A.J.," she sighed.

She shone the light toward the noise coming from the chute she had slid through. She strapped on her utility belt and felt the butt of her auto.

Miller's body tumbled out of the darkness.

"I told you to stay with the kids," she said. "Plus, you scared the bejesus out of me."

"I called you," Miller said. "You didn't answer. The Lord sent me to rescue you."

"Have you ever been in here before?"

"This is the Devil's Den. Why would I enter Satan's lair?"

"Look."

She focused her light on the skeleton. Clothes clung to the bony frame. A white bonnet was fitted over the back half of the skull. From the long, plain dress that covered the bones from neck to ankles, she guessed she was looking at the remains of a Mennonite woman, probably late teens or early twenties. She knew of no reports of missing people, but then, not everything was reported to the law. Communities took care of themselves, and didn't need any government intervention.

She photographed everything from different angles with her phone. "Know of any persons in your congregation who suddenly left?"

Miller said, "No." After a long pause, he added, "Well… maybe."

A knife stuck upright through the mid-section of the remains. It had passed through the third and fourth rib and stuck into the backbone. Laying on a piece of soiled and torn material, a rock sparkled in the flash in her beam.

She pulled a glove from her utility belt and slipped it on. Then, she picked up the stone. As she threaded the jewel through her fingers, colors reflected green, silver, blue. In this low light, her eyes could be processing the light incorrectly. She would have to examine it again when she returned to the surface.

She tucked it into her shirt pocket. Then continued to search the bones.

Clutched in the skeletal hand was a stained note.

Coup removed the piece of paper and read it to herself. Afterward, she shoved it in with the gem.

Then she yanked the knife. The blade was coated in blood rust, the handle worn with use. The initials, S.M., had been carved on the hilt.

"Recognize this?" She held the weapon in the light so Miller could see it.

"Never saw it before."

"It has your initials on it."

"Lot of people have my initials, even our governor."

"You made an identical knife for my daddy. He said no steel has a better edge."

Miller didn't answer.

Coup rolled up the hem on the dress. At one time, the fabric had been blue, with white piping. She aimed her flashlight and read the monogram out loud, "Aletha Miller."

She directed the light into Miller's face. "Your wife's name."

Again, Miller said nothing.

"Let's read what's on this note. 'My dearest Simmons, I must give my heart first to the Lord. As for you...'" Blood had washed out the rest of the writing.

She remembered her dad saying Miller was their main suspect and there'd been rumors of Aletha leaving Miller. If she had, Miller would have been banned from the church. Ridiculed. People had killed for less. "Was she leaving you?"

"No."

"Your knife, your wife, and a letter." She let out a long sigh. She did not want to do this, but it was her job. "Miller, I am arresting you for the murder of your wife." She read Miller his Miranda rights, then cuffed him.

Three

Somewhere in the back of Miller's brain, he heard Coup talking to him, but it was jumbled. He didn't want to hear her anyhow; he was trying to process the skeleton in front of him. Was it really his wife?

Thousands of questions and memories clogged his mind. The last time he'd kissed Aletha, her lips had tasted like the apples she'd just eaten. Her smile that last day he'd seen her had been as full as the morning sun. He ran his hand across his face and was surprised he was sweating. The temperature in the cave was cool. What had he done?

He wiped his palm on his trousers' leg.

It was a pair Aletha had made for him. This morning, he had found them at the bottom of a box. He shouldn't have worn them. Something had told him bad things would happen if he did, but she'd made them for him the afternoon after they had returned from town.

A white cap was tied to the skull of the skeleton. She had needed a new one and they'd gone shopping at the mercantile. He'd wanted her to purchase a blue one, but she'd responded by saying, "My appearance must not entice others or tempt them to have impure thoughts."

But the thing was, Aletha didn't need a blue head covering for the male members of their congregation to lust after her, most of them had wanted her for years and considered him unworthy of her love.

But when it came to her trying on the long dress, she had compromised with him. She'd picked a pale blue outfit but allowed the trim and her cape to be white. When she'd worn the dress, his heart had come to life. The cape had been to conceal the form of her body, but all the extra material had done was to make him count his blessings to God for steering him toward this woman.

But then the Lord took her away.

He remembered the day she'd gone missing. He'd wanted to hike to Devil's Falls for a picnic, to spend the afternoon with her in the quiet of the forest, where the only sound would be of water cascading over the rocks.

But she'd been behind on her scripture reading and studies and had wanted to do it in solitude in her special place of meditation, known only to her. Just her and the Almighty.

She'd never wanted to go to the falls. The name alone meant it was an evil place. He'd adored her naïveté. "Stay away from temptation," had been her motto.

How had she ended up in this cave? And with his knife in her chest?

The church leaders had already excommunicated him, ruined him, so they couldn't harm him anymore. God couldn't even punish him with damnation because taking his sweet Aletha from him was worse than any malediction.

"Miller? Miller, do you hear me?"

Coup was yelling at him and shaking his shoulder, which brought him back to the present.

"Yes, I hear you."

"I'm taking you in." She turned him away from Aletha's body. "When we get to the jail, you get to make a phone call. Are you listening?"

"I didn't murder her."

"That's not for me to decide."

He turned his head for one more look. He wanted the image of her body to be burned into his memory.

"Do you have anyone you can call?"

There was only one person he knew. Someone who'd been a friend once.

But currently, the man was the meanest, nastiest, son-of-a-bitch on the plateau. Or anywhere in Tennessee. "I want to call Fat Bear."

"You know how to sour the sweet tea, don't you, Miller?"

Four

Coup checked A.J.'s vital signs again. Everything was normal, but the boy was still unconscious. Him and his damn fainting spells.

In the dim light, she turned to Miller. She had to convince him to choose another person for help because Fat Bear was a reprobate. There had to be someone else in Miller's life he could trust. "Are you sure you want Fat Bear? He has no legal training."

"He has other knowledge. The wolves speak to him."

"Don't bet your life on Cherokee lore." She waited for a response.

Miller stayed quiet.

She had two choices about A.J. They could all sit in the cave until he regained consciousness—an option she didn't care for because the place was giving her the creeps again thanks to those damn sorority girls—or she could have Miller help her pull the boy to daylight.

Damn it to hell.

"Here's what we're going to do. I'm going to uncuff you. You will grab A.J. by his arms and drag him out of this hole. If you give me your word as a Mennonite you won't run away, I won't arrest or cuff you in front of the kids."

"The church says I am no longer one of them."

"Forget the blasted church, Miller. It's in your blood."

"If the Lord tells me to run, I must obey."

"Do you want your ankles cuffed together?" She wouldn't have made the offer of not arresting him in public to anyone else on the plateau. But a Mennonite's word was solid. They weren't wired the same as the rest of the human population. These people never reneged.

The dampness of the cave stopped her thinking and caused her to shiver. In the glow of her light and with his stooped stance, he looked like he was seeking divine intervention. Did he forget he was in Devil's Cave, a hell hole, the site of his wife's murder? She doubted the hand of the Lord reached into these depths.

"I will help if you agree to go get Fat Bear."

"I'll do that only if you give me your word."

"I suppose the Lord wants me to attend to the boy's needs and see he gets the proper medical care."

"Say it."

"You have my word."

"Give me your knife and sheath."

He slid his knife off his belt and handed it to her.

She tucked it into her pants beside her flashlight holder.

Miller climbed into the chute they had tumbled through, and squirmed around so he could back out. Pieces of rocks and dirt tumbled onto her. Once Miller was in place, she grabbed A.J. by the shoulders, pinning his arms up, and heaved the boy toward Miller.

The man locked wrists with the boy and pulled him into the chute. Then he started skootching back for the journey to the entrance.

"While you're backing out, think of someone else you can call. Maybe the mayor. Can you count on him in a pinch?"

"I gave you a name."

"Fat Bear is not good for you." She doubted he was good for anything. Except trouble.

After thirteen minutes of knee scrapping and head banging into pencil-thin stalactites, with Miller pulling and her pushing the lad, they broke into the warm, welcoming sunshine. She had hoped the bright light would cause A.J. to regain consciousness, but, to her dismay, he didn't.

Nikee-Dee started crying again when she saw A.J. Seems like girls cried over boys from the cradle. The girl needed some of Momma's sweet tea.

The other kids yelled, "Hurray!" and pranced around in joy with huge grins. Some spouted that they knew A.J. would be saved. Even Mrs. Warren yelled, "Praised be to God!"

Coup pressed her thumb on the black radio clipped to her shoulder. "Dispatch, this is Coup, requesting assistance."

Static crackled out of the speaker.

"Dispatch. Helen, do you copy?" She knew Helen was in the office. Helen always was, even brought her own lunch every day on the off chance an emergency occurred. "Anyone?"

More static.

Damn this state. It had more dead zones than the moon.

She handed the keys to her squad car to the oldest boy in the group. "Hurry back to the parking lot and use the car's radio to contact the police station. Have them send Rescue."

The boy took off before she could finish, but, still, she yelled after him, "And leave the siren alone!"

"Run fast," Nikee-Dee said between sobs.

"Look, kids." Coup addressed the group. "A.J. should be fine."

The effect of the coolness of the cave had left her body and the heat of the sun caused her to sweat again. To shorten the rescue time, she decided to get everyone up to the top of the bluff, but it was a thousand feet up, steep in some places, and she wasn't sure if she and Miller could carry the boy out.

"Any ideas on getting A.J. out of here?" she asked Miller.

"Okay, kids." Miller seemed pleased. "This is your lucky day. Someone get the tarp out of my backpack. We are going to build a travois."

Coup watched him in disbelief. Miller knew there was a chance he could go to prison for murder, but he rallied the kids as if he was teaching them a new game. He had the girls lay out the tarp on the rough ground, then fold it lengthwise in half, while the boys gathered hickory sticks thick enough to create a frame.

Miller had one of the boys use his knife to poke holes at one end, then the boys used longer sticks for the sides and thick vines to tie the material into an almost triangular frame. Then the Mennonite showed them how to lift the injured kid with their arms under his neck, shoulders, back, and legs, and place him in the center of the tarp.

"Just like in the westerns when the Indians move their camp, except I'll be the horse," Miller said. He tied the free ends of the tarp to his belt. "Let's move. I'll go last."

Coup watched the kids follow Debbie Warren and double-time up the narrow limestone trail. "Get going," she said to Miller. 'I want you in front of me. Remember your word."

He looked at her, misery in his brown eyes. "There's a steep incline and you'll need to lift the bottom."

She slogged her way past ferns, wild ginger, and blue phlox. Her legs ached.

After a several yards, with the pre-teens well in front of them, Miller spoke again. "I'd never go back on my word."

She felt like crap. The man could have refused to help, could have played dumb, and left her with the burden of the children's safety and A.J.'s rescue. Maybe being the third generation of rural cops, or as a third-generation country sheriff, she had seen too much, heard too much, and no longer trusted anyone. Was that why she had no one in her life? Did she need to be so hard on Miller?

She shook her head to toss the thoughts out of her mind. *Keep focused on the job.* It was what her commendations said she did well. "I know a criminal attorney in Nashville. He's good."

"I've committed no crime."

For the forty-eight minutes they stayed quiet. When she stepped out of the forest of hickory, oak, poplar, and sweet gum trees onto the dirt and gravel parking lot. A.J.'s dad, Robert, was pacing around his van. A white, boxy truck with the zig-zag red stripe of Fire Rescue was just pulling up. A black-haired, female EMT in her starched shirt and trousers did a quick pass of an ammonia inhalant under the patient's nose to bring him back to the world.

A flood of relief went through Coup's body. Her knees wobbled and she sat on the bumper of her squad car.

A.J. started talking about his adventure and his encounter with the Devil. "I fought the horned and tailed demon. I used my karate. Wish I'd had the rifle Mr. Miller let us fire."

Even as the EMTs strapped him to a gurney and slid him into the ambulance, A.J. babbled away.

Robert looked relieved when his son talked nonstop.

Debbie Warren loaded the rest of the kids into the van so they could follow the rescue vehicle.

With everyone gone, she and Miller were alone.

A barred owl called for its mate. A red fox peeked out from the base of mountain laurel as if asking what she planned to do next.

Miller walked over to her with his arms held out, wrists together.

"Get in the back of the car," she said after opening the door. "Give me your keys, I'll have a patrol person drive your rattle trap to your home."

"Thank you for the respect," he said.

"Did you let A.J fire a gun?"

"Black powder, similar to what Davey Crocket used."

"Are you nuts?"

Miller remained silent.

The short ride to Monterey's single-story police station seemed like it lasted for hours. She hated the silence. The tires on the pavement were a constant dull hum. Upon entering the station, she ushered Miller into the cell. The shutting of the iron grill cell door on Miller seemed to echo into eternity. It was if the universe cried, saying she had made a mistake.

Miller sat in the corner on the aluminum bench bolted to the concrete floor, his back against a block wall and uttered two words, "Fat Bear," before closing his eyes.

Those words wouldn't leave her thoughts. Fat Bear didn't own a phone. She'd have to drive to his residence to speak to him.

She cranked up her dark blue Dodge Durango squad car.

Leaving Monterey, she drove north on 70N, a two-lane road built on top of Avery's historical trace upon which he had led settlers to the Promised Land—land given to anyone who would farm and stay in the area, opening the west to the growing population of the new nation. And, in her mind, this *was* the promised land—the most beautiful part of Tennessee, deep green forest and blue skies stretching beyond the horizon.

Turning into the Whispering Pines development, she headed to Fat Bear's domicile. Of all the neighborhoods on the outskirts of Monterey, this one had to be the worst. Built on the bluff, beautiful homes were surrounded by thick woods. But some of the residents brought their bad attitudes, self-righteousness, gossip, and biases from other states to turn this Homeowner's Association into a cat fight. And Fat Bear, although a native Tennessean and part Cherokee, was the most miserable son-of-a-bitch she had ever met. The man had more complaints filed against him than any other person in the neighborhood. More than anyone in the city. Plus, he was the major suspect in several petty crimes of fences being torn down, roads blocked by fallen trees, and the discharging of firearms.

She turned again onto a narrow gravel road, and, as she approached Fat Bear's driveway, several people stood alongside the road, demonstrating.

Their focus was on a man in his fifties whose hair was as black as the inside of Devil's Cave. He was of medium height, average weight, but sinewy, and stood in front of the protestors like an unyielding hardwood tree, his skin the same color as the clay on the ground, his eyes, blue and deep, gave him a haunting look or a man full of mysteries.

Fat Bear.

Mother of sweet tea, how was Miller friends with this brute?

Five

John Kole stepped back and admired the progress on the stone wall he was dry stacking. The white sandstone with red iron streaks gave a nice accent to the front of his wooded property and complemented his single-story stone house. Even though his home wasn't visible from the road—the way he wanted it—he knew it matched aesthetically. The craftsmanship would be the envy of his nosey neighbors, unlike the homes of those transplants who preferred stucco or brick, styles from where they used to live, not true mountain dwellings. They needed to stay away from his home and with this wall, they'd get his drift.

Four eastern bluebirds glided to the top of his creation. They pranced and chirped as if praising his efforts.

He drank from his dented, blue aluminum water bottle. The rising humidity caused large wet patches to form on his T-shirt. It stank so bad he doubted if washing it would remove the stench. He'd have to toss it. The lone, white, jagged cloud drifted in the distance, "No rain today!" The leaves on the evergreens drooped; he would, too, if this heat endured.

The birds stopped singing and flapped away. Twelve women marched toward his lot. Battleaxes was a better term. The self-proclaimed committee for a better Homeowners Association. Dobermans, they called themselves. The majority were Floridians, and they were the most miserable group of people he had ever met. Some carried white cardboard protest signs stapled to new, wooden dowels.

A woman in her mid-sixties stepped ahead of the crowd. Her

dyed-blonde hair swayed to her waist as if she were still a teen going on her first date. Her tight jeans sported those foolish so-called-fashion holes at the knees. Silver collar tips reflected the sun off her button-down blouse. She had accused him of ridiculous things in the past and was the Doberman's pack leader. Even when her mouth was at rest, large, bleached white, teeth were visible. He referred to her as Fang.

"We are here," she said, "to inform you that this wall is a violation of the covenants."

"I'm not in your prissy HOA," he said. He had just started this project this morning.

"Yes, you are."

"Check your plot maps."

"Those are wrong. The surveyor made a clerical error when he transcribed his notes to the county record."

"It stands."

"Not for long." She pulled a piece of paper from her front jeans pocket. "We hired an attorney, and he drafted papers to proposition the court."

"Which lawyer?"

"My husband." She straightened to a proud posture. "In Miami-Dade, he was often sought after."

"I'd tell you to send your weasel-faced husband over for a lesson in Tennessee law, but since he's married to you, I'm sure the poor fool has suffered enough."

"You, sir, are a vile person and do not belong in our community."

"I was born in this house." He thumbed at his home.

"Nevertheless, take this wall down."

"Pound sand."

A murder of crows landed behind him, cawing. His grandfather had taught him that, when the Great Creator sent crows, it was always a good sign—although, for him or the HOA, he wasn't sure.

Pushing her way out of the crowd, a black-haired woman

with a silver streak in her hair—which made her resemble a skunk—held her placard high, where it twisted in the soft breeze. It read, "Go Home."

"Sherry, let me hold your sign," Fang said.

Stepping within a few feet of him, Sherry said, "We don't want your kind here."

"And what *kind* is that? Decent people who mind their own business?"

"Half-breeds."

The crowd behind her chanted, "America is for Americans."

It wasn't the first time someone had spoken a slur to him. Hatred wasn't dying on this mountain. As more non-Tennesseans moved to the plateau, it seemed that respect was an old, useless attitude.

"Ma'am," he said. "This conversation is over. Time for all of you to leave."

"I have warned you," Fang said. "The HOA has spoken. The consequences are on you."

He heard an irritating honk and spotted the sheriff's car. The cop crept through the crowd to park on the side of the road between them and him. "Did you call the cops?"

"No," Fang said, "but I'd bet she's here to serve papers on you."

His grandfather's voice from a long-ago time entered his head. Grandfather had been the spiritual leader and had told him to have his property declared sacred Cherokee land.

He hadn't.

The spirits were now punishing him.

Coup stayed in her vehicle. He knew her tactics: observe, then act.

Knowing her, she might observe him all damn day.

The chugging of a diesel engine approaching from the opposite direction of Coup grabbed his attention. A John Deere front-loader lumbered toward his property. Sitting behind the wheel was another woman, wearing jeans, a dirty, short-sleeved shirt, and a straw hat on top of her stringy, gray hair. As she bounced on the yellow seat, she smiled and lowered the front scoop so it was a foot off the ground. The green tractor with the yellow wheel hubs headed for his new stone wall.

"Turn that thing around!" he yelled to the driver.

She replied with a raised finger, then turned the utility loader into the swale in front of his wall. The engine grinded and shot black smoke as the twenty-inch rear tires flung mud from the drainage depression flattening blue-and-yellow wildflowers under the treads.

Kole walked over to the driver's seat of his brown side-by-side and pulled a 12-gauge shotgun from the mount between the two front seats. Then he aimed the barrel at the front tires.

He waited. Technically, she was on the right-of-way which belonged to the county.

Keep coming.

The tractor tires bit into the earth and nudged forward.

Ten feet.

Five feet.

One foot.

He squeezed the trigger. The recoil felt good on his shoulder.

The *boom* echoed through the trees, sending the crows skyward.

The ladies fell to the ground. Several cried out in fear.

Smoke wafted out of the muzzle.

The shredded front tire of the tractor fell off the rim.

"Drop the gun, Fat Bear!" Coup yelled as she jumped from her vehicle, her service auto drawn and pointed at him.

He met her stare, then pumped the remaining two shells out of the magazine. Then he picked up the red, ten-shot casings and placed both the gun and the ammo on the black seat of his side-by-side.

"Arrest him!" yelled the tractor driver. "He's a madman. His kind don't belong here."

Kole placed his hands on the warm, metal frame roof and spread his legs on the gravel driveway.

Coup walked behind him, kicked his legs farther apart, then bent his arms behind his back and cuffed them. "Don't go anywhere, Cherokee."

"My name is John Kole," he said.

"We have a list of charges," Fang said as she pulled a pink sheet of paper from her back pocket. "Enough to lock him up for good."

"It's time for you good citizens to disperse," Coup said.

"We want justice!" someone in the crowd yelled.

"If you don't leave," Coup said, "I'll arrest the bunch of you for demonstrating without a permit."

"This is a private road," Fang said.

"Nope. County road." Coup holstered her Remington. "Now move."

"What about my tractor?"

"I suggest you don't drive it on private property anymore."

"I was in the swale."

"With intent to do damage," Coup said. "Scoot."

Damn Dobermans thought Kole. A bunch of salivating dogs. For a year, they had been harassing him. Maybe the blown tire would cause them to rethink their racial views.

After the crowds dispersed, Coup said, "Do you stay up late thinking of ways to make my life harder?"

"Not me. I mind my own business."

"Sure." Coup peeked into his side-by-side. "It's your lucky day. I'm not going to charge you."

"For what? Discharging a gun on my property? That's not a crime in this state."

"How about destroying a tire?"

"I'll buy the bitch a new one."

The crows returned and landed on the top branches of nearby evergreens. A few squawked.

"I'm here on official business."

"Aren't you always?"

"I have a man in custody for murder."

"Get him a public defender."

"He asked for Fat Bear."

Kole wished he could escape the name his grandfather had given to him. "A proper Cherokee name," he had said. Grandfather had wanted him to follow the old ways and become a spiritual healer. "Who requested me?"

"Menno Simmons Miller."

"You arrested a Mennonite? God, you're cold," he said. "Or dumb."

"Get in the car. I'll give you a lift to the jail."

"You're talking about the hermit who lives on Rattlesnake Mountain?"

He received no answer.

"Tell Miller, good luck."

Coup frisked him. "John Kole, I'm placing you under arrest for dangerous discharge of a firearm."

"Have you lost your mind? I'm on my property. This is a false arrest."

"When we get to the jail," she said, "you can tell Miller yourself."

"Your daddy must be proud."

Six

Kole stopped to inhale the scent of the blooms of the two thick-trunked, magnolia trees that shaded the entrance of the police department. The white flowers gave the illusion of a pleasant and peaceful place.

He knew differently.

The sheriff escorted him into the jail and to Miller's cell. The room, like the whole building, was institutionally cold, leaving inmates feeling hopeless and alone.

As they walked past Coup's office, he noticed two of the trees' blooms sitting on her desk in a mason jar.

Coup uncuffed Kole and said, "Talk to him."

Miller slept on a steel bench with a faded green Army blanket pulled up to his chin.

Kole planned for a quick talk with him. He'd tell the Mennonite, "Too bad." He wasn't the right guy to represent him. It'd take five minutes tops, and he'd be gone.

"When a prisoner is interviewed," Kole said to the sheriff, "isn't he supposed to be moved to an interrogation room?"

"Don't have one," she said. "It's not a big jail."

"What about a chair for me?"

"Nope." Coup walked to her office.

"No privacy here. You'll be able to hear every word of our conversation. What about attorney-client privilege?"

"Request a tax hike and I'll build you a suite." Coup slammed the door to her office.

Kole smelled the coffee brewing in the lobby. Some Tennessee joe would come in handy about now. The half-moonshine mix might help him let Miller down easy.

"Wake up, Miller," he said. "The sheriff wants to hang your butt."

"Hell, I do *not*!" she yelled. "Just doing my job."

"Thanks for the client confidentiality."

"I'm awake," Miller said. "It was quiet until you pissed off Coup."

"You're going to be charged with murder."

Miller sat upright. The springs under the thin mattress creaked rusty notes. "I know."

"You need someone in the legal profession. And it's not me."

"Fat Bear." Miller place his head in his hands. "Your name was the only one I could think of."

"Don't call me that. And think harder."

Kole walked to the corner of the room, his back sideways to the rest of the lockup. The exposed block wall grated against his spine. A grayness filled the room, and it closed in on him. He'd been in public toilets larger than this. It wasn't a cell, but a cage. Miller deserved better. "I know the Mennonite congregation," he said, "They're a tight bunch of people. Your sect never requests outside assistance. Your people take care of each other."

"They won't help me."

Miller's reply had been abrupt; Kole wondered why. "Did you ask?"

Miller rubbed his hands across his face as if wiping away a bad memory. Then he stared at the unpainted floor. "I was excommunicated. As far as those holier-than-thous think, I was never a part of them."

"Who's the pastor?" Kole asked. "I'll make a call on your behalf."

"Don't waste your dime."

To Kole, it seemed Miller had made his peace with the Lord and was ready to get the big injection. The man must be guilty.

Kole focused on the same spot Miller was staring at. Gouges were cut into the cement where the metal post bedframe had been dragged across the floor. Kole found nothing in the image to help him escape this predicament.

"Fat Bear—"

"I asked you politely not to call me by that name."

"I know your grandfather." Miller stood, walked to the opposite wall and back, then sat back down. "To repay a debt, I had to give him my word to always refer to you as Fat Bear."

"I don't follow his ways."

"You and I have a common trait. We are both loners."

"Then you understand why I don't want to get involved."

Miller looked directly at Kole with watery eyes. "You have the knowledge and the blessing of the Spirits."

"I drink your moonshine. The Great Spirit doesn't approve."

His grandfather had taught him that the spirits had blessed him at birth. During their walks through the dense forest or across tall-grass meadows, his grandfather had pointed out how bucks, hawks, snakes, ravens, and crows were symbolic and spiritual representatives of specific sources of power, and they served as messengers, guardians, protectors, and healers. At times, Kole felt an insight into nature he couldn't explain.

"Just as your forefathers had their sweat lodges and cleansing ceremonies, you have your own ritual with the earth."

"It's called getting drunk."

"But you have visions when you do." Miller paced the floor twice, then slumped onto the bed. "Only a loner can experience these insights."

"The Cherokee ways are not the same as the Mennonites'."

"As loners, you and I are granted wisdom by the Lord through unconventional methods."

"Don't expect me to tend to your still while you're in the big house. I'm walking out. Find someone else."

Like in the past, this was another situation where Kole felt the Spirits were punishing him because of his ancestors. He wasn't a pure Cherokee. His grandfather, when he'd come of age, had married a white woman who'd been given to the tribe when she was young as a peace offering. They'd had one child, his dad—who'd also married a white woman. Kole, at best, was a quarter Cherokee. How could his grandfather come up with the idea that Kole should follow the customs and be a shaman?

"Did you choose to be Cherokee?"

"No."

"As I did not choose to be a Mennonite. We were both born into lives against our wills."

"Don't use psychological babble shit on me."

"We did not choose our beginnings, true?"

Kole wanted to leave. Miller was one of those people you don't argue with because he could twist anything into being the Lord's will.

"You are correct." Kole turned to the cell door to yell for Coup to let him out.

Miller jumped from his bed and ran to get between Kole and the cell door. "What life did your grandfather require of you?"

"To be a shaman. But no one could attain the knowledge of earth, wind, fire, and water like him. Plus, I didn't want to."

"My wife, Aletha, did not choose her life; she was thrust into it. She was a soul who should have been sent elsewhere in the world, not on top of a mountain, to a group of people who retained some customs from five hundred years ago."

"The Mennonites can believe and act any way they want; it doesn't affect me. They are a better group of people for their strict adherence to the teachings of the Bible."

"I know you were once an attorney for the Cherokee."

A sadness passed over Kole. "Don't dig up the past."

"You defended a young girl against a murder charge."

Acid ate into his stomach lining. The memory of her trial flooded his mind. She'd been raped and found guilty of murdering the scum of the earth who'd done it to her. It'd been his first case. She'd been Cherokee and he'd wanted to impress Grandfather and be respected.

"I represented her poorly," Kole whispered. "She hung herself in the holding cell."

"And wasn't it her daddy who did the killing?" Miller asked.

"Confessed right after the trial, but it was too late to save her. He died of cancer a week later. Said the Great Spirit punished him."

Kole gazed at the gray walls, waiting for the depression to leave him.

It didn't.

"I'm no good, which is why I cannot defend you."

"You rejected the Cherokee ways because of this, but you still believe in the Great Spirit. I was tossed out of the church, but still believe in God. Aletha was taken from the living, but she is still with us. She comes to me on autumn's blue moon. I did not kill her." Miller grabbed Kole by the shoulders, a tremble in his voice. "Call on the Great Spirit to guide you. For Aletha's sake, find the truth."

Another wave of coffee aroma swept through the cell. Kole needed something stronger. Some of Miller's brew. Straight and neat.

His vision blurred for a second, but, in that moment, he saw himself standing on the edge of a bluff, looking down a thousand feet into a darkening forest. Crows were perched on sweetgums and hickory trees, their white eyes watching him, a path he didn't want was laid out for him.

Damn birds.

His heritage obligated him to help anyone who requested he beseech the Great Spirit—the one lesson Grandfather had taught him that he would always honor. "What time is your arraignment?"

Seven

Kole fired up his side-by-side as Coup stuck her head in the driver's open window and handed him a copy of her legal briefs.

"You better study these before the proceedings. Also, when we see the judge, don't cross me, don't be disrespectful, and don't embarrass Miller, me, or yourself. Your reputation precedes you, so, be as sweet as Momma's tea."

"When are you up for re-election?"

She slapped the hood of his vehicle, then jumped into her car.

Miller was sitting in the back seat with his head bowed.

Small town legal system Kole remembered when he'd been chasing his degree and had been assigned as an assistant to a Monterey case. A man had been arrested in the morning, tried in the afternoon, and taken to the hanging limb that evening.

Justice was swift in Monterey.

That was why most perps liked to be arrested outside of Monterey's jurisdiction, especially Cookeville, where the system traveled slower.

Monterey was known for their brand of justice. If a person was innocent, he got to go home for dinner. The guilty were not so lucky.

Following Coup, Kole mashed his gas pedal to the floor to maximize his speed to forty miles per hour—and it still wasn't enough to keep pace with the sheriff for the eight blocks. Speed limits were probably just a suggestion to her.

He was relieved when they arrived promptly at Monterey's

municipal building. He'd get inside, stand before the judge, then be off since, because it was a murder charge, the judge would deny bail for Miller.

And with Miller behind bars, the Mennonite wouldn't bother him, so he could concentrate on getting him exonerated.

If he could. A shudder ripped through him. He hoped this didn't turn out like his last case. But this one was different. It was a fact that Mennonites had never been known to commit any type of crime—they were the most peaceful people God ever created—and his gut told him Miller was not guilty. His head, though, said otherwise.

Twelve years had passed since the killing. The murderer could have moved away, died in a car accident, or a hundred other things. Would he or she be bold enough to stick around if they were still alive to revisit the scene from time to time? That was a gloomy prospect at best.

Kole pulled into the asphalt parking lot, two spaces down from Coup, thinking it wise to keep his distance from her at all times. The half windows in the pink, brick one-story building reflected the afternoon sun with a golden hue. The letters on the structure's sign looked like silver bars.

As he walked toward the entrance, he thought, *Four thousand square feet of civilization intrusion.* His grandfather had held a cleansing ceremony before the bulldozers had scrapped the place Cherokees had once gathered for their sacred hunt.

He hadn't passed any spirit animals on his drive over, which was odd. And not a good sign.

Coup ushered Miller through the glass front door, then turned to Kole. "Is your vehicle street-legal?"

"Let's not keep the judge waiting," he said.

They stepped into a brown-tiled foyer, a window to pay taxes on the right and the water department on the left. He followed Coup and Miller down a narrow corridor beside the tax department to an assembly hall. The air felt stagnant as if the room had been sealed off since the place had been built.

Miller jangled the handcuffs that bound his arms behind his back.

"Uncuff him, Coup," Kole said.

"*Sheriff* to you," she said while she freed Miller.

The assembly hall held about fifty people at capacity, but they weren't making it to double digits today. The metal chairs looked cold and lonely to Kole.

"Miller, sit here." Coup pointed to an end chair on the front row, then said to Kole, "Front and center."

"Are you in charge of seating?" He raised an eyebrow.

"I'll get the judge. Mind your words."

Miller sat and, after a few moments, stared at the American flag tucked in the corner. "Remember, I want justice for Aletha," he said to Kole.

Kole studied the file Coup had given him. It contained five pages—two on today's events at Devil's Creek Cave and three pages on Aletha's disappearance.

The mayor walked in and announced that, since the city was short-handed, he'd be filling in as needed. He whispered a few words to Miller, then sat in his leather, high-backed seat behind a solid hickory desk on the platform.

To Kole, the man looked pale, as if he hadn't been in the sun for months; Kole didn't like people who spent more time indoors than in the forest because they lost the essence of the earth. The mayor's charcoal slacks were wrinkled, but the collar of his pin-striped, blue shirt was starched stiff. He wore a matching sports jacket and no tie. Kole couldn't remember the last time he'd worn a jacket—or if he even owned one. And he figured the stiff collar would poke the man's chin when he nodded off.

The mayor stood and announced, "The Honorable Judge McAlister. All rise."

Kole stood as the judge limped in with sparse white hair that was uncombed and in stark contrast to his black robe.

A short woman with her black hair in braids, wearing a red dress and tanned Cherokee boots, followed, sat in the second row of chairs, then set up her stenograph.

Coup waited beside Miller. After the judge sat in the center chair on the platform she said, "We can be seated."

"Let's begin." The judge rapped his gavel. "Where's Dewayne?"

"Your Honor," Coup said, "the D.A. has been delayed, and will be for some time. I am to stand in for him."

"Is he still fishing?" McAlister asked.

Coup shifted from foot to foot. "I've done this in the past."

McAlister looked at the mayor. "When is this city getting a real defense attorney?"

"It's a small town, Your Honor," the mayor said.

"Miller, you can request a delay until Dewayne arrives, if you wish?"

"We can proceed, Your Honor. I have faith in Fat Bear."

"I don't like it, but since there are no complaints from Mr. Miller, we will continue."

Coup sat in her chair. "I am requesting no bail. This is a murder charge."

To Kole, it felt as if the temperature in the room dropped fifteen degrees, yet, sweat still ran down his back. He hadn't expected Coup to be so forceful. Her off-duty, apple-pie friendliness had disappeared.

McAlister's face looked as hard as plaster. "Rise when you speak to the court." he said. "As a matter of fact, why don't the three of you stand for the whole hearing."

Kole rose at the same time as Coup and Miller.

"Your Honor," he said, "Miller, my client, is not allowed to sit by me."

"Because we have no bailiff or extra patrolmen," Coup said.

Kole waited for the judge to intervene, but he remained quiet.

"My client is a trustworthy Mennonite. If he gives you his word, he won't flee. Their community is a pillar to God, and it's never been tarnished."

"Fat Bear," McAlister said, "how's your grandfather?"

Kole cringed, but didn't react with words. "He's fine, Your Honor."

"He's an honest man. Can I say the same about you?"

"You'd need to ask others."

"Miller is no longer a member of the church," Coup said. "Excommunicated. They booted his ass—er, sorry, Judge. His butt."

"He's a valued member of the community," Kole said.

"A loner is what he is. Lives on top of Rattlesnake Mountain. There's no congregation up there," Coup said.

She was correct. Cougars, foxes, and wild hogs roamed the area, so no one hiked to the summit—too many stories of people not returning.

And not from falling off the bluff.

"Your Honor…" Kole shot a stern gaze at Coup. then faced the judge with a smile. "Mr. Miller is such a great asset to the people of Monterey, he even helped Ms. Warren supervise the children today for the Davey Crockett event."

"He let pre-teens fire guns," Coup said.

"I fired my first rifle at six," Kole said. The clacking of the keys on the stenograph caused Kole to raise his voice a notch. "Nothing wrong with pre-teens learning firearm safety. Besides, the mayor recommended him."

"Correct, Your Honor," the mayor said.

Coup stepped closer to the front table. "Hell, the man is a moonshiner."

"Enough!" Judge McAlister shouted. "Step back, Sheriff."

Kole had done his best. He'd painted Miller in a good light. Was it enough? He didn't think so. Coup could be right - have Miller locked up because it didn't make sense to let an accused murderer roam the mountains. Even if Miller said he would not flee, he could hide in the mountains for the rest of his life and never be found. The Mennonite knew how to live off the land.

Guilt raced through him for letting his own feelings stop him from presenting the best defense for Miller.

McAlister smoothed his robe. "Miller makes a fine shine, don't you think, Mayor?"

The mayor nodded. "The best in Tennessee."

"And though I don't believe in the Cherokee ways, your grandfather was a great shaman, which I believe you are, too, Fat Bear. If your spirit animals told you to walk away from this, you would have."

He wished he'd run from this.

"Since you didn't, you must believe in Miller's innocence, as, apparently, does the mayor. A shaman knows things ahead of time."

Kole wasn't a spirit man, and he didn't want to follow in his grandfather's ways. He wanted to shout this to the judge. But didn't, because matters would be worse for Miller.

"Fat Bear, approach the bench."

He did, cautiously because something felt wrong.

"I am releasing Miller into your custody."

Damn it to hell. "No, Your Honor. I'm not equipped to be his sitter."

"My mind is settled. Don't interrupt. Miller is to be in your presence at all times."

"Your Honor," Coup said, "I must protest."

"You will keep your mouth shut. Your father never interrupted me. Take a lesson, missy." Judge McAlister slammed his gavel. "Adjourned."

Coup walked over to Kole, then whispered in his ear. "I'd like to call you some names, but my momma said that a lady doesn't use those words."

Kole knew he had made an enemy with Coup. He'd have to remedy that. He watched everyone leave except Miller.

"I hope you can cook," Miller said. "Jail food isn't fit for the devil."

Kole kicked the chair he had sat on, then shoved Miller to walk in front of him. "Bread and water for you."

He felt like a fog had drifted off the mountain and engulfed him. How the hell had this happened? What was he supposed to do now?

Eight

Coup slammed the municipal building's door shut, then marched to her car. She jerked the driver's door open, jumped in, grabbed the steering wheel, then yanked her hands off it. Her hands stung. "Momma's sweet tea," she said, examining her palms to see a shade of cherry red spread across them. The afternoon sun had baked the inside of her car, so sitting in the driver's seat just long enough to crank the A/C to the coldest setting, flipped the fan on high. Then she stepped out of the sauna.

Seeing the Mayor's car brought on a smile. Her car might be an inferno, but at least the birds hadn't pooped all over it as they had on his car.

Fat Bear and Miller had exited the building and were headed in her direction. This was a good time for her to set Fat Bear straight about Miller and the investigation. Besides, she wasn't getting back in her car until it cooled.

"Fat Bear, a word."

The asshole grimaced.

She didn't care. He'd better get used to her calling him by his Cherokee name because she intended to do it a lot to show him who is in charge. The half-breed was trying to set a murderer free and right under her nose, to boot. She'd be damned if she was going to let that happen.

"Sheriff," he said, "I'm busy. I have a murder to solve."

"I don't know how you convinced the judge to release Miller into your custody. But if either of you step out of line, I'll lock you both up."

"Sheriff?" Miller started.

"Don't say anything." Kole stepped between Miller and Coup.

She nodded to the mayor's car. "Did you have your grandfather cast some voodoo spell on the blackbirds, so they'd crap on his new Cadillac?"

"Please," Kole said. "Do not disrespect my grandfather or his beliefs. It's not voodoo. You call your deity, God, we call him the Great Spirit. And it's ravens, not some tail-wagger."

She checked herself. She had a lot of regard for Fat Bear's grandfather and the Cherokee culture. But how did Miller's release happen?

"Sheriff," Kole said, "I'm not happy with this arrangement either. I'm no babysitter. And if I have to keep an eye on Miller, how do I go about finding evidence to clear him?"

"And I don't want to be a prisoner in his house," Miller said.

"Keep quiet, you," Coup said.

From the way Miller stepped back, maybe she'd been a bit too loud or too stern. But both of them need to know she wasn't a pushover. But, still, she didn't need to be a bitch about it.

"You are not solving a murder case." She inhaled deeply then released the breath little by little. "By law, I will share my findings with you, whether the facts convict or exonerate."

"I don't see you working on it. You've already convicted Miller in your mind."

"Your job is to defend him." She balled her fists, then opened them. Her palms were still tender.

"And I will."

"And just so we're clear, do not contaminate my crime scene."

"I have the right to examine where the incident occurred."

"When you plan to visit the site, call, and I'll assign an officer to accompany you."

"Since I'm Miller's legal representative, I expect to have the full cooperation of your department and all privileges of being his attorney extended to me."

"And you'll have it." She glanced at the mayor's car again and had to chuckle. Her patrol car was spared, which was good news. But this case brought mixed emotions. She liked Miller and, deep down, thought he hadn't knifed his wife on purpose. However, she was sworn to uphold the law, so in her polite voice, she said to Fat bear, "We both have a job to do. And that is to ensure justice is served. Send me a request so everything is above board."

"Ready? Here it is. I'll be at the cave tomorrow with or without one of your representatives."

She didn't like Fat Bear. Too arrogant. And he seemed angry for being a Cherokee.

"Tell you what, Fat Bear. I'll escort you myself."

Nine

Ready for action, Savannah-Jo Hunnicutt stood outside the Whiskey Bent Saloon, the honky-tonk happening place in Nashville. It was Steampunk night, and everyone would be attired in the time period of Victorian England. With the white lightening flowing, the atmosphere would be hormones-on-legs.

The retro-futuristic convention had started in the morning. It'd been advertised as, "Moonshine, Ruffles, and Steam." It was just her style, and she had a ticket for the three-day event. It would be like stepping into an H. G. Wells or Jules Verne novel. Tonight was kick-off night with a meet-and-greet—or, rather, a who-do-I-want-to-bed. She'd have her choice of anyone. However, her sights were on just one—Trixie. Their work schedules had kept them apart for the past month. Savannah-Jo chose this costume to delight Trixie and for them to have a sensual evening.

Stepping inside the brick, three-story building, she felt the hot, sticky, sweat filled air.

"Savannah-Jo, over here!" An invite from the end of the wooden bar, which seemed as long as the state of Tennessee, came from Trixie, her sometimes roommate and part-time lover. And hopefully, her midnight dance partner. She felt the heat rise in her.

Patrons raised a glass as she pranced across the floor. Her black-on-black, double-bustle skirt gave a good view of the inside of her legs and bloomers. She could feel their eyes roam from her hips to her knee-high, gear-buckled, cross-laced, four-inch heel boots. Molten lust was in the air, and she loved it.

Trixie stood beside Sean, who leaned against the bar. She knew him and loved it when he'd take Trixie and her to experience spooky tunnels, stock car races, and hand gliding.

"Join us," he said.

The noise level of the packed bar muddled his words. She read his lips more than heard him. She squeezed between him and Trixie, edging Trixie closer to the stuffed brown bear mounted on a raised platform like he was climbing across rocky terrain.

Sean kissed her check while she planted one on Trixie's lips.

"Peppermint," Trixie said. "Reminds me of last Christmas Eve when you wore it."

"How are the twins tonight?" he asked.

Sean liked to refer to Trixie and herself as twins. They weren't, but could pass themselves off as fraternal sisters, a game they liked to play to tease the young corporate types. Both had shoulder-length, brunette hair, hers dyed, Trixie's natural. Short, she had to wear four-inch heels to be of average height. Trixie wore flats. And they were skinny, without an ounce of effort.

"It seems the way you two are dressed," Savannah-Jo said, "that *you're* the twins."

Both Sean and Trixie were dressed as Victorian English gentlemen. From their gray top hats down to their black leather boots.

"The black dress gloves and the silver-plated canes finish off your outfits nicely," she said.

"I think it's our black tailcoats." Sean did a twirl. "Matching brushed-cotton trousers, silk puff tie, and the stiff, high collar. I feel important."

"For me, it's the silver vest," Trixie said. "Only, I had to get one a few sizes larger to be able to button it. Big boobs get in the way."

"I don't mind," Savannah-Jo said.

"They never get in my way." Sean's grin was as big as his hopefulness.

"And you…" Trixie smiled. "Nice white silk shirt. White, hun? Are you innocent? I can see your charms poking out."

"Glad you approve," she said.

"Enough," Sean said. "Too much fashion talk." He turned to the female bartender, who had brown, shoulder-length hair with blonde streaks. Her black tank top showed plenty of enhanced cleavage, which, combined with her smile, encouraged generous tips. The woman stood in front of a glass mirror with the restaurant's name—Three Drunken Earls—in an oval logo painted on it, four shelves of whiskey, bourbons, and moonshine below it.

She paused to breathe, her corset too tight. The country music blasted through the room from three male guitar players. They were not dressed in steampunk, but in their country duds, cowboy hats low over their eyes.

"Have you heard the news?" Trixie asked.

Sean nodded. "They found a skeleton."

Savannah-Jo hadn't watched TV in a week, and the radio in her Lexus was satellite. The world could have ended, and she wouldn't have known. Skeletons? Unusual, thus a breaking story. The public didn't react to murders anymore; every third day in the city someone was either shot, knifed, or beaten. "How is that news?"

"Because it happened in Monterey," Trixie said.

"Up on the plateau." Sean tried to spin his cane. It hit the side of the bar, and he caught it before the silver tip bounced on the floor. "Inside a cave."

"Who cares? The town was once a summer destination. Now, it's a ghost town." She wished she'd worn her black, thigh-high hose. Maybe they would hide the sudden trembling in her legs. She slid onto a bar stool and hoped no one questioned why.

"I heard the bones have been laying there for twelve years," Trixie said.

"What time should we meet in the morning?" she said, trying to change the subject. "Which booth do we want to see first?"

"And a Mennonite," Trixie said. "Who would kill a Mennonite? They are the nicest people in the world. I had so much fun at their sorghum grinding day. They dress funny, though."

Savannah-Jo's stomach twisted as if a python had cinched around her waist. "Where are our drinks?"

"Here you go." Sean handed her a tall, thin glass with an orange peel stuck to the rim.

She gulped the mixture of rye whiskey and Earl Grey tea. It burned down to her toes. "How would they know it was a Mennonite?"

"By her clothes." Trixie sipped her drink. "This will get me in the mood for tonight. But two of these will knock me on my ass."

"When can I join in?" Sean had a huge smile.

"Not tonight, sweetie," Trixie said. "Just me and my girl."

The conversation paused. Savannah-Jo felt flush and sipped her drink. The cool cocktail offered no relief, and she was squashed between the two of them. With Sean's musky cologne and Trixie's citrus-scented body spray, she didn't want to inhale.

The female bartender tapped Savannah-Jo on the elbow. "Is the Drunken Earl too much for you, darling? I could make you something else, a Shirley Temple, maybe?"

"Bitch," Savannah-Jo said under her breath. But if the bartender had noticed, did Trixie and Sean also suspect something troubled her? Her night turned to crap in that instant. "I'm fine," she said to the bartender. "How about cranking down the AC or do you get off seeing sweaty bodies?"

More people crowded at the bar. All she could see were gray top hats and black bustles. The band pounded out two more songs about broken hearts.

"That's about the same time I remember my dad saying a train was robbed." He shrugged when both women looked at him. "I lived there as a kid."

"Another urban legend," Savannah-Jo said. "Sean, are you going to pick us up in the morning? And what time?"

"No, it's not an urban legend." Trixie's cheeks reddened from her drink. "I remember reading about it in the company files. You know, it was a slow day, so I was looking for something interesting."

Both she and Trixie worked as investigators for Boyd's Insurance and Recovery. And she wished Trixie would stop talking about the news and talk about tomorrow's event or their work.

"What was stolen?" Sean leaned in close to her.

"The file didn't list anything," Trixie said. "Just an entry of two items, unknown articles, valued in the millions. Pretty weird. I thought it was a fake file. Something to screw with the new people."

"Some file," Sean said. 'It could be paintings, carvings, jewelry. Almost anything."

"It's still an open case," Trixie said. "Wouldn't it be exciting to search for it?"

"Search for what? We don't have a clue about what to look for. Besides, Boyd would never give you the assignment," Sean said.

Trixie set her empty glass on the wooden bar. "This has gone to my head. We need to leave if we want to play tonight. Your place or mine?"

Savannah-Jo was glad Trixie was ready to go, but she needed to think, not play.

"Boyd's tough." Sean finished his drink. "That was a waste of good whiskey."

Savannah-Jo had learned, in the first month of her employment, that the owner of the company wanted all profits and fame. He loved his name in the headlines. If it was above the fold, he gave out bonuses. Plus, he had swatted her a couple of times in the copier room and suggested they should have dinner together to discuss her career. She always put him off. She, not Trixie, needed to be involved in this case. And to convince Boyd, she'd use his advances to her advantage.

"I'm off," Sean said, then disappeared into a sea of Victorian England.

"Are you ready?" Trixie asked.

The past can ruin your future went through Savannah-Jo's mind and it frightened her. "I need another drink."

Ten

Kole's grandfather's raspy voice broke the silence in the bar. "Fat Bear, we need to talk." He pulled up a wooden chair and sat across from Kole. Grandfather wore his blue, long-sleeved tribal shirt which fit snug over his body, hiding his muscular arms. His broad chest was still as solid as a mountain. A narrow black cord was used as a tie and, just below the neck, a blue-and-yellow painted bone clasp, which resembled the outline of an ancient canoe, held it in place.

Pure Cherokee, and always would be until his grandfather died. Kole dressed more American, in jeans, a short-sleeve shirt, and work boots. He wanted to fit in with society, but he was trapped between the two worlds. Alone.

Kole sipped his beer and stared at his grandfather. The man didn't smile. Short gray hair peeked around his black hat with its lone eagle feather sticking out the side. Kole didn't want to be bothered but knew from past discussions that it was easier to listen than try to dismiss the ninety-year-old man.

He was glad there were few customers in the bar tonight so no one would ridicule them. Grandfather often attracted trouble when around people who cared little for the environment. Plus, by sitting in a darkened corner, the roughnecks might ignore them. He hoped the single pool table would occupy the locals.

Glancing around the inside, he saw that, besides him and grandfather, five other people occupied the building. The ex-con bartender and his blonde wife waitress were both on the other side of the bar, while the three Mexican men stood at the counter. No one looked in their direction. The air was still thick with the smell of cigarettes, whiskey, and women's perfume from last night's activities.

"Why do you poison your body?"

Kole bit his lip. The sadness in his grandfather's squinted brown eyes sank Kole's heart. He had disappointed his grandfather by not learning the Cherokee ways and refusing to follow in his grandfather's footsteps. "Hard day. A beer a day is supposed to be good for you."

"Not for a Cherokee." Grandfather shook his head. "A fox visited me at sunrise."

Grandfather had a story to tell, or, as he would say, a warning or tiding. He should have known this was why he'd come. Kole leaned back in his chair.

"The fox ran to me," Grandfather began. "I have never seen one move so quickly. It's a bad sign."

Kole drank his beer from the long-neck bottle. "Yes, I know Grandfather. You have instructed me well. You can get to the point."

The old man gave him a hard stare, his chin held higher than usual.

"Forgive me, Grandfather," he said. Kole loved this man and felt terrible for the interruption. "I disrespected you. Please go on."

"The fox is a messenger of danger, sickness, or death. This one was a male and without his skult. Forlorn."

It had been a while since Kole had heard the term skult. People now used the term harem to describe a male fox's group of females.

"I believe it was a death warning he brought."

"But you are well liked. No one would do you harm."

"Fat Bear, not for *me*. For you."

Kole felt the blood rush to his face, then he shrugged his shoulders. It wasn't the first time someone wanted him dead. But who? The only people he'd angered in the past few days were the POA Dobermans. They were old ladies. He dismissed the idea they'd kill him.

"I heard of your actions this afternoon."

"Those POA ladies are a nuisance. Radical, yes. But mostly harmless."

"You have ears, but do not hear. Listen to nature. The songbirds do more than sing."

Did Grandfather know about Miller?

The hissing of airbrakes being applied outside came through the walls. A few minutes later, the heavy steel door to the bar opened, then slammed shut. A truck driver entered the establishment. The man was as huge as the cab of an eighteen-wheeler and dressed in an old pair of jeans which shone from use. His speckled beard stretched down and covered the top button of his green flannel shirt.

"You have inserted yourself, into matters of no concern to you," Grandfather said,

The trucker pounded his boots on the concrete floor. Muddy footprints streaked the pine floor as he walked to the bar. "Whiskey!" he shouted. "Neat. Fill the glass up."

"We are not keepers of the Mennonites," Grandfather said. "Like us, they have their own society and laws."

"I have no idea why Miller requested me."

"Because you are like the fox. You possess regality and loyalty."

"Not to the Mennonites."

"And pride."

The trucker downed his drink and ordered another. When he turned from the bar, the man sneered as he looked in their direction. He then walked to the pool table and set his glass on the chipped rail. He racked the balls, selected a cue stick, then chalked it.

"Separate yourself from this matter," Grandfather said.

"And the fox told you all of this?"

Grandfather stiffened. Kole knew he crossed the line again. The sunspots on the old man's face hardened.

The cue ball hitting the yellow number one sounded like an overhead rafter cracking and splintering.

Kole turned toward the sound and noticed the trucker had rolled up his sleeves. On his right lower arm was the name P. H. Sheridan, the man who coined the term, "The only good Indian is a dead Indian."

"Grandfather," Kole said, "we should leave."

"We talk first. Do not concern yourself with the trucker," Grandfather said. "Your pride in your case is much more than in the fox."

"I had no choice."

"It will not end well for you. The fox is a wise friend."

The trucker towered over their table. "You Cherokees don't belong here."

Kole studied the man who was over six feet and easily two-hundred-fifty pounds. His arms and legs were as thick as wheel axles. An old cut over his left eye suggested the man liked barroom fights. His shirt and jeans were soiled with grease and smelled of diesel.

"I belong wherever I choose," Kole said.

"This is the 1838 Bar." The trucker dropped his glass to the table, splashing the remaining whiskey onto Grandfather. A stain splattered his shirt. "Do you know what 1838 means?"

"The street address," Kole said. "Or don't you know how to read a map?"

"It was the year," Grandfather spoke slow and reverently, "when General Winfield Scott and his seven thousand troops finished removing the native tribes from their beloved hunting grounds."

"Praise Scott," the trucker said.

Kole's anger coursed through his veins. But he was no match against this man.

The bar owner, waitress, and the three Mexicans turned to watch.

"It started in 1830." Grandfather spoke to the trucker and the Mexicans. "It was called the Cherokee Removal Act. Sixteen thousand of my ancestors were forced to march to the Oklahoma territory. Four thousand died. The Trail of Tears."

One thought went through Kole's mind. *Please, Grandfather, don't anger the man.*

"Well, he forgot two." The trucker opened and closed his fists.

"We'll be on our way," Kole said.

"No." Grandfather stood. "I bow to no man."

The trucker pulled a long blade from a leather sheath on his belt then pointed it at Grandfather. "Time for me to do a little scalping."

The Mexicans ran out the door. The owner and his wife disappeared into a back room. They weren't going to get involved.

Kole jumped up and swung his chair across the trucker's chest. Pieces of wood flew in different directions.

The trucker lunged at grandfather, his knife level with Grandfather's heart.

Grandfather sidestepped him, grabbed the man's beard, and pulled him forward. Then grandfather body-slammed the trucker into the wall. The weight of the man splintered the pine paneling.

As the trucker fell, grandfather pulled the knife free.

Kole grinned. He loved his grandfather. The man knew how to start a fight and how to finish one.

Grandfather jammed the knife into the tabletop, then turned to the trucker. "I did not become old by being stupid. You, however, may not see next year."

The trucker wiped blood from his forehead and stayed seated on the floor.

Kole walked over to the beaten man. "A word of advice. Don't engage a Cherokee in a knife fight."

"We go now," Grandfather said.

Outside the bar, the stars filled the sky. A warm breeze blew up from the valley onto Kole's face. It would be another hot day tomorrow.

"One more thing," Grandfather said. "Later, I noticed the same fox mounting another fox. Not the right time of year for this mating."

Kole remained silent. He didn't want to second-guess him.

"The fox is also an intelligent and wise friend. You are going to have sex with someone you shouldn't."

Kole watched Grandfather walk away to disappear into the night. The man was like mist.

But Kole laughed. *Everyone* he'd had sex with was a mistake. His past girlfriends and three ex-wives proved that point. They either had significant others or asked him for diamond rings. He was definitely not getting involved ever again; he couldn't afford the alimony.

Eleven

In the heart of Nashville's financial district stood a twenty-six-story building made of steel and glass. Boyd's Insurance and Recovery occupied the top floor. Savannah-Jo paused at the open door to Roger Boyd's office to confirm in her mind what she wanted: two percent of the firm, a partnership, and the Monterey case.

And if she had those three, she could start her horse rescue farm. Too many horses were being neglected or destroyed and the economy downturn and rising price of feed and hay were tanking the ranchers. Plus, as part of her rescue plan, she hoped to start a farrier school—another skill which was fading away, but in great need.

"Good morning, Savannah-Jo," he said with a smile as bright as the morning sun that lit up his office.

A *suite* was a better description, with the solid oak, kidney-shaped desk in front of the floor-to-ceiling, blue-tinted glass and a seating area on the opposite side of the room. It included a round, cherry table and four cushioned chairs, along with a wet bar, private bath, and changing area. Percolating Kopi Luwak coffee filled the suite with caramel and chocolate scents. She wanted all of this.

Boyd sat at his desk. He was the sole owner of Boyd's Insurance and Recovery. With a net worth of over a billion dollars, he hired many lady friends.

His clothes reflected the money, all hand-tailored from a small town in Italy. And that designer agreed—for the price to build a battleship—never to duplicate the style. Boyd had been customized to set him apart from other executives. Soon, her fashion would be from the same cut.

She could tell by the glint in his eyes that he took in her appearance from heels to mascara. Her negotiating outfit consisted of four-inch blue pumps, borderline between clubbing and office wear, shimmery black hose, a blue skirt which liked to ride high, and a white blouse with four large buttons. Walking toward his desk, she undid the top one.

"What brings you in?" Boyd straightened the manila folders on his uncluttered desk, then pushed two of them aside. "I thought you and Trixie were attending the steampunk convention?"

The room had a feeling of warmth and welcome, unlike Boyd's heart, which could be cold like last winter's freezing temperatures.

"My career is more important."

Boyd leaned forward in his high-back executive chair then adjusted a photo on his desk.

Photos of his tanned body and sun-bleached hair hung on a wall, showing him mountain climbing, scuba diving with sharks, and hang gliding. Fifty years of age and he liked to conquer nature and women.

She had a hunch about what he was thinking. He had already made advances about bedding her. And if she decided to be one of the mares in his vast stable, it would cost him a hefty paycheck. She wasn't like his regular bimbos.

"For an advancement, you need to make a significant recovery."

"Good. I want the case in front of you."

He jerked forward. "You've read the contents?" He smiled and leaned back. "Of course, you have."

"I heard about the killing in Monterey."

"Why do you think they're related."

She sat in one of the cushioned chairs facing him, then propped her heels on the edge of the desk and crossed her ankles. No reward for him yet. "One, we have a train robbery—we think, anyway; the file is vague. Second, a two-point-three earthquake occurred the next day. The event blocked the entrance to the cave referenced in the news. Three, a Mennonite is killed during the same period. I would venture to say the day of the quake."

"As you said, nothing in the file."

She pointed to a set of louvered doors. A hum came from the other side. "I know about your supercomputer. How it monitors all publications, blogs, and podcasts worldwide, looking for keywords and phrases. What does it have tucked away in its data banks?"

"Nothing. Five-hundred-million-dollar investment, and all it does is eat electricity."

"You don't have a clue what was stolen?"

"The only thing that came out of that mine was coal."

"Plus, hematite and limonite."

Boyd cocked his head.

"Iron in layman's terms." She smiled. "Besides my P.I. certification, I have a master's in geology."

"No rubies, crystals, or diamonds?"

"Nope."

"But aren't diamonds and coal made from carbon?"

"Different process." She relaxed, ready to recite a lecture given to her once. "Coal has impurities in it. Diamonds don't. Coal forms near the planet's surface at a low temperature. Diamonds come from the mantle, which is at a high temp."

"So, the great barrier to the westward expansion of the colonist has no mineral value?"

"Just coal. And the studying of what happens when two continental plates collide, forcing the inner guts of the earth upward." She pantomimed with her hands, one plowing into the other, with her fingers forming a temple, then opening skyward to simulate an explosion.

"An eruption, maybe?"

She pondered the statement. "Diamonds have never been discovered in Tennessee. Yes, there were plenty of fault lines where magma could seep upward. And no, it hasn't happened yet."

"What about being pushed close to the surface?"

"When the Alleghenian Orogeny occurred and formed the Appalachian, the Allegheny, and the Cumberland mountains, it could have pulled stuff from down deep, but it's unlikely, and never proven." She felt giddy. "Rare, but possible."

Boyd frowned. "Too much of a long shot."

"I have no big cases at the moment."

"Little recoveries still bring cash into the business."

"I don't think the firm will suffer if I take some time off."

"How much time?"

"Two months."

"Nope."

"One month."

"We need guaranteed income."

"What if I use my vacation time?"

"You won't find anything in two weeks."

Boyd could be a hard ass at time, but Boyd was Boyd, and she knew what his second enjoyment in life was.

"Long time since your name was in a headline."

He rubbed his chin, a dead giveaway she had his interest.

"And the last two times were from my recoveries. Which you took credit for."

Boyd sat still, except for his thumb tapping one finger, then moving to the next one as if he was mentally counting.

Clouds blocked the sunshine, darkening the room. A chill replaced the warmth.

"Okay," he said.

"Good." She sat upright. "However, I want to be a partner. I want to own three percent and have my own office like this one."

"Time for you to leave."

"Have I ever lost a recovery?"

"This one can't compare to the piddling I've given you."

She took a deep breath. "If I find it, how about that partnership and an office?"

"I'll find it myself. You're good, but not this good."

How dare he say that. She was damn good, better than he

ever was. He purposely held her back. He didn't need another headline-grabber on his staff. "When was the last time you recovered anything newspaper-worthy?"

"Don't forget who you are speaking to. I can terminate your employment anytime."

The bastard.

She calmed herself, walked to his office door, closed it, then locked it. After looking through the glass plate wall into the gallery and seeing no one, she lowered the white blinds to guarantee against roaming eyes.

When Savannah-Jo sat on his desk, her skirt rose high on her thigh—as planned—revealing the blue fringe at the top of her stockings.

"We both know we like each other. Our offices would be adjoining and designed to block out the world. Like now."

"You're overlooking one problem." He stood and removed his jacket, then draped it over the back of his chair. "The mine went belly up. No more coal, and a penniless holding company. No one to pay a finder's fee."

This was more than she could have hoped for. "Sounds like finders' keepers. Two items went missing. One for you, one for me. A win-win."

Boyd undid his silk tie and laid it across his jacket. He unbuttoned his shirt. "Deal."

She laid on his desk sideways and propped her head with her arm. "But first, a memo declaring my partnership."

"My word is good."

His words were squat. Savannah-Jo undid another button on her blouse, revealing her full cleavage. "That's what the next button costs."

He sat back down and typed on his keyboard. "Partnership only."

"Everything." She toyed with her blouse. "And you get a complete package also."

"If you recover the goods, two percent, adjoining office, and lots of nights working late."

"Since you are making the agreement conditional, maybe I should, too."

"Sounds like you're worried you can't recover the items."

"I think these last two come with an office." She ran her finger along the edge of the next button.

"Will we always be compromising over every issue?"

"Negotiating."

The printer ejected a sheet of paper.

She checked to ensure it was printed on the company letterhead, then watched him sign it.

Sliding off his desk, she sat on his lap causing his chair to swivel so they faced the windows. The view from the top floor overlooking the Cumberland River was magnificent, the air clear enough for her to see her future.

Two percent… so easy.

Twelve

The sweet scent of butterscotch wafted over Kole as he stepped into Monterey's police department. An image of vanilla ice cream covered in a honey-colored, thick syrup swept through his mind. His stomach rumbled.

He shook the thought from his head. *Stay focused. Examine the evidence. Forget everything else. Coup or no Coup.*

"Morning, Fat Bear," Helen said from behind a dark pine counter in the reception area.

Three, five-inch-tall orchids with icy green blooms dominated a black laminated shelf behind her. Her brown hair was cut in an old-fashioned page-boy. Helen, in her forties, sported a different look every month. This one looked reserved. He wondered if Nashville had a medieval festival in progress.

"I brought you donuts." He handed her a rectangular, pink box with assorted temptations. "They're from Pete's."

"Coup isn't here."

"No problem. I came to see Dragging."

"He's in the back at his station. But Coup says you can't roam about. I have to escort you to wherever you want to go." She pushed her chair away from her desk.

"You don't have to." He waved his hands for her to sit. "Have a donut or two while they're still warm. I promise not to wander."

She opened the box and selected a chocolate-covered, jelly-filled, with red, white, and blue sprinkles. "I guess this once would be okay." She ripped a chunk out of the donut.

The man Kole wanted to see guarded the evidence locker

and was named after one of the greatest Cherokee leaders—war chief Dragging Canoe. Anyone who met the man, Cherokee or not, he'd tell the history of his namesake.

Dragging sat at a tiny wooden table in front of the small evidence locker no larger than a double closet, with a walk-in safe. Dragging logged detailed notes about everything that went in and out, and who wanted to see what was in a thick black notebook, its cover worn from constant use. The calm in the room created a sense of reverence. In some respects, the department was still in the '50s.

Dragging resembled the great chief, with his dark tanned skin which looked like the soles of moccasins. He wore a red, buttoned shirt and jeans over his six-foot frame, and people claimed his prominent nose was more sensitive than a bloodhound. Dragging took pride in his heritage and honored his namesake with a shaved scalp except for a shoulder length mullet of black hair at the back of his head.

"I need to see the evidence in the Miller case," Kole said.

"Not without the sheriff's permission." Dragging's voice was hard and cold like a winter wind. The man's eyes showed no warmth.

"I've got it here somewhere." Kole fumbled in his shirt and, front pockets of his jeans, and, lastly, the back pockets. He laid his wallet and keys on the desk. Not finding the imaginary notice, he sighed. "Must have left it at home."

"Too bad."

"You know I'm representing Miller, right?"

"The woman-killer?"

"Accused."

Dragging nodded.

"So, I have the right to see everything pertaining to the case." Kole stepped to the side of the desk.

Dragging stood and blocked his path to the storage locker. "Coup says if you try to bully your way past me, I'm to lock your ass up."

Kole stepped back. It would be easier to pass through a brick wall than try to get around Dragging.

It seemed suspicious that Coup didn't want him to see the evidence unless she was present. Was there something she didn't want him to discover? Did she plan to show him only what she wanted him to see? It didn't fit her personality to do so.

But there were too many ifs. He needed to see all of it. Or was it simply from the run-in he'd had with her years ago when he'd dynamited a dam someone had built upstream on his creek.

How could he appeal to Dragging?

"They treat you good here?" Kole asked.

"Better than they treated my ancestors."

"I know what you mean. My neighbors are trying to oust me." In 1775, an unscrupulous land speculator cheated the Cherokees out of their sacred hunting grounds, which comprised most of Tennessee and southern Kentucky. The white settlers poured over the steep Cumberland Mountains, razing the land and killing a majority of the wildlife in their westward movement. Chief Dragging Canoe had defended his people and land in a bloody, eighteen-year war. The odds were against him—outnumbered and out-gunned—and he died in 1792, a defeated man.

"You piss people off."

It was a statement, not a question. Kole grimaced. "You are a member of the Wolf clan, and I'm the Paint clan. We should band together. Help one another. Like the time before the settlers."

"I am Anivayah. You are Anivadi." Dragging's voice rumbled down the hallway. Then he smiled.

Dragging had used the Cherokee words for their respective clans. Membership was decided at birth, passed from mother to child since time began. But Dragging had smiled. He had accepted Kole. He knew their clans were close, tradition and blood demanded they work together.

"Fat Bear," Dragging said, "I cannot let you pass. My job would be in jeopardy. If I lose it, I will disrespect our people."

"I'm not asking you to bring shame onto you or our people."

Dragging crossed his arms.

Kole thumbed toward the front of the building. "I forgot to tell you—I brought donuts. Helen has them."

"I hate donuts."

Dragging's words made Kole take a step back. He thought everyone loved donuts. Now what? How could be appeal to the man?

It came to him. Dragging concerned himself with matters close to his heart the same as Grandfather. "I see someone vandalized the Standing Stone monument with orange spray paint." Kole referred to a twelve-foot-tall limestone rock which, at one time had marked the boundary between two Indian tribes. Today, it was a popular picnic site.

"A disgrace to our people."

"And it's right in front of the library. Bold criminals to do such a crime in a popular place."

"People who want to erase our heritage."

"I wanted to let you know that I plan to restore the monument since the city doesn't have funds to do so. I'll use my own money." He hadn't planned to do so, but it could be the item to persuade Dragging to let him inside the evidence locker.

Dragging stood there for what seemed hours before he said, "I have to use the can."

Kole watched Dragging walk to the restroom and step inside. After a few minutes, he guessed Dragging would be busy for a while.

An overhead fluorescent light flickered, throwing a greenish-white glow on rows of metal shelves. Three white storage boxes sat on the center rack. Inside the room, it was cooler than a butcher's freezer.

Monterey didn't keep much. County budget money was hard to get allocated to small towns. Thus, everything had to be sent to a more secure area to be digitized. Everything was transported to the neighboring town of Cookeville. Once a week, on Mondays—unless weather kept the authorities from coming up the mountain—whatever Monterey had was moved to the headquarters.

He found the "Miller" evidence box labeled with a black Sharpie and opened it. Inside were two items, both in plastic sleeves. The first one was a letter. It started with, "My dearest Simmons."

The handwriting was faint. It sounded like Aletha was going to leave Miller. That was out of character for a Mennonite. They married for life and stayed married even after death. The Mennonites believed marriage was a scriptural ordinance and not to be entered lightly. It was the same as Christ and His love for the church. Then again, that hadn't worked out well for Him— He'd been nailed to a cross.

Or did the letter mean something completely different?

He paused and listened. Helen was chit-chatting on the phone. Dragging hadn't emerged from the bathroom.

Kole fumbled with his phone. The damn thing had several functions and apps, half of which he had no clue how to use. He found the camera icon and snapped three photos of the letter.

The other item was a jewel, shaped like a diamond, but when he rotated it, blue and green colors flashed. It reminded him of the ocean when Grandfather and he had gone fishing in the Florida Keys.

They had anchored their skiff in the flats between the string of islands and the mainland. Standing in waist-deep water, they'd cast their lines as the morning sun had peeked over the horizon, causing an orange hue to creep over the flats.

Grandfather had caught the first fish, a tarpon. The animal's scales had reflected the harsh sun rays the same as the diamond he held in his hands. He'd been awed by the animal's beauty and how nothing could surpass nature. The horror of the dead Mennonite came to him, along with the realization that, at times, the cost of something magnificent was everything.

Kole placed everything back into the box and closed the lid. There wasn't much. The knife seemed to be the only damaging evidence against Miller. What was it that he didn't know? He needed to see the murder scene.

Time to leave and talk to the Mennonite. On the way to the front door, he knocked once on the restroom door.

Thirteen

A mid-morning, humid wind blew into the Plateau Café when the front door swung open. Coup stood by an old "Visit Rock City" advertisement, turned and saw a short woman with long, brunette hair stepping inside. The woman wore heels, tight-fitting pants, and a clingy blouse. Coup recognized Savannah-Jo Hunnicutt upon sight, since she had pulled her internet profile.

Coup waved her over. "You must be the investigator from Boyd's."

She had proposed to meet at the café in hopes Savannah-Jo would feel more at ease and maybe learn more from her. The woman had heard about the diamond and, although Savannah-Jo didn't state it, Coup knew she wanted to claim it. Her momma's tea would sour before that happened.

Coup had questions for Savannah-Jo. She felt that, if she knew where the diamond originated, how Aletha happened upon it, why the woman would swallow it, the answers would lead to the murderer. Was it Miller or not?

Beyond that, she wasn't sure what she was after, other than concrete evidence to back the prosecutor's case or leads to someone else. She liked Miller, even though the Mennonite community didn't. Maybe that was the reason she hoped he was innocent. For Miller, she'd put her feelings aside because justice was her job.

"Coup," said a middle-aged, black-haired waitress, "I'll have your order out faster than a squirrel after a nut."

The sun reflected off a window from across the street and

shot a beam of bright white through the café. Coup blinked. A flash of white blindness burned into her brain.

Sweetness, not now, she thought. She clenched her eyes and waited. Dizziness filled her. When she was about to empty her stomach of her morning breakfast, the spell passed. Damn side effect of her surgery.

Sheriff Couper motioned toward an aluminum table with a red-and-white checkered cloth in the diner's back corner.

As Savannah-Jo walked to the table, the scuffed pine floor bounced under her. She paused to look at the wall covered in historical pictures.

The floor creaked and pitched. Coup suspected the termites ate well.

"Apples are being harvested." Coup sat and crossed her legs. "So I ordered us tea and apple pie."

Savannah-Jo nodded toward the pictures of black-and-white photographs of Monterey in the '40s and '50s of downtown, the depot, and Tennessee Central disembarking passengers that lined the plywood walls. "Don't see any differences in the structures from then compared to now. This town is stuck in time."

Coup gave her the most pleasant smile she could muster. "You're wearing a nice fragrance."

"Thank you. Only one shop in Nashville carries it."

The waitress placed white porcelain cups and saucers with blue butterflies hand-painted on them on the table. She headed back to the kitchen.

"Are you from the plateau?" Coup asked.

"No, born and raised in Nashville."

"Your accent reminds me of people who have lived here for generations."

Savannah-Jo pulled her arms to her side.

To Coup, Savannah-Jo's trembling lips told her something bothered the woman.

Savannah-Jo handed Coup her business card—white, rectangular, thick cardstock with pink edges and glossy, raised black letters. "Boyd asked me to interview you in person."

"How is he? I haven't seen the old goat since my daddy passed. I hope he's doing as well as ever. Do they still call him the goat, or has that passed with time?"

"I've never heard of anyone referring to him in that fashion," Savannah-Jo said. "It has come to our attention that you've come across a Tarpon Diamond. I'd like to see it."

"As would a lot of people. But it's evidence in a murder case, so, as much as I'd like to show it to you, no."

"It belongs to us, and I've come to claim it."

"I would have thought the mining company owns it. Which is who?"

"Cumberland Rock and Sand, and they went under."

"Big loss to the town when they closed." Coup studied Savannah-Jo's face. The woman looked away and placed a hand over her mouth to stifle a yawn. There didn't seem to be any empathy in her. "If they are no longer in business, then it goes to the state. And in a few months, darlin', you can see it in Nashville's Natural History Museum. They offer tours. Something the law doesn't permit me to do."

The waitress returned, poured their tea, then placed slices of pie in front of them. "I'll check on you two in a bit."

"About twelve years ago, Boyd's Insurance and Recovery paid the claim from the train robbery," Savannah-Jo said.

"Interesting." Coup uncrossed her legs. "No robbery was reported to the city, county, or state police. But Cumberland Rock and Sand reported it as stolen to Boyd's?"

"Maybe they just reported it as lost." Savannah-Jo leaned back in her chair. "I'll check with Boyd."

"Ask him how a mining company loses a diamond? Did the owner have a hole in his pocket and it fell out?"

"I wouldn't know." Savannah-Jo shifted in her chair.

"Or did a thug jump the president of the company and steal it?"

"I wouldn't know." Savannah-Jo crossed her arms.

"And how did it end up with my murder victim?"

Savannah-Jo glanced around the room, inhaled a deep breath, then relaxed her arms.

"Are you telling me everything?" Coup's eyes narrowed. She felt Savannah-Jo was holding back. She didn't like it when people did. "But you know for sure it belongs to your company?"

"Yes."

"Then I need to see your proof of ownership."

"We are in the recovery business," Savannah-Jo said sternly. "Our firm finds works of art, precious jewelry, lost manuscripts and documents, anything insured for at least a million. Once we recover the item, the client pays us."

"That's right nice of you." Coup sipped her tea. "Write me a check. I found it."

"I could interpret your request as wanting a bribe." Savannah-Jo reached for some pie, tasted it, then pushed the plate away from her. "Boyd's Insurance has filed with the state rights of ownership for anything recovered from the robbery."

"Look, sweetie," Coup smiled again, "first you have to prove the item was stolen or lost from the train. Then, the state can notify me of your ownership. But it seems you can't even tell me if either occurred."

"I'm here on professional business." Savannah-Jo sipped her tea. She set the cup down and pushed the saucer over by the pie. "From one career person to another, I am asking, politely, to see the diamond. Then, if it matches our description, we'll file the paperwork with your office. If it doesn't, I'm out of your hair."

"Was it just one diamond? Or, you wouldn't know?"

Savannah-Jo clenched her jaw. "I'm not here to butt heads. I was hoping for some courtesy from your department."

Coup drank the rest of her tea and then forked a piece of warm pie packed with apples and cinnamon.

"You leave me no choice." Savannah-Jo hardened her words. "One last chance or I'll have a court order on your desk in the morning."

"You are as sweet as a honeybun, aren't you? My office is

down the street. You can't miss it. It has 'Police' written on it in large letters. The courier may deliver it there."

* * *

Savannah-Jo was disgusted with her interview with the sheriff. The cop had played her. She had underestimated Coup. From here on, she'd be better prepared and on her toes. And get what she wanted from the bitch.

She needed a new plan and a place to stay.

She drove her red Lexus convertible down the main street to the Imperial Hotel, a big difference with the roads in Monterey compared to Music City. This municipality had two lanes, instead of four, open routes instead of traffic jams, and had passed the designation of Dullsville years ago. Just one other vehicle was on the road, and it was a semi hauling cows.

She pulled across the street from the two-story, red-brick hotel with a white balcony and wicker rocking chairs. After popping the trunk, she removed her two suitcases and wheeled them inside to the reception desk. The hotel had a rustic country feel. Nice, if you liked living in the past. But she preferred neon bars, fine dining, and spas.

Inside, the place had polished, dark wood floors, a large oak counter for check-in, and a grand staircase as wide as the street she drove on. Not what she'd expected.

"Welcome," said a man behind the counter, speaking with a British accent, "to the Imperial Hotel."

She guessed his age at around fifty due to the white puffs of hair behind his ears in an otherwise black mane. He wore a black suit with a red tie. Probably the only man in this hick town who wore a suit.

"King size room," she said, "for an extended stay."

"We can accommodate your request." His blue eyes lit up. They were the same color as the deep mountain sky. "You may have our last room."

"Really? The place doesn't look busy. The whole town seems quiet."

"For now." He handed her a registration card to complete, then leaned across the counter and whispered, "In four days, there will be a murder trial. Lots of people coming to town to watch it."

"I heard about it on the news."

"Yes," he continued in his hushed voice. "A Mennonite is accused."

"Does he have a name?" She already knew the answer, but she'd learned long ago to first ask a few questions to gauge their response to the truth. Then, when she dug for more information, she'd know if they were lying or not.

"Memmo Miller. He has a dubious background. And his attorney pulled a fast one and was able to get him released."

"No?" She drawled out the word. "This town has a murderer roaming the streets?"

"Accused murderer," he said. "We mustn't jump to conclusions, but the whole town thinks he did it. Miller is in the custody of his attorney."

He took her hand, looked around the room, then focused on a closed door. "Management doesn't like us discussing anything with customers unless it's about encouraging them to have dinner here at the hotel."

"I'm just a single girl." She moved closer to him to where she could smell his musky cologne. "The news said Miller's attorney is John Kole. Does he have an office in town or is he an out-of-towner?"

"He's local and goes by the name of Fat Bear."

"Such an unusual name."

"He's Cherokee."

Time to ask a question the news hadn't revealed. "Does he live in town?"

"No, up in Whispering Pines. But I'm sure he's on Rattlesnake Mountain at Miller's place, going over their defense strategy."

This man was a wealth of information and willing to share.

A resource she could use and manipulate. For instance, the lay of the land.

The sting from Coup dissolved. Savannah-Jo felt elated; she was back on top.

She glanced at his brass nametag. "As I said earlier, *Reggie*, I'm by myself and starving. I hate to eat alone. What do you say? Will you have dinner with me?"

"Why don't I show you to your room?" He grinned.

"So nice of you."

Fourteen

Kole stopped his side-by-side in front of a dented, buck-shot-riddled "No Trespassing" sign. His plan was to fetch Miller and have the Mennonite show him where Coup had found the body. From this point, the gravel road ended, and two ruts cut by run-off started. It was the shortest route to the man's home. Hardwood trees blocked the morning light, causing the air temperature to drop ten degrees. The hairs on his arms stood at red alert. Dense foliage formed thorny, green walls seeking unsuspecting skin to slice. Miller's house was three more miles up the steep incline. To drive or walk?

In places, the drive looked uneven and sloped enough that if he angled his vehicle wrong, he'd roll it over, or, worse, rip the undercarriage apart. Best to walk.

As he opened the door to step out, a timber rattler poked his triangular head out of the shrubs. The snake flicked his tongue several times before crawling across the ruts.

Kole eased the door closed. The snake, thicker than his leg, looked to be five feet long and its brown body displayed black, zig-zag stripes. Rattlesnake Mountain lived up to its name.

Miller had walked this yesterday, after dark, with no concern. The man must have a guardian angel looking over him. Kole didn't have that amount of faith in any deity to guard him against rattlesnakes.

He closed the driver's door and decided it was best if he drove.

He had wrestled with his grandfather's advice about not

getting involved since leaving the bar. The spirit animals had visited his dreams last night and were on opposing sides. The only thought they'd shared was that it wasn't going to end well. The choices they'd presented had been limited.

The antelope had appeared first, and, after a minute or two, ran into the mist. He'd run also if he didn't love this area, the mountain views, the coolness of the waterfalls. He'd drive his side-by-side out of the state and never return, skirting what the Great Spirit had thrown in front of him. But then he'd never see Grandfather again unless he crept in with the shadows. No, that wasn't in his fiber.

When the badger had emerged in his dream, he'd known from his teachings that it'd been a good sign, and usually meant protection. But for whom? If he believed Miller was guilty and didn't attempt to find the truth, he'd be protecting himself. Why should he bear the burden of having to prove a man's innocence? He could float like a leaf on a gentle stream and whatever happened, happened. But there were too many wrongs in life to begin with, and it wasn't in his makeup to watch another occur.

The vehicle hit a pothole hard, which jarred his side-by-side. The impact forced open the passenger door and slammed it into a tree.

Damn, he'd been driving too fast. He was remembering his dream and not concentrating on the terrain. This murder was consuming him.

He stared at the door for several minutes. It was wedged into the trunk, and he'd have to get out to close it.

Sitting high in the vehicle, he focused on the ground for snakes. He wasn't worried about the mature ones. They'd learned that injecting venom required great energy, which was best exerted in times of danger. But adolescent rattlers hadn't learned that lesson. They'd strike and pump a man full. Grandfather had taught him to respect all life. Killing was not respecting, there were other was to get out of danger. Kole wondered if his grandfather ever met a rattle-shaking, coiled-to-strike, pissed-off snake. If he had, maybe the rule would be ignored for those buggers.

For the time being, danger didn't seem to be lurking about.

He jumped out of his side-by-side, then hastened over to the damaged door. He wiggled it free, then tried closing it. With relief, he heard it snap closed.

After getting behind the steering wheel, he engaged the transmission, and the vehicle crept forward.

What bothered him the most was Grandfather's warning. Trouble was hidden on this mountain top. The look on Grandfather's face had indicated lives were in danger—the type of peril where only evil could walk away.

He'd decided the animal spirits had reminded him that he had an obligation to Miller… and to do the right thing.

Fourteen minutes later, he pulled in front of Miller's tiny cabin.

The pine siding house was propped on concrete blocks and the flooring sagged between the lichen-covered supports. A front porch with no railing stretched across the front. A table and rocker pieced together from tree branches and trunks sat off to the left, gathering dirt.

A half-dozen chickens clucked as they roamed around the side, picking bugs out of the tall mountain grass. The home was inside a clear-cut area forty or so feet from the tree line. Probably to protect the dwelling from fires.

On top of the rusted, slanted, tin roof were hand-made solar panels—a hint Miller did have a few luxuries. Kole wondered if those luxuries included indoor plumbing.

He heard sheep *baa*ing from behind the house, along with the grunting of hogs. The oldest of security systems.

Miller stepped out the front door, wearing the same clothes he'd worn yesterday.

"Get in," Kole said.

"Where're we going?"

"To enter the bowels of Mother Nature."

Miller frowned. "I'm not going anywhere, and especially not near someone's bowels."

Kole reached under the dash and pulled out a Smith & Wesson .357 magnum revolver. Then he stepped out of his side-by-side, aimed, and fired.

The echo rolled down into the valley.

Fifteen

Coup returned to her office, drained from meeting with Savannah-Jo Hunnicutt. The lady was definitely a city person—a career woman—who used every option, tool, and asset she had to work her way up the cooperate ladder. She respected assertive women, ones who had goals, and a plan to fulfill them, but something was off with Savannah-Jo. Coup wasn't sure of the woman's true purpose. There was something else besides recovering and returning antiquities.

Inside the building, she passed Helen at her desk, who was on the speakerphone, listening to a woman's voice reporting a cow strolling down the state road and could the sheriff round it up. She hurried past.

Before entering her office, she checked the crypt. Dragging was at his desk, reading what looked like an ancient document. All was quiet. She smiled and took a few minutes to relax and breathe, before thinking about the Tarpon Diamond.

Diamonds, sapphires, rubies, and other gems women and men adorned themselves with were an obsession for some. She, however, would like about a hundred acres with a brook running through it, lots of pasture, a herd of mustangs roaming on it, and a crew to maintain everything. Maybe someday, when she retired. She smiled again. It'd never happen. She'd never quit being sheriff. Her daddy had passed that trait onto her.

She glanced down at her desk. Fed Ex packages, courier pouches, and regular mail were piled on the right, and daily and weekly reports on the left. Helen was good at her job. More than a dispatcher; she was the office.

In the center of her desk was a standard white envelope with her name typed in bold caps on the front.

Coup settled into her chair. Strange that Helen hadn't alerted her to the special correspondence.

She picked it up. No return address or stamp.

Coup slit it open and read the single enclosed sheet.

Only one person ever wrote her death threats.

She buzzed Helen. "Is Charlie Walker still in the county pen?"

"No," Helen replied. "He was released two weeks ago and preached his first sermon last Sunday since his six-month stint."

"Let me guess. It was on how moonshining isn't a sin but doing God's work."

"His Freedom Christianity congregation is growing, and they love him immensely."

Coup flipped off the intercom. Charlie sent her a death threat every month, usually using the postal service. The man had control of the English language and wrote with metaphors and flourish.

This letter lacked those details.

Helen knocked on the doorway frame. "I'm going to Cookeville for my first oil change."

"Still loving the new car smell?" Coup said. Helen had bought a new Honda Accord. One as blue as a deep pool of water at the base of a waterfall.

"Come outside. I want to show you the remote start feature."

Coup followed Helen out the door, still carrying Charlie's letter. She wanted to ask Helen when he had dropped by. But first, she'd let Helen revel in her happiness. Each day she had to witness a new feature of the car. Yesterday was the giant backup screen.

She could tell Helen was jubilant. The woman had trotted out the front door. By the time Coup stepped outside, Helen was on the opposite side of the employee parking lot and had the black fob in her hand, pointing it toward the waxed-buffed car.

Coup heard the distinct double *beep* of the door unlocking, then another single *chirp* to start the car.

The *whoomph* of an explosion filled her ears and a blast of hot air hit Coup and pushed her backward. She hit the ground hard. The world spun and became hazy.

Red and orange flames leaped upward. The trunk popped open, and the hood flew into the street. Fire engulfed the car. The smell of burnt rubber filled the air.

Heat scorched the parking lot. Bells and sirens rang from somewhere.

Through the black smoke, she found Helen lying face up, burn holes in her clothing, her hair singed, her scalp exposed near her forehead. She checked for breathing and heartbeat.

Nothing.

Someone yelled, "Call 9 1 1!"

Coup dragged Helen to the grass and started chest compressions.

"Breathe, Helen," she said. "God dammit it, breathe."

Sixteen

Kole paused in front of the entrance to Devil's Cave. The hike from Miller's cabin had been done in silence because of the gun discharge incident. The cool air blowing out of the cave's dark tunnel felt refreshing on his face after the August heat. But, along with the breeze, was a hint of dampness, something earthy, and the lingering scent of rotting flesh. He wondered what he'd find in the bowels of the earth.

What he wanted to find was something, *any*thing, that would lead to Miller's innocence. A back door would allow the killer to slip in and out of the cave unnoticed. But why kill the Mennonite woman in the first place?

He needed to work fast. The judge wanted the trial to start in four days.

"You didn't have to kill the snake," Miller said. Sadness coated his words.

"I counted twenty-one rattles on his tail." Kole had a tough time understanding how Miller had become attached to such a deadly snake. One lunge from the seven-foot reptile and a man would be dead before he felt the bite.

"He was old."

"Still deadly and he was coiled to strike."

"He could have been cold."

"In this heat? Not likely." Kole pulled two midnight blue flashlights from his backpack and tossed one to Miller. He pointed to the black hole in the mountain. "You first."

"I will fear no evil." Miller slid headfirst down the shaft.

Kole had explored many caverns, caves, and mineshafts. He'd

even fished in a lake three hundred and forty-seven feet below the surface. But this one gave him shivers from head to toe. His spirit animal wouldn't venture in here. No benevolent spirits roamed below. The cave looked like it had seen its share of evil and smelled of more than one painful death.

He touched the knife buckled to his belt. It'd been a gift from Grandfather and blessed with morning smoke on the spring equinox. He doubted it would deter whatever he met in the darkness.

A weak laugh passed his dried lips as a feeble attempt to encourage himself. Still, he shimmied in behind Miller.

He pushed aside basket-sized rocks. Their rough jagged edges indicated they'd broken loose recently. Holding his breath, he tried to sense any trembles in the ground, a hint of something passing through the substrate. He hoped this wouldn't turn into a tomb.

After leaving the shaft, he crawled into the larger room where Miller stooped in a circle of bright white light.

"You can stand a little," Miller said.

Kole did. The front of his shirt and pants were covered in muddy slime. *Get a grip.* He didn't say it out loud, not wanting Miller to know he was uncomfortable in this pit—not that that would be a surprise to Miller. The Mennonite knew him well.

"This is where we found my beautiful Aletha. Her skeleton eye sockets now haunt my dreams every night."

Kole panned his light in a back-and-forth pattern. With each sweep, he pointed the beam deeper into the cavity.

"And I'm not sure if I want them to go away or not." Miller's words were slow and heavy with sadness,

Kole felt for the man. For years, the community had told Miller Aletha had run off with another man to escape their restrictive lifestyle. But his faith strong had been strong that she hadn't. Then he learned someone had murdered her, and society thought he'd done it. For a man of God, Miller had had his share of tribulations. "Maybe you should picture her on better, happier days. What did she look like on your wedding day?"

After a pause, Miller said, "She'd placed purple irises in her hair. The purple to signify the holiness of marriage."

It didn't seem to Kole that the image of Aletha on her wedding day perked Miller up any. His words sounded more depressing.

Kole continued into the darkness. He saw no signs of anyone venturing this far back, including the sheriff or her detectives. After counting three hundred and eighty-seven steps, he stopped. A foot-high pile of what looked like dark brown grains of rice lay in front of him.

"Bat guano." Miller knelt, then pulled a bag from his pocket. "Rose enthusiast love this crap. They'll pay thirty dollars a pound for it."

"I'm not hauling shit out of here."

Miller scooped some into a baggie.

Something flashed in Kole's light. "Stop."

Inside the pile was a lipstick tube. The base was pitted and patched with orange, and rust spotted the cylinder. "Take a picture of this," he said to Miller.

"How about a video?" Miller pulled out his cellphone, then a bright white light washed across the possible evidence.

After a few seconds, he said, "Done."

For a man whose religion shunned modern conveniences, Miller was avant-garde.

Using a handkerchief, Kole picked the silver tube up and twisted the base.

The waxy substance slid out. The tip was a dirty brown, but, further down, the true color emerged. "Know anyone who wore purple war paint?"

"Jerimiah," Miller said, "Chapter four, verse thirty, 'And you, O desolate one, what do you mean that you dress in scarlet, that you adorn yourself with ornaments of gold, that you enlarge your eyes with paint?' No, my Aletha would not use such devil's instruments."

Kole didn't see the harm in women's beauty products. But he

also knew the Mennonite women wouldn't do anything to cause impure thoughts in men—at least in public. And for some reason he couldn't explain, he wondered if Coup ever wore any. If she did, it wasn't obvious. "Anyone she may have been friends with?"

"No one in our congregation."

"Outside of it?"

"We keep mostly to ourselves."

Yes, they did. Kole slipped the handkerchief-wrapped tube into his backpack. In the recess of his mind, he remembered reading how the inside of each tube had a serial number which could be traced to the manufacturer, then to the store that sold it. Would that help in any way in learning who had dropped it here and when? He hoped this find would play out and not dead end into the crapper.

Kole walked farther into the cave.

The slow, steady drip of water off the ceiling helped him count his steps. The floor had a steady downward slant, and the rocks were polished smooth. This hole in the earth often flooded.

He swung his light back and forth, looking for cracks and cervices where the water flowed.

He found none, which confirmed his suspicions that the water flowed out the cave's mouth and into Devil's Creek.

"Miller," he said. "Did it look like it might rain today?"

"Cumulonimbus clouds were forming."

"Are there thunderstorms in the forecast?"

"Let's pray not, or we might be swimming out of here."

"My thoughts as well." Kole stopped. The prudent action would be to turn around and trot out of here. But he wasn't done searching. Cold air brushed against his face. The only reason the wind blew would be because of a back entrance. He wanted to find it.

He recalled a cave-in had occurred at the entrance years ago. Folks still talked about the day the ground shook, and some had thought the Second Coming was happening. Did the four-point-oh shock happen during or after Aletha's murder?

"When do you think the earthquake happened?" he asked Miller.

"Right after Aletha was knifed and killed."

"How'd you deduce that?"

"The Lord punished who did it. I'm sure we'll find their body somewhere in here. The Lord loved my wife. He'd condemn the person with a long and painful death."

"Don't tell the prosecutor you think those two events happened at the same time, or she'll use it against you."

Kole came to a pool. It stretched out in front of him as far as his flashlight reached. He stepped into it.

The water felt cool like the first snow of winter. He sloshed forward and sent ripples washing into the rock walls. The ceiling rose above them another nine feet. The bottom felt as smooth as the dry area had. At his feet, the water was clear. Small pebbles glinted back at him. He scanned his light across the still surface, looking for changes in water color—blue or green shade indicated depth.

He found none, except for brown stains. Pointing his light up showed the ceiling covered in bats.

Miller pulled him back. "Give them a wide berth."

"Afraid they'll bite you?"

"No." Miller shone his light on a single bat. Its nose was blanketed in white spots. "Pseudogymnoascus destructans. A deadly fungus. Don't get any on you."

For a man who lived in isolation and never had never gone beyond the eighth grade, Miller's intelligence was something to be marveled at.

Kole sloshed through the water, keeping close to the side, and an eye out for fungus droppings and a change in water color.

He doubted they'd fall into a chamber. He surmised the water would drain out of where a well shaft might lay. The thought caused him to test the floor with each step.

After another fifteen minutes, they came to a waist-high ledge.

Kole tossed his light onto it and pulled himself upward. It looked like the tunnel went another twenty feet or so, then stopped.

"Looks like a dead end," he said.

Miller shined his light into the darkness. The beam yellowed.

Kole put his light on top of Miller's confirming the tunnel ended. He saw nothing but pocked and cracked limestone. The coolness of the breeze felt more robust against his body, and he didn't believe they were at the end. The only explanation was that the walls were like Swiss cheese—minuscule holes by the thousands let air pass through the rock.

Then his light flickered.

"Guess it's time for fresh batteries." He slid off his pack.

"No. Your spirits are talking to you."

"Then ask your God what they are saying."

"Proverbs say a scoffer seeks wisdom and finds none." Miller took his light and shined it in different directions. When he aimed the light upward, the beam flickered again but showed an opening. "You should trust the spirits."

Kole studied the opening. "Unless we are going to experience rapid weight loss, neither of us are getting by in that hole."

"But you found the back door," Miller said.

Kole was pleased. One part of his theory was in place. He continued to gaze upward. The shaft twisted to one side, but it looked like a halo had formed at that point. "A teenager could do it."

He pulled a flare from his pack. "I want you to back out of this cave and climb up the side to where you think this hole exit. I'll give you twenty minutes before I light it."

"Injun send'm smoke signal." Miller headed back to the entrance.

Damn. Miller knew that Kole didn't like the word injun. Next time he'll shoot the Mennonite instead of the snake.

Seventeen

Leaving Kole below, Miller climbed outside Devil's Cave. The air lost its earthy smell and now had a hint of pine, which reminded him of the day he'd proposed to Aletha. They'd been in a cluster of millennial trees, with the red cardinals filling the crisp morning air with their slow trills.

He looked up at the mountain's steep incline. It appeared impossible to climb and he wondered if the Romans had thought the same thing when they'd gotten a look at Masada. When the conquerors had reached the top, all they'd found were dead bodies.

The image of Aletha seeped into his mind. Seeing where his lovely wife had been murdered brought back the sight of the hollow eye sockets in her skull. Reality had set in. The haunting was no longer confined to his dreams. What was next?

He found footholds in the weathered rock to hold him, and he used spruce trees to pull himself upward on the rocky terrain. At times, he had to use out-cropping, and the limestone bit into his hands and legs as if he was being punished for long-ago sins.

Of which he had many. Some, he asked forgiveness for, which was granted. And for others, he hoped the Lord looked the other way.

After what seemed like hours, he reached a narrow, flat strip of land on the side of the mountain. By tracking the yellow sun across the sky, he knew only fifteen or twenty minutes had passed. He'd never noticed this bed before, but guessed it was what remained of an old railroad line.

Waist-high green grass and wood ferns had taken ownership of the even ground. The route followed the bend in the hillside, which perched on a drop-off and gave him an expansive view of the valley. He marveled at the deep blue Tennessee sky. Aletha had always said they would see this again in heaven.

The pain in the palm of his left hand caused him to examine it. He saw a small puncture wound seeping blood. The ooze looked dark red against his cracked skin and reminded him of Jesus's nail-pierced hands. He pulled a soiled handkerchief from his back pocket to wrap the laceration.

Seeing the blood brought a thought to him. Could he kill the person who murdered Aletha?

He felt a fever rush through him. She'd been knifed, and, most likely, hadn't died immediately. She would have bled out— a slow, painful way for her life to end. He could see her in his mind, laying prone on the rough rock, saying one last prayer. And, knowing her loving heart, she'd been seeking forgiveness for the one who'd stabbed her.

Tears came to his eyes. He didn't wipe them away, allowing them to cake in the dust on his face.

Whoever did this to his wife was no person, but an evil beast. He *could* end the life of such a creature.

Would he use his hunting rifle and fill the murderer's limbs with holes, a final shot into the chest? Or would he be filled with rage and break the person's neck like a worthless stick? No, he would extract an eye for an eye, and plunge his longest, sharpest knife into the evil heart.

He paused and said, "Forgive me, Father, for my unholy thoughts," and then said for all to hear, "Deuteronomy, chapter 32, verse 35, 'It is mine to avenge, sayeth the Lord.'"

He didn't feel any better. Was God's justice swift, and the person already in hell, being punished? Or was the person still alive and enjoying the fruits of the earth?

He eased along the railroad bed. A short piece of rusted iron was embedded in the ground, disappearing into the soil after several steps. He was unsure what to do.

Aletha would want him to live in peace, which he did, and forgive others, which he didn't. But all doubts on Aletha actions have been answered. He thanked God she hadn't run off into the land of darkness.

However, a man was the head of his family. His role was to provide, protect, and love, to guide his family in living a just and God-fearing life. He also remembered another Deuteronomy verse: "Justice, and only justice, you shall pursue, declared the Lord."

He saw a puff of gray smoke spiraling upward, staining the sky, looking like an old man with a long, weathered beard, anger hardened on the face.

Then red flames and smoke rose out of the ground too thick for him to see through it.

The fire was an answer to prayer, and, with relief, he knew what to do.

Eighteen

Kole looked upward and studied the narrow tunnel that created the cave's back door. It frustrated him that he could not shimmy through it.

If he could climb, then he'd prove that there was another way a human could enter or leave the cave. Thus, if an earthquake had occurred when Aletha had been killed, and the tremor had closed the front entrance, someone who knew the cave—or was desperate—could have escaped, thus the reason no second skeleton was found.

He had to know if it was possible. It could help Miller's defense.

How could he prove Miller's innocence? The only fact he really had was that Aletha had been killed in this cave with Miller's knife, a fact the prosecutor would bring up and hammer the jury with. And since there was no exact time of death, he couldn't prove Miller had been elsewhere when she'd been murdered.

Water droplets hitting the underground pool echoed around him. Pointing his flashlight toward the sound, he watched tiny concentric circles ripple to the edges, as if—as his grandfather would say—the cave was trying to tell him something?

Or was the dripping water a ground spirit telling him to be patient?

Miller had suggested the earthquake had occurred seconds after Aletha had been killed. The murderer had found the back opening to the cave, then crawled through it, and escaped to freedom with no suspicion of what he had done.

Two gigantic assumptions.

He shined his light up into the hole, twisting the beam in different directions, hoping to see a way to scoot out. The smell of fresh pine needles filtered in from the outside, the fresh air encouraging him.

Damn it. He had to change one assumption into fact—that someone *could* leave the cave by a second way.

He was going through that opening.

Grabbing a rock, he pulled himself upward into the opening by bracing his boots against the rock sides. Turning his body onto his side enabled him to continue and slip past a bulging stone. Stretching both arms in front of him elongated his body, which allowed him to squeeze into the narrow hole.

The passageway looked to be about thirty feet in length. He spotted a dim glow at the far end.

Digging his toes into the limestone, he formed a niche, pushing, and squirming as hard as he could.

He gained a foot, maybe two.

At times, he found a handhold and pulled. Repeating the process of toe and handholds, he made progress. A feeling of satisfaction overcame him. He was going to be able to breakthrough. But, even with the sweet breeze, sweat formed on his face.

He snaked his way several more feet. The flow of the air was stronger and full of grassy scents. He swore he could see blue sky and green trees looming over him, yellow trilliums dipping downward. The sweet-sweet-sweet song of a warbler drifted down to him as if encouraging him to bust through. He was close.

Wiggling his boot, he searched for another foothold. Confident he'd found a solid one, then dug his heel in and surged forward.

A crack of rock splitting and dislodging boomed in his ear. His boot no longer sat on something solid but dangled into nothingness. Then, with no time to react, his body contorted and fell, banging against one side, then the other. Pain ripped into his leg.

Something dug into his side. He craned his head and looked

down. Blood covered broken needle stalagmites, sharp formations of rock with razor edges and stiletto points. And, by the darkened stains on other pieces, he wasn't the first to have been sliced.

Stain colors revealed much, Grandfather used to say. On one of their hikes through the rough country, Grandfather had shown him how to use a native herb and rub the plant onto the stained object, then roll it in the sunlight beside hot coals from a campfire to determine it was human or not, an art not accepted by forensic science, but Kole knew by testing the theory when he had accidentally cut himself once that it was very accurate. And common sense dictates that bright red was recent, dark or black showed aged, and gray indicated an ancient death.

In the dim light, he must have missed them when he wiggled his way through the tunnel. And now, one spearing his leg.

He let his body slide down the hole and onto the cave's floor.

Blood soaked his pant leg and ran down to the top of his boot. Using his knife, he cut the jeans. A four-inch gash oozed sticky hemoglobin. He pulled back the skin flap and flicked out pieces of rock. One piece had his blood and staining from long ago. Fumbling through his backpack, he found his first aid kit, then tossed the broken stalagmite into a side pocket.

"Oh hell." He sucked in a breath, biting back a scream as he poured a disinfectant into the wound. After his breathing returned to normal, he placed gauze over the gash, then wrapped his leg with duct tape.

He washed the blood from his hands in the water and then tested his leg.

He could put weight on it and walk. It was going to hurt like hell for several days, not to mention, leave another ugly scar. He had several on his body, and they all came with an unpleasant story.

Disgusted with his failure and the injury, he proceeded with the original plan and removed the plastic off a flare. He examined the black ignitor surface and, satisfied it was intact, scratched the cap across it.

A red flame shot out, giving the cavern an eerie glow.

Shielding his eyes with one hand, he used the other to toss the flare up into the tunnel. It lodged itself about halfway up the hole, hissing and flickering there.

He sat on the damp ground. It wasn't long before he heard Miller yell, "I see the smoke!" Then, a few minutes later, "Found the second entrance to the cave! I'll meet you at the cave entrance."

Kole favored his leg as he retraced his steps out of the cave. Every twenty or thirty steps, he applied pressure to his wound to relieve some pain. The bleeding had stopped, but it felt like a piece of the stalagmite was still lodged in him. He'd let Grandfather tend to it. Maybe even let him perform a healing ceremony.

A thought came to him as he waded through the underground pond, and it stayed with him as he crawled through the tunnel to daylight. If he was going to have a scar, and if the murderer had escaped through the back entrance, would he have been scared also?

The rock had been stained from blood from a long time ago. The beam from the flashlight had made it difficult to determine its age, but outside in the natural light, he might be able to tell because, as Grandfather would say, "Nature reveals nature."

He finished his thought as he stepped outside of the cave. The afternoon sun shone brightly. He blinked several times, giving his eyes time to adjust. But there was something else besides the harsh sunlight—a bluish-gray reflection halfway up the tree line. Not of nature, but man-made.

Instinct forced him to drop facedown onto the ground.

A rifle shot shattered the silence.

He lifted his head just enough to see that, above moss-covered rocks in front of him, his worn hat with a large caliber bullet hole in it.

Neither he nor Miller had brought guns.

He started to hyperventilate, his heart banging against his ribs hard enough to crack them, and his spine tightening as if being crushed like a boulder had landed on him.

Who wanted him dead?

Nineteen

Coup stood outside the historical mansion of T. J. Birdwell. Any monied Tennessean who was second-generation or more knew the history of the white, two-story home built by an American officer in the Revolutionary War, purchased by the first Birdwell who'd moved to Nashville after the War of 1812. The second set of Birdwell's had enlarged it after the Civil War. They'd added the wrap-around porch and eight double sets of white Grecian columns. They'd also invested in the railroad.

The home and history impressed Coup, but it wasn't her taste. It didn't give off welcoming vibes, and she wondered if the house reflected its occupants. She hoped not.

The current Birdwell had been the CEO of the Tennessee Central Railroad at the time of Aletha's murder.

Coup had researched TCR's old timetables; the schedules—times and days of the week—had stayed the same. And, interestingly, there'd been no special runs listed. But then, why had the silver-domed train made a special run that night—something that hadn't happened before or after, unless the events had been removed from their files. Someone had to orchestrate all of it, from the midnight ride to the coverup. She decided to start with Birdwell, since most of the upper management from that time had passed away. Coup wanted answers about that train.

She walked up the double flight of marble stairs that were wide enough to hold a cottage. The sun's reflection from the polished stonework forced her to shield her eyes. The sweet scent of honeysuckle filled her lungs.

After a few heart-pounding seconds, she opened her eyes, and, with relief, found her sight had returned to normal. She pulled a cord by the ten-foot-high white double doors, and a bell tinkled inside. The house had no modern doorbell. The antebellum house felt a hundred years out of time and place.

A young black man, attired in a black suit, white shirt, black tie, gray vest, and white gloves, answered the door. "Yes," he said, stringing out the word.

"I'm here to see Mr. Birdwell."

"And you are?"

"Sheriff Coupland of Monterey. I guess you didn't recognize the outfit." She had pressed it early that morning while drinking her coffee. She skipped a full breakfast because she never felt at ease dealing with the upper class. Monterey was made up of rural, hard-working folks doing manual labor like farming, ranching, and mining. Most didn't have much, and what little extra they earned, went into the plate on Sunday mornings or toward helping a neighbor.

"Do you have an appointment?" The man stood concrete still; tornadic winds couldn't knock him down. "He has a full day of meetings in town."

"This is a polite social call about a murder."

"Should I call the law firm where Mr. Birdwell serves on the board of directors?"

"Did you not understand when I said, 'polite social call'? Or do you want me to show up with every squad car from our city?" She hoped he didn't call her bluff. Monterey only had one department vehicle, and she had driven it here.

With a facial expression that said, "Commoners," he replied, "Please wait here. I will see if Mr. Birdwell is home and available." He closed the door.

Coup stared at the wood grains in the door in disbelief before shoving a loose tendril of hair behind her ear. Rude, arrogant, and he had a disregard for southern manners, not to mention the law.

What to do? Open the door, walk in, and demand to see

Birdwell? No. If he were home, he'd just disappear somewhere in this mansion. She couldn't do a room-to-room search.

Should she get a summons and have him appear in her office? Nope. He'd send an army of lawyers.

Maybe an arrest warrant. That'd work… except she had no charges to bring against him, bless his little old, stinking heart.

She waited and tried to tamp down the anger rising in her.

It seemed like twenty minutes had passed before the door opened again, but it was less than three when she checked her watch.

"Follow me," said the same man who'd first greeted her. "Mr. Birdwell is relaxing in the arboretum." He started down a long hallway. "Please watch your tone and pick your words wisely. This is a genteel household."

She rolled her eyes. "I'll try not to track in any dirt."

The floor was made of cedar planks laid diagonally. Both sides of the wide passageway opened onto rooms as large as her house. She passed a library, a study, a ballroom, formal dining room, and, finally, came to the back of the house that looked upon an arboretum.

"Wait here," the butler said, then offered an aloof smile and approached the pool. "Sir, the sheriff." Then he turned and walked, stiff-legged, back into the house.

The front part was enclosed in glass, with marble surrounding an oversized swimming pool. Blue-and-gold macaws, green parrots, and yellow songbirds perched on orchid-covered tree limbs in the steamy mist. Lianas grew on trellises and stretched across wood beam archways over a bubbling hot tub surrounded by banana trees.

Cement dolphins on both sides spit water into the pool. Birdwell breast-stroked to the shallow end, which was crescent-shaped with a set of concrete steps. Once waist deep, he used a brown cane to help him navigate out of the water and into an oversized cushioned chair.

"Please join me," he said.

She stepped onto the concrete patio that surrounded the pool.

"I don't believe I've had the pleasure." He shook her hand, then motion her to a matching chair. Brown skin clung to his eighty-two-year-old boney frame. Parts of his scalp peeked through his white hair.

"Sheriff Mary Beth Coupland," she said. "From Monterey."

"I'm assuming your uninvited presence has nothing to do with a request for a donation to the Policeman's Benevolent Fund."

"It doesn't. It's police business." Birdwell was being polite, as dictated by his society, but letting her know her unannounced visit was an annoyance and unwanted.

"Then I must inform you that no such discussion can take place without the presence of my attorneys."

"Just a few quick history questions."

"Call my secretary to set up an appointment. I'm sure we can meet sometime next year."

She didn't like the rich or powerful; they acted above the law, and everything was on their schedule.

She exhaled and calmed herself as much as she could. "I only need five minutes of your damn time."

Birdwell shifted in his chair. From the expression on his face, she figured that a woman had never talked to him in such a bold manner.

"I knew another Sheriff Coupland whose speech was just as salty," he said. "Any relation?"

"My father."

"I see." A flash of anger swept across his face, then it softened and was replaced with sadness. "I'm having an early lunch, if you care to join me. I have a debt I need to repay to your dad. Please agree to my invitation."

Her dad had never mentioned anyone owing him anything or had ever spoken about the Birdwells. Her curiosity piqued, she replied, "I am a tad bit hungry."

"Excellent. Charles will show you where to change into something more appropriate."

"No need. This is police business, and I should stay as dressed."

"I guess I wasn't clear earlier. For business, attorneys must be present. For a social luncheon, on the other hand, require something other than a uniform."

"I don't carry an extra set of clothes in my trunk."

"You'll find Charles prepares for everything. He is quite resourceful."

"This is highly unusual. I must decline."

"From what I know of your father, he would not feel this would tarnish your reputation and would approve."

How were Birdwell and her father connected? "Then just this once."

"Charles!" he called out.

"Follow me, miss," Charles said.

Where the hell had he come from? This doorman spooked her.

"I'll change also," Birdwell said, "and meet you back here in, say, fifteen minutes?"

"Splendid."

She followed Charles down a wide hallway she hadn't noticed before. They seemed to head toward the far side of the house—the servant's quarters from another era, she assumed.

But she was wrong.

They entered a spacious room with vaulted ceilings and bay windows. Tapestries hung on the walls, depicting the history of the house and grounds. Several oversized, stuffed chairs and day beds filled the center of the room, and floor mirrors were placed evenly apart.

In another time, this was where the ladies would have gathered to relax and shed their gowns and ill-fitting corsets after a formal dinner. Where they could have gossiped in private before the final evening drink.

Charles stepped into a walk-in closet larger than her house and studied assorted ladies' clothes hanging on the three walls. He pulled a yellow sundress and matching flats, then set them on a day bed. "These should fit you nicely," he said, then closed the door as he left.

It had been a while since she worn anything frilly, and the one-hundred percent linen was cloth she could never afford. She was surprised by how well it fit and couldn't help a smile from forming. Charles sure knew how to size up a woman.

Once changed, she opened the door.

Charles was waiting. "I'll have your uniform placed in your car," he said. "You may keep the dress as a gift from Mr. Birdwell." He then led her back to the pool area.

Birdwell, wearing slacks, an open shirt, and a jacket, stood beside a round glass table with two metal chairs. He addressed a black woman standing off to the side. "Jasmine, refreshments, please."

Some old southern traditions wouldn't disappear until another generation of old money died—*if* this country was lucky. "You knew my dad?"

"Quick story. I had business on the plateau." He held her chair for her, then sat opposite her. "Traffic was light, and I was ahead of schedule and decided to drive on Route Seventy to go up the mountain. I'm sure you know the road."

"A two-laner full of sharp curves. It has beautiful overlooks, but the asphalt is crumbling, and you must proceed with caution at certain mile markers."

"Exactly. Well, that day, black clouds came over the mountain from the east suddenly and brought a downpour—four inches in an hour, I was told later. With the wet road and no visibility, I went over the embankment and plunged six-hundred and fifty feet."

She inhaled sharply, wondering how he survived.

"Not to bore you, so I'll make this short. Your dad was the first one on the scene, pulled me out of my car, and rushed me to

Cookeville Medical. As he pulled me out, the car tumbled the rest of the way down the mountain, hit a boulder, and was crushed. If not for your dad, I'd be dead instead of having a limp. I vowed to repay the debt to him, but never had the opportunity. I'd like to pay my debt to you. Ask your questions."

"My visit concerns a murder that happened twelve years ago."

"Not sure how I could be connected to it in any way."

"I believe the Tennessee Central unknowingly played a part."

The macaws squawked when Jasmine returned carrying tall, frosted flutes on a silver serving tray. She placed the drinks on the table, along with dishes of crab salad. Then she departed as silently as she'd arrived.

Birdwell held his glass up for a toast. "To Tennessee."

"Tennessee," Coup said. Her throat caught on fire as the brown liquid slid down, causing her to scrunch her face.

Birdwell must have seen the reaction on her face as he said, "It's called Lynchburg lemonade. Made with the finest Jack Daniels has to offer."

"They forgot the lemons."

"Jasmine," Birdwell said, and it seemed like she stood at his side before he finished saying her name. "Ms. Coupland will have to return to work after our lunch. Please bring her something more suitable." Then he said to Coup, "My apologies."

"My fault," she said. The burn in her stomach matched the heat on the porch, which was thick, and she was thankful for the loose dress. "Back to my question, please."

"Are you accusing one of my trains of running over someone?"

Coup told him about finding Aletha's skeleton and the diamond.

Birdwell slipped on a pair of dark sunglasses as sunlight beamed into the room while she talked about the midnight run of the railroad and the myth of it being robbed.

He didn't comment but stabbed the crab meat with a fork.

To be polite, she followed his lead, and they ate in silence. The meat was full of oceanic flavor. She reminded herself not to gobble it down.

Jasmine returned and set a glass on Coup's side of the table then removed the other one.

"A single diamond, you say," Birdwell said, grinning.

She guessed he wasn't good at poker… or *was he*? "Should I have found more?"

He shrugged. "I couldn't say."

"You know something I don't?" She inhaled. He knew something, but what was it? Was it that the train was robbed, and he knew the people who did it? And had he ordered justice to be served to those people? It wasn't uncommon in those times for the community to have blood on their hands.

"From twelve years ago?"

"Yes."

"You expect me to remember everything from twelve years ago?"

She raised an eyebrow.

"Well, I suppose I could check the records, but I'm retired. I no longer have any pull with the company. Maybe a search warrant would be better suited?"

Jasmine returned with seared tuna sprinkled with a dark, thick sauce. She refilled their glasses, then carried off the empty salad dishes.

Coup sipped her sweet pink lemonade. There was no trace of alcohol. She hoped Birdwell was not offended by the change of her refreshment because these people based everything on manners. She had to comply with their culture before she could expect any cooperation. If she played nice, her gut told her Birdwell clearly remembered the midnight run and, he wouldn't have to check any files.

"Yesterday, I had an insurance property retriever in my office. A very nice Nashvillian, like y'all are, here in our capital."

Birdwell smiled.

"She thinks someone robbed the train but declined to tell me of what."

"And you think it was this diamond?"

"Forensics can't tell me precisely, but, yes, I think both events occurred within a few days of each other. Possibly within a few hours." She sampled the tuna. Flavors flooded her mouth. The rich knew how to eat. The lemonade seemed to enhance the red filet.

Jasmine trotted back with a cheesecake dessert. The maid seemed to appear and disappear out of thin air.

"You must think this diamond is worth quite a sum for the Central to make a special run to retrieve it."

"I can determine that it has a terrific value, but not enough to justify the run. But if it is one-of-a-kind, a collector would pay all expenses. Plus, the value could rise with time."

Birdwell shook his head. "I don't see where the Tennessee Central did anything illegal."

"They didn't."

"And all the officers and employees would be held blameless?"

"Unless one committed the murder."

"Of course. But that would not taint the other employees or the company."

The man loved his train company. He'd want the best for it. "Picture this, Mr. Birdwell—what if the Central helped solve the crime? The company and the man behind it would be local heroes."

"What do your friends call you, Sheriff?"

"Coup, my daddy's nickname for me."

"Daddy's love their little girls. However, Mary Beth is a lovely name too."

"Most times, Coup seems to fit."

"My friends call me Thomas Jonathon."

"After Stonewall Jackson?"

"It was a tough delivery for my mother. She almost died. Said it was like shedding a brick."

Coup restrained herself from laughing. She bet his mother said "shitting," but in polite society, one must not use such words. "She must have thought you'd stand tall against opposition."

"We have something in common," he said. "Names that are not flattering."

She held up her glass. "To names we live with."

He nodded, then drank.

The butler appeared, still as stiff as an iron I-beam. "Sir, it is time to prepare for your next appointment."

"Thank you," Birdwell said.

Coup stood when Birdwell did. She held out her hand, disappointed in the waste of time since the visit had turned into a dead end. But she *did* get a new outfit… except she had no idea when she'd ever wear it again because Monterey didn't have garden parties, and she couldn't remember her last date. "Thank you for lunch."

"The pleasure is all mine," he said. "It would be nice if the Central got some limelight again, but I fear those days are in the past; the railroad is no longer glamorous."

He placed his hand on the small of her back and led her to the front door.

Charles opened the door and stepped aside.

"Please return for cocktails someday," Birdwell said. "We'll have some old fashions."

"I would like to do so." As she crossed the threshold, she felt Birdwell's hand sweep across her hip and ass. Did the old man just cop a feel? Disgusting. When and if she returned for cocktails, she'd ensure others were present. Didn't want him trying to bed her.

"My debt has been paid. Thank you for the opportunity to do so." He closed the door.

She had the feeling he had dismissed her. That Birdwell and the butler had arranged that, after a certain amount of time had passed, the butler would announce a phony appointment. This angered her. The stinking rich lived by their own rules.

One thing she noticed was that the heat in the swimming

room was hotter than where she stood. If Birdwell liked the heat, with his money, why didn't he move to the equator?

Halfway to her car, she stopped. Something was in the pocket of the dress.

She pulled out a torn piece of paper with a scrawled number two on it. He'd paid his debt, all right, the sneaky bastard. There were *two* diamonds.

Who had the other? The murderer?

Or, if Aletha had had one, did Miller have the other?

Twenty

This portion of I-40 between Nashville and Monterey was as straight as a bullet coming out of a rifle. Cattle pastures, spotted with fat Angus cows, lined both sides of the interstate. Coup gripped the wheel as the speedometer zipped up to eighty-three mph, the fast speed clearing her mind of Birdwell, Miller, and the diamonds and she focused on one person. Helen.

She keyed the patrol car's mike and Dragging answered.

"Give me some good news," she said.

Dragging was slow in responding. Patches of black asphalt dotted the pavement as the tires hummed on the four-laner. "I can't."

The lack of good news felt like a boulder had dropped on her head. Then anger swept through her. The son-of-a-bitch who did this to Helen better enjoy his next quart of whiskey because she would bring the wrath of a tornado down on him.

Dragging continued, "Helen is critical, but stable and unconscious. Lots of machines connected to her."

"I'm headed to Cookeville Medical." She watched the needle slap one hundred. "You work with the tech guys. I want to know everything about the bomb in her car."

"I alerted Grandfather."

"Good." Grandfather, chief of the Cherokees on the plateau, would call on his ancestors' spirits to guide them. She didn't believe in everything they did, but every Cherokee would be on the lookout.

She pulled into the first rest stop, changed out of her dress from Birdwell, and back into her uniform. Fifteen minutes later, she tapped her hat to the guard stationed at Helen's door then walked into the hospital room. She was pleased with the guard the local sheriff placed at Helen's door. His muscles pressed against his starched uniform; she figured this giant man could play the front line for the Tennessee Titians by himself. Then she focused on Helen.

She sucked a harsh breath when she saw the mass of tubes and machines hooked to her friend. The low beep-beep of the monitors sounded mournful. With all the flowers packed in the room and with their floral scent could not displace the cold and the gloom out of the room. The closed drapes stopped the sunbeams from penetrating the gray cloth. The room lights were dimmed, almost as dark as the heartless creature who'd done this to Helen.

This was too dreary for Coup, so she started to pull the drapes aside to let the sunshine in, turn the lights brighter, but then decided against it. Helen needed sleep to heal.

Before she sat in the tan, cushioned, chair beside the bed, Coup had to see the doctor and get some happy, yellow flowers.

At the nurses' station, she found him. "Frank don't sugarcoat it or give me a bunch of maybes," Coup said to the doctor.

"The blast hit her hard," he replied. "The trauma caused multiple organ failures. She's on a ventilator and we've sedated her to give her organs time to recover. Is that straight enough for you, Coup?"

Coup steadied herself against the counter. She liked his bedside manner; no dancing around it. It reminded her of her father's forwardness. "Her room is too gloomy and needs some cheeriness. Thank you, doctor. I'm off to the gift shop."

First, she called her friend, the sheriff of Putnam County, and thanked him for his choice of officer to guard Helen's room. Then she bought every yellow flower in the hospital's little store.

She placed the different floral arrangements in Helen's

room. While setting a small vase near the monitors, she noticed a note on the bedside chair that hadn't been there earlier.

She unfolded the torn sheet of white paper. It read, "NO MORE WARNINGS."

"You son-of-a-bitch," she whispered.

She walked over to the guard. "Did anyone enter this room after I had stepped out?"

"The doctor and a nurse."

His answer gave her no comfort.

After placing the note into her pocket, she sat in the chair and held Helen's limp hand. Sorrow swept through Coup. "Helen, your job is to get well; *my* job is to get the bastard who did this to you." Coup inhaled. What she had to say next wasn't going to be easy. "He gave me a warning, Helen, and I'm so sorry I didn't take it seriously." Coup stopped to suck back the tears. "This is my fault. God, I'm so sorry."

A few minutes passed while she composed herself before she was able to speak. "That scum of the earth contacted me again. This creep is watching me. He wants Miller convicted of murder, so, I'll have to act like I'm trying to hang Miller instead of finding the true killer. But don't worry; your room will be guarded all the time."

Coup hoped Helen could hear her and have some comfort. The plants that Coup had brought in gave the room some cheer. Cold air blew from the ceiling vents. The yellow tulips and daffodils fluttered with the artificial breeze.

"I will act like I'm gathering evidence against Miller. This should appease the killer and keep you safe. But I'll feed the information to someone who can do the investigation for me. I don't know who. Dragging is good at his job, but he doesn't have the skill set of a detective. I can't ask anyone from the police department to assist me, so who can I get?"

Coup stopped talking.

Monterey had been a quiet town. Once the shootings and hangings of five decades ago had all ceased, people had come to the plateau for sightseeing and hiking. Homeowners hadn't even locked the doors to their homes.

Not anymore. She'd have to develop protocols to protect her staff and the homeowners.

She felt Helen's hand twitch. Coup looked at her face. Helen's eyes popped open, and her hand pointed to her chest. Coup noticed a small white board and marker tucked into the bedding. She curled the marker into Helen's hand and held the board closer.

"Use Fat Bear," Helen wrote, then her eyes slowly closed.

The beeping of the monitors continued, but they no longer sounded mournful.

"Great idea, Helen. He'll do the work and never suspect I'm using him." Coup grinned.

Twenty-one

Coup stood on the rickety front porch of Miller's cabin and looked first at the rattler with the missing head, then at the rutted, pot-holed road she'd used to arrive here. The bottoming out of the undercarriage caused her butt to ache and twisted her backbone, which, to her, was enough reason to convict Miller. Finding the other Tarpon Diamond in his firetrap house would seal the case against the Mennonite.

She had a feeling some would call women's intuition or being aligned with the earth's vibes that she called listening to her gut instinct. No matter what it was called, she knew she'd discover something of enormous value here, maybe even, the second diamond.

This case brought her sorrow and happiness. Sorrow, because she liked Miller, as did most of the non-Mennonite community. He seemed God-fearing and law-abiding, but a loner. However, what kind of man would kill his wife for a collector's diamond? The kind whose days should be numbered. Which was the part of the justice system she liked.

In four days, the trial would commence, and she wanted the evidence locked down solid, tighter than a mason jar lid sealing preserved apples.

She peeked into a front window. The house was quiet.

"Miller, you around?"

A soft breeze rustled the branches on chestnut trees, and the popping of fish catching insects came from a nearby pond. But there were no human sounds.

"Memmo Simmons Miller!" She cupped her mouth to funnel her voice to cut into the trees. "It's Sheriff Coup!"

Still nothing.

Maybe this was good? She'd take advantage of the opportunity of him not being home, search the place and be gone before Miller returned. Probe anywhere she wanted without having to listen to Miller about any improprieties. Not breaking the law, she was doing a wellness check.

Miller wasn't known for straying far from his home. How much time would she have? Five minutes, half an hour, a whole afternoon? Then she remembered that he and Fat Bear were going to inspect the crime scene. Afterward, they'd return here to discuss the case. It would take them a maximum of four hours to hike down to the cave, roam around, and come back. She knew Miller liked to start his day at 6 a.m.

She checked her watch. Damn. Her trip to Nashville to see Birdwell had cost her a lot of time. They'd be back in thirty minutes.

Before walking into the wooden house, she glanced at the snake again. He was the biggest one she'd ever seen. If she had shot the rattler, she would have put two bullets into him.

Stepping inside, she gasped. The place looked bleak. It was a three-room house, and she was standing in the living room. She pushed aside hanging beads to peak into the bedroom. Beads instead of a door… was he an ex-hippie?

The bathroom, thank goodness, had a door, and an all-purpose room, which included the kitchen against the back wall with a wooden table to eat or work on, and, in front of her, a couch with worn sheets draped over it to hide the coiled springs, as well as a hand-crafted rocker built from rough wood. An antler chandelier hung over the table with a single bulb and two empty sockets. The place had the earthy scent of sawdust.

Miller lived in poverty.

But this simple house would be easy to search. Still, she needed to hurry—in and out. She should leave before he returned, especially if Fat Bear was with him.

That guy bothered her. He acted like he was above the law. Not all the time; mostly when he was on his property or in the backcountry, but that didn't make it right. She smiled thinking how he'd shot out the tires on the woman's tractor who'd been about to plow his fence down.

There was a man with some balls.

Time to get to work. She checked the obvious places first—lighting fixtures, drawers, the commode tank. Then she opened the freezer and found no ice or ice trays.

She'd found nothing and it'd cost her a fifth of her thirty-minute search time.

Something large, thudded outside. Was someone coming up the trail? Had Miller and Fat Bear returned early? She eased over to the window facing the woods behind the cabin. A trail was cut, but no one was on it. Then she saw a tree limb fall to the ground with enough force to feel it in her boots. Old trees were dying. Her dad referred to those fallen branches as widow-makers.

She returned to her search. Seventeen minutes remained.

She would examine behind the picture frames next, but Miller had nothing hanging on the walls except for a crucifix made out of small tree branches hanging above the stove.

Seeing the religious symbol made her realize everything in the house was constructed out of poplar trees, the kitchen table, couch and chairs, rocker, bed frame, walls, and the roof.

His home had minimal furnishings, almost spartan, but that's how some of the Mennonites lived; they didn't own anything elaborate or fancy that would tempt them to seek more flashy items instead of staying focused on God.

The way everything was arranged suggested this home had once had warmth, a woman's love. Miller had tried to keep it and not let it fade away.

How many people have had that kind of love in their lives? Would she find it one day?

Miller was talented when it came to carpentry. Which upset her. Damn him. She'd have to find an unexpected place to hide the diamond. And if Miller cut the trees, planed them, and polished the grains, then he could tuck a hidey-hole out of sight.

She had checked everything above the flooring, thus dropped to her knees.

Miller may be poor, but he did seem to take pride in his living quarters and swept the floor often. She ran her hand along the smooth floorboards, feeling for a crack or splintered wood. Using touch, more than sight, she worked along the boards.

Her digital watch indicated eight minutes left. She began to feel this search was useless.

She wouldn't have to leave; Miller had the right to be present during the search. But she had learned that she worked better when no one was around.

She'd chance five more minutes.

After creeping three more feet, she felt something out of place. One small plank was slightly higher than the surrounding ones. Not by much, a paper width's difference.

She pried up the loose board. Inside, packing material covered something. Something that had to be of great value. She was glad she'd trusted her gut instinct.

Outside, the sound of a side-by-side hitting one pothole after another echoed off the trees. She replaced the board.

"Miller," Fat Bear said, "fix this damn road."

"Oh hell," passed her lips.

Twenty- two

"You just laid there?" Kole said to Miller while driving them back to the cabin. He had already demanded to know when the Mennonite would fix the road to his house. Some of the potholes were deep enough to swallow a semi-truck.

"You said to stay put."

"Someone tried to take my head off!" he yelled at Miller.

"God blessed us with a nice day. The grass looked comfortable, and I couldn't resist the temptation to take a nap. Thus, I did as I was instructed. Like a sheep under the watchful eye of the shepherd."

Miller's voice was calm, unemotional, which frustrated Kole.

"But when I heard the shot, I came running," Miller said.

"And you saw nothing?"

"That's right."

"*Nothing.*" Kole emphasized the word. "A man as skilled as you in exploring these mountains and living as a hermit for the past twelve years, and you didn't see anything?" Kole had searched the area where he'd reasoned the shooter had made his stand. He'd found zip. No shell casing, no flattened grass, no cigarette butts, or footprints… as if a ghost had fired at him. Grandfather would have been disappointed at his inability to track.

"You paint me as a backwoods, law-breaking hillbilly, but I'm not. I am a man of God, living in His paradise."

Kole rounded the last curved inclined, then pulled beside Sheriff Coup's vehicle, parking near the porch. He shook his head as Coup approached them. "This day is getting more and more damned." His blood simmered.

"You just made my day," Coup said. "You can be present as I rip this fire hazard apart."

Kole slipped out of his side-by-side and adjusted his hat. "Do you plan on harassing my client?"

Coup, with a smirk on her face, shot back, "Doing my job."

"With too much pleasure."

"Miller," she said, "get over here and tell Fat Bear what I will find in your cabin."

Miller walked to them. They stood like the three points in an equilateral triangle.

"Sheriff," Miller said, "you're speaking in tongues."

"What's this all about, Coup?" Kole asked.

"I'm about to blow this investigation apart and send Miller to see Old Sparky."

Kole knew the reference to the electric chair. It'd been built in 1913, but it had been a while since the state of Tennessee had used it. During the last execution, it had malfunctioned, with sparks and flames shooting from the restraining cuffs, thus giving it its morbid nickname.

Coup looked past him, then down the road as if she was searching for someone.

"Sounds like you've already convicted him. Should I get the jumper cables out of my car, and we can juice him here?" Kole regretted his words, still angry from the morning's shooting. Coup was known as a fair and a good cop. He shook his head. "Sorry, I was out of line."

"That was your first and last pass," she said, then her voice softened, "but I assume Miller is difficult, at best."

Miller walked over to the dead snake. The diamond-patterned skin was torn in three places. White meat pulled out at one end, stretched to a small hole in the ground. The crows had already picked at it. The rattles no longer sang out warnings. "Everyone says, 'Have a blessed day.' I don't think this is one of them."

"Not for the snake." Kole scanned the grass, looking for other rattlers.

"Tell him why I'm here, Miller," she said.

"I have no idea," the Mennonite whispered.

"You should cooperate and change your plea from temporary insanity to a fit of rage."

Miller knelt by the snake, brushed off some insects, then coiled the remains. "I'll bury him when the two of you leave."

The air blew warm on Kole's face. His leg hurt and he touched it to see if it was still bleeding.

"What happened to you?" Coup said.

"I banged my leg. It's nothing."

"Sure." She turned away from Kole. "I imagine Miller's got some concoction to rub on it so gangrene won't set in. It'd be a shame if you lost it."

"I need to consult with Miller. Time for you to leave."

"No problem. After my search."

Tilting his head, Kole asked, "For what?"

"There are *two* diamonds. Aletha had one, and I'm sure Miller has the other."

"Sheriff," Miller jumped up with a clenched fist, "if I had a diamond, do you think I'd be living here?"

"What's going on?" Kole said.

"Let me spell it out to you two non-conformists."

Kole felt his stomach twitch. The forest around him fell silent. There were no birds flying overhead, not even a vulture, which he expected to see peering down at him. No squirrels ran from tree to tree or deer peeked through the foliage. Even the breeze had stopped. Nothing wanted to be a witness to what Coup was about to say.

"Aletha and Miller came upon two diamonds," Coup said. "Maybe they found them, or someone gave the gems to them, or they stole them; it doesn't matter at this point."

"All conjecture," Kole said.

"They were in the cave and started to disagree. To prevent Miller from getting them both, Aletha swallowed one."

"More conjecture. Not facts."

"Facts, Fat Bear. Important ones."

This jarred him. What made Coup think Aletha had swallowed one and why hadn't she shared this theory with him before? Coup was hiding her cards.

"Miller gets mad—worse, he is furious about what she did," Coup said. "He stabs her to cut the diamond out of her."

"You're crazy!" Miller shouted. "I'd never hurt her."

"But, for some reason, something, possibly the quake, or someone spooked him, he ran off, unable to retrieve it. So, he waited until he could reenter the cave. He'd had to wait twelve years, but he's a patient man. Just like Job in the Bible, right Miller?"

Miller stared at her in disbelief. "I risked my life to go in there to rescue A.J."

Kole pointed a finger at Coup. "This is a wild tale."

"A true tale. And when I search Miller's house, I'll find the second diamond."

"No!" Miller yelled. The word stretched out and echoed down the mountain. "She can't enter my home."

"You heard him, Sheriff. Miller is not consenting to a search." He over-emphasized his smile at her. "Too bad."

Coup pulled a sheet of paper from her breast pocket, rolled it tight with a point, then jammed it into the rip in Kole's hat. "There you go, darling." She stormed to the front porch.

Miller jumped in front of her.

"It doesn't have to be like this," she said to Miller. "Cooperate and things will be easier. Please step aside."

Miller ran to Kole, fell to his knees and pleaded. "Don't let her do this."

Kole pulled the paper out of his hat, unrolled it, and read the contents. "She has a search warrant."

Miller cried out, "Please don't, Sheriff! Please!"

"You're hiding something, Miller." Coup pushed the door aside and entered the cabin.

"There's nothing in there that has to do with my wife's murder," Miller said.

Kole wasn't sure how he felt. Anger for Coup's derogatory comment and actions, or surprise Miller admitted he was hiding something, like the diamond. Or helpless that he couldn't legally stop Coup. He had to do something. Anything.

"Come on," he said. But Miller was already ahead of him.

Coup knelt at the trick floorboard. With her knife, she pried it open and laid the piece of wood aside. Mustiness rose and filled the room of times past.

"You've already tossed the place," Kole said, "haven't you?"

"Stay out of there," Miller said.

She reached inside, and Miller grabbed her hand.

"Easy there." She flicked her wrist and freed her arm.

"This is personal," the Mennonite said.

"Miller, I've already asked you nicely. I know it's painful, but it'll be over soon," she said. "Fat Bear, get your client under control."

Kole helped the defeated man to his feet.

"Stop her!" Miller screamed. "Please!"

"Hold tight," Kole said.

Tears trickled down Miller's cheek as he clung onto Kole's arm.

Coup pulled a pink bandana from her pocket, wiped the sweat from her forehead, then undid the top button on her shirt. She snapped on a pair of lavender latex gloves. After examining the dark space, she reached in and pulled a bundle of worn envelopes out of the hidey-hole. She reached deeper and pulled out more. Then, one last time, she stretched her arm in and felt the sides and corners. With a sigh, she withdrew an empty hand.

"I don't see any diamonds," Kole said.

Coup unbanded a stack, pulled a sheet of yellowed paper, then read it.

At first, a smile spread across her face. Then her eyes

narrowed as if she was in pain, and her face turned red with embarrassment. And then, bundling the stack, she gently placed them back, and covered the hole with the plank.

Standing, she walked over to Miller and put her hand on his shoulder. "I didn't expect that," she said. "If I had, I wouldn't have read them."

Miller sat at the table, his head in his hands.

"What are those?" Kole asked.

"Intimate, very intimate, love letters between two teenagers." She lowered her head. "I imagine they are worth more than diamonds to Miller."

"You heartless bitch." The day's frustrations burst inside of Kole, and he saw red. A burning from ancient times consumed him. Some sort of justice needed to be done. The morning events had fired a madness in him, and he could no longer control his actions. He picked Coup up and slung her over his shoulder.

"What the hell!" she cursed.

He carried her out of the cabin. Her fists pounded his back, and her legs thrashed against him. He opened the driver's door of her squad car and dumped her into the seat.

"There's something wrong with you. I used to think you were fair. I was wrong. Get out of here," he said, and turned to walk back to Miller.

Coup gunned her car and bounced down the road.

Miller started to laugh. "You are dumber than Nabal who was disrespectful to King David of the Old Testament. He died a fool's death. Coup won't forget what you just did."

"Damn," Kole said in a whispered, long sigh. "I'll end up in a federal prison."

Twenty-three

Coup sped to the 1838 Bar. Each pothole, slow driver, or farm tractor she encountered on the narrow, secondary roads added fuel to her anger. She needed to talk to someone, and Paige, a trusted friend since primary school, would hold her secrets. Once she shared what happen with Paige, her best friend would agree that Fat Bear needed to pay for his inappropriate actions before nightfall.

She stormed into the drinking establishment, went straight to the bar, then ordered a whiskey, neat.

Paige, the barmaid, rolled up her long-sleeved, silver-blue cowboy shirt. She took the order and returned with a sweet iced tea.

"Tough morning?" Paige asked. The barmaid wore skinny jeans. A loose ponytail held her long, blonde hair, while her face glowed without lipstick or eye shadow. Her fingernails were painted neon purple.

Paige told the patrons she was twenty-two, though she could pass as a teenager. For the last five years, Paige's pretend age hadn't changed.

Coup surveyed the room. The lingering smells of beer and whiskey floated around the room. The ceiling fans mixed in the scent of "I'm available" perfume. She didn't want anyone to know about her mishap with Fat Bear. Normally, there was no one in the bar this time of day, but now, a young Mexican man in a white dress shirt, blue slacks, matching jacket, and tie was shooting pool by himself. He seemed intent on his game as his musky cologne fogged the room like a dense cloud.

"What's his deal?" Coup asked.

"He plans to ask his señorita to marry him. Has the last-minute fears and doubts. He's not sure what her answer will be."

"He thinks the answer is in a game?"

"If he runs the balls, she'll say yes. That's what he told me."

"Some people pray, some burn incense, but he plays pool. I've seen it all."

"What brings you here in a huff?" Paige asked.

"Fat Bear crossed the line this time," she said.

"The handsome, rough-looking Cherokee?"

"That's the bastard."

"Isn't he Grandfather's favorite?"

"Yep." Coup sipped her tea. It was awful. It had so much sugar that the drink was more of a white paste than anything refreshing. "He claims *not* to be Cherokee, so I should enforce the law."

"What'd he do?"

"Manhandled me."

"As in, grabbed you?"

"Threw me over his shoulder and dumped me in my car." Coup was embarrassed and leaned into Paige to tell her the complete story.

The more she told, the more humiliated she became. Her face felt flush. She wasn't sure if it was the warm room causing it, or the anger still boiling inside her.

Then she heard the series of clacking pool balls, and watched the man leave with a smile. If only she could predict the future by some solitary game.

"Everyone around here likes Fat Bear, even though he's a loner."

Coup sipped her tea. The sugar rush pulsed through her body. It'd still be too sweet even if she poured it into a bathtub of water.

"You could arrest him or shoot him," Paige leaned against the counter, "and no Cherokee would vote for you in the next election. You could lose."

At this moment, that'd be fine, Coup thought. But what other job would she enjoy? Bartend with Paige? Unlikely. Coup liked the outdoors. Maybe she could try her hand as a trail guide and nature interpreter. But dealing with tourists was just as bad as dealing with drunks, poachers, and Fat Bear.

"Did I tell you Savannah-Jo, the bitch from Nashville, was in here and wanted to know if I knew the train courier's name? Told her I had no idea."

"Thought he moved," Coup said. "Wasn't his name Rueben Crawford?"

"He did. Stayed away about a year."

Coup repeated the courier's name. He had to been involved with the Tarpon Diamonds.

"Then she asked about Miller and Fat Bear."

"What kind of questions?"

"General ones. I got the feeling she might be wanting to get cozy with Miller. Asked about him the most." Paige said.

Coup rolled her eyes. "Down-and-out women go for anyone."

"You'd *think* she could find a guy in the big city."

"If she comes in again, direct her to Fat Bear. Maybe she'll drag him away. That'll save me a lot of headaches. Let the man be gone. Hell, I'll even pay for the wedding."

"Back on the Fat Bear topic, I see." Paige smiled. "He must be occupying space in your head."

"I'd inform Grandfather of his poor citizenry if I could figure out how to mention it to him. I don't want Grandfather thinking I can't solve my own problems."

"Honey, I'll tell him," Paige said. "Grandfather comes to see me every week. He's such a darling."

"I don't want to hear it." Hell, were Paige and Grandfather getting it on? "Screw the election. Next time, I'll handcuff him on the spot and throw his Cherokee ass in the slammer. Let *him* fume instead of me."

"Next time?" Paige raised her eyebrows. "The Coup I know would have already done it."

"I still can."

"Tell me," Paige leaned over the counter and whispered, "what was it like having a nice, strong man wrap his arms around you and sweep you off your feet? Bet it felt nice, real nice."

"Screw you, Paige. Hell no. Not Fat Bear."

Coup shoved her iced tea onto the counter, then stomped out of the bar to the sound of Paige's giggle.

Twenty-four

Kole watched the spiral of dust caused by Coup's spinning tires settle to the ground. A sense of dread seeped through him, knowing Coup would soon bury him for his outrage. And because of those actions, he may have jeopardized Miller's defense.

He turned and faced the Mennonite. "You know nothing of the second diamond?" He hoped the Mennonite said *No*. A *Yes*, would mean he'd been involved in his wife's death. An even more troubling thought came to him, how did Coup know there were two Tarpon Diamonds? What else did she know that he didn't? He needed to get a step ahead of her. Where to start?

Miller broke his thoughts. "I didn't know about the first one."

Kole stood outside of the cabin. As the Mennonite caressed the worn letters in his rough hands, Kole felt sad for Miller. With Coup tossing the guy's home, and then had come the embarrassment, awkwardness, the pain of sorrow, and knowledge of Miller and his wife's passion, Kole felt the home should have some respect and privacy given back it, so, he remained outside. "Tell me again about the day Aletha disappeared."

Miller inhaled a deep breath, then released it. "I'd rather not. Haven't I experienced enough pain for one day?"

"Once more." Kole studied the man, Miller's shoulders slumped, and his eyes reddened. "I've missed something."

"What you're missing is your walk with the Great Spirit."

"Please."

"She went to the cave to meditate and was never seen again."

"So, no one met her there?"

"Not that I know of. I never went with her. I worked every day, all day, except Sunday. A lady who lives in Whispering Pines, the head of their HOA, said Aletha ran off with someone."

Miller referred to Fang. Kole knew her—junkyard dogs had better temperaments. "So, Aletha had no male acquaintances?"

"She was a faithful wife. Being in that cave was a time of prayer and meditation for her."

"I wonder why the cave?" Kole sat on the steps beside Miller. "Why not here on the porch?"

"Solitude."

A hot, dry wind swirled up from the holler. It, too, had the same loneliness to it that Miller's house did.

"Your knife in the cave is damning evidence. How do you think it ended up there?"

"I gave it to her." Miller's jaw hung slack. "This is a dangerous mountain. All kinds of wild critters. Shouldn't everyone carry a knife?"

Kole reached to his side and felt the blade Grandfather had given him. He had stated that the knife was a friend to all Cherokee men, and they depended on it. The night Grandfather had given him the blade, the sky had had a full moon and been packed with stars. They'd both pounded on a single drum for hours for the protection of the bearer. "No disrespect but praying in a place called Devil's Cave seems hypocritical."

"It's dark and quiet. A place to hear the Lord's voice in the wind and dripping water. Just like in a tabernacle."

A crow landed on the peak of the roof and cawed. Kole looked up. The bird stared at him and cawed a few more times. The black feathers stood boldly against the blue sky. The bird hopped to the roof's edge, flapped its wings, then flew into the forest that was as dark as Devil's Cave.

Grandfather had taught him that these birds were messengers, usually bringing hope or good luck. But, often, the receiver of the dispatch didn't know which until after the event. What the recipient thought was bad could turn out to be good and vice versa. Nature talked to him. No matter how hard he tried to ignore the old ways, they kept returning to him. At times—like now—he felt Grandfather's beliefs seeping into him, even as he tried to block them.

Kole didn't want to admit what had just happened. But he choked down his pride, and thanked Grandfather silently for the message.

"Aletha was the only person to go missing," Kole said. "And now we know she didn't."

"She wasn't the only one," Miller said.

Kole stood and stretched his back.

"I forget when, but it was close to the same time Aletha disappeared," Miller said.

"You Mennonites like to live secretly."

"Not one of us. A local girl. Same age as Aletha. I met her once—didn't like her. She was worldly, and wanted to visit Rome, Paris, and London. Why would someone want to visit those sinful places when they live in God's country?"

"It's a curse." Kole looked at Miller. "I, too, would like to see the sunset on a different mountain range."

"You need to listen to your Great Spirit."

He should have left this mountain a long time ago. Then he wouldn't have to deal with the Dobermans or this case. Maybe he should have run off as a child. "Did they ever find her?"

"Don't know. That same HOA woman who spread untruths about Aletha said the local girl ran off with the train courier. He was worldly."

"He's missing also? This town has a lot of missing people."

"No, he came back."

"And the girl?"

"Parents found work elsewhere. I guess she went with them."

"Monterey is a quiet town, well, except for twelve years ago when Aletha was killed. Then nothing unusual happens. Life is normal. But, in the past week, they found Aletha's body, Helen's car explodes, and someone tries to put a bullet in my head. Then we learn there are two diamonds, and Coup is hell-bent on convicting you. We need to pay this train courier a visit."

"He should know if any diamonds were on board. Speaking of diamonds," Miller said, "Coup's like a diamond—sharp, hard, strong, tough. Pretty, too. What do you think?"

"You need to focus on her actions. She's going to fry your ass. And I have no thoughts about the bitch's prettiness."

He glanced at the pocketed road Coup had used when she bolted away. The dust cloud had long ago dissipated, and the stones lay peacefully along the ruts.

When he'd had her slung over his shoulder, she had felt really nice. Her skin had radiated the scent of the pine and poplar trees, like a Cherokee woman.

Miller grinned at him as if he read Kole's thoughts.

Damn Mennonite.

Twenty-five

Coup set her GPS for the train courier, Johnny Carlson's house. It was less than ten minutes north of Monterey, the land of leave-me-alone. A place where the locals applied their own form of justice with the hot end of a gun. This part of the plateau changed from grassy, green pastures to hard, bone-breaking, jagged rocks. She wondered if the courier would be as unfriendly as the hard limestone terrain.

The road was a gravel path a car-width wide, and the immediate landscape consisted of mountains with deep, drop-off ravines packed with ash, black oak, hackberry trees, and rhododendrons. If she drove over the edge, no one would ever find her at the bottom of the thick forest because the leaf litter would cover her in a few days.

The navigation system announced, "You have arrived," so she stopped the car, then stepped out. Smoke from a wood fire filtered through the telephone-pole-high poplar treetops like a whispering fog. The jagged outcropping towered over her on the driver's side of the road; the other side dropped five-hundred feet into darkness.

Thirty-five feet or so in front of her, she found a flat, patchy area of broom sedge and purple wildflowers the size of dimes that someone used as a turnabout. She didn't trust it. With her luck, the edge would give way and send her to her Maker.

Standing there on the packed dirt, she spied a white travel trailer a few feet below. Rust covered the dented top and looked like sad tears as it streamed down the algae-covered sides. A pathway of flat rocks led to the single front door. Plywood was nailed to the window opening.

Fifty-five-gallon drums on both sides of the entryway overflowed with white kitchen garbage bags. Mingled with the household trash were car bumpers, an engine block on wooden supports, and oil containers sitting in black sludge.

A man in his sixties, with a head of white hair, opened the rotted door. His hiking boots were worn and scuffed, his jeans still clung to some blue in spots, and curly silver hair covered his tanned chest. "I got a twelve-gauge behind the door, so you'd best you take your business down the road."

Coup shifted her hip so he could see her badge. "Have a few questions." She walked to the door. "Can I come in?"

"No."

"Mr. Carlson, we can talk here or at the jail." She'd said *jail* instead of *in town*. The man had seen the inside of the cell a few times and she bet he didn't want to experience it again. She also decided to act syrupy-Southern, the way country boys like to hear their women talk. It might open him up to give some answers. She held her laughter for the role she was about to play. "Sugar," she smiled, hoping to change his demeanor, "just a couple of questions to put to bed an old inquiry."

"I warned you, bitch." He pulled his cut-down shotgun from inside.

Coup telescoped her truncheon. She whacked his wrists, sending the gun clattering to the floor, and then hammered the cylindrical metal rod across both of his knees. It pushed him backward.

To send the message home, Coup stepped inside and slapped the baton across his forehead.

Carlson sat on the mildewed carpet in a daze.

"Sweetie, you fell and bumped your head. Here, let me help you up." She lifted him from under his arms and slumped him into an oversized, torn, fabric-cushioned chair, the only one in the building. She ejected the black shells from the shotgun and tossed them into his dish-filled sink where flies hummed. Then she leaned the weapon against the side wall.

Carlson winced when he touched his forehead. "Bitch, I'm bleeding," he said when he saw blood on his fingers.

She handed him some paper napkins from the kitchen.

Wind gusted through the ravine and shook the trailer. She swore she felt it inch toward the edge, about to plummet them over the side.

"What you need is some sweet tea. I'll fix some while you tell me about the great train robbery."

He grunted.

She found a dented metal pot, filled it with tap water from the sink. The sulfur smell of the well water was strong. Rotten eggs didn't come close to describing what came out of the calcium-caked spigot. She sat the pot on a propane stove. She hit the burner igniter. After a few seconds, the flame flickered blue in the burner.

"That bump on your head caused you to have amnesia. Oh, dear. It was twelve years ago, and you were a courier guarding some diamonds."

"Some chick clobbered me on the head like you just did. Don't remember a thing."

She found two tea bags. They looked used, but she dropped them into the boiling water. Mason jars were the only glasses she could find, so she wiped them clean with her shirt because there was no cloth or towel in the kitchen that she could trust to be clean.

There was no TV in the tiny living area, and no window A/C unit. The inside must boil in August. A single bare bulb lamp sat on an old wooden box. From a dirty window, she saw a yellow gas generator which must power what little electricity he needed. The door to the bathroom hung lopsided and a putrid smell escaped from the room.

"Tell me what happed before someone bopped you."

"I was hired by Central to accept a package in Monterey,

lock it in the safe, then give it to an officer of the company in Nashville."

"I'd hate to see you fall again." She poured sugar into the jars and poured the tea on top. "Don't skimp on your narrative. What was in the package?"

"Can't you leave me alone? That happened a long time ago."

"I'd love to, sweetie, but I must fill out this inquiry. Paperwork, that's all I do these days. Not even sure if anyone reads the stuff. But if I don't, someone's panties will get wadded up."

He sighed. "Two diamonds. When held under a light, they reflected different colors."

"When did you get hit?"

She opened the refrigerator door. Inside was beer in brown bottles and silver cans. A head of lettuce was melting. She dumped tannic-colored ice from the fridge into the jars, then handed him one. She left hers on the counter. No way she'd drink or eat anything in this hazmat trailer.

"I signed for the package. Took a peek before I placed them in the safe. Turned and saw this girl, and *wham*! I was out cold."

"How old was she?"

"It's hazy." He drank his tea and settled into the chair.

"You said *girl*. Pre-teen, middle teens, what?"

"Maybe middle teens. It happened quick."

"Your record states you like underage girls."

"Long time ago. Docs cured me. No feelings for them anymore."

"I believe you, honey. What doctors?"

"That's all I know. Don't remember anything else. She hit me."

"Did you give her a reason to do so?"

"No. There're crazy bitches out there. It was after midnight. What teen is out at that hour?"

"Maybe we should go downtown."

"Please believe me." His voice broke. "I can't go to jail again. I live out here to be left alone."

"Nothing more to share?"

"I was told by the railroad to never talk about the diamonds or that night. And I haven't."

"Sweetie, you just did."

"Just go. I don't know anymore."

Coup stepped out of the trailer. She thought about jumping into the nearest creek to wash the stink of the place off her.

She slid inside her squad car. Carlson was a good actor. It had been a while since she'd seen one as good as him. She needed to check a few items, then return. And figure out who the girl was.

He knew more.

Twenty-six

Savannah-Jo had parked behind a green dumpster at the base of Rattlesnake Mountain in the side lot of a gray-clapboard country store with wagon wheels and a hitching post out front. She guessed the building had been built in the '40s or '50s. She had a great view of the two-lane road and saw that bitch of a sheriff fly by. But Savannah-Jo didn't start her car. *Be patient.* Kole needed to pass before she headed up the cliff.

An hour later, he did.

She turned her engine over, then began the ascent to Miller's. This was going to be so easy. The plan was to get what she needed and be back at the hotel in less than two hours to have a delicious meal and maybe some bedtime conversation with Reggie. The Brit was very informative.

She pulled her Lexus to within three feet of the cabin's front steps where Miller sat. A frown appeared on his face. Dumb hillbilly. People loved her. Well, the ones in the city, at least.

"I'm Savannah-Jo Hunnicutt," she said after sliding out of her car and extending her hand.

"It's been a long and rough day, lady. I'd like to be left by myself."

"I brought beer, wine, and bourbon. What's your pleasure?"

"If I'm right about your visit," Miller said, "you want me to talk about the diamonds. Seems that's what's on everybody's minds these days. Greed. False idols. No fear of the Lord."

A chill went through her. The mountain top became still. The setting sun turned the sky red behind the dense forest, and deep shadows filled the road behind her. Nature was building a black wall around the cabin.

"Let's start with Aletha," she said.

"Then we need some shine."

"Only if it's smooth. No turpentine stuff."

"Lady, I make the best."

Miller stood and walked about fifty feet past the side of the cabin to a small patch of green grass.

She watched him kneel to the ground, lift a trap door, then disappear into the earth.

After several minutes—about the time she thought she should check on him—his head of black hair appeared. He closed the secret door, then smoothed the surrounding grass.

Carrying two quart-sized mason jars of clear liquid, he motioned for her to follow him into the house.

To her, all the furnishings were home-crafted, including the cabin itself. She and Miller sat at a rough-hewn table in the kitchen area. The place felt like a poor coal mining, Appalachian shack. "Did you do all the handy work?" She hoped she didn't get splinters where she couldn't reach.

Miller shoved a jar toward her. It bounced on the table in a few places. "Blessings from the Lord."

She didn't know if he meant his home or the shine.

He nodded at her and raised his jar.

She twisted the metal lid and noticed the absence of rust. That was a good sign that the contents would not kill her immediately. She held the jar to her nose and sniffed. Maybe a hint of botanicals. Not much. This stuff was pure shine. She sipped. "Oh, this is smooth."

"Angels have blessed it."

It took about half of the jar for her to coax Miller into saying what he knew, from the day he'd gone into the cave to help the bitch sheriff, his arrest, and Fat Bear representing him before the law. The information he offered didn't differ from what Reggie had shared with her, but Miller gave her a description of inside the cave. The detail stunned her.

Fat Bear, not *Kole*, was how Miller referred to the Cherokee man. Interesting. Pieces were coming together. What the two of them knew and what they didn't know. The moonshine went down too easily. She acted like she took a mouthful swig at a time, but she paced herself and sipped it, barely letting her tongue get wet.

Miller acted like he was drinking fruit punch

"Were you in the cave today?" she asked.

"Why would you think that?"

"It hasn't rained today, and the ground around your home is packet dirt and rock, yet your shoes are muddy."

"I was." Miller gulped from his jar. "I need to find who killed my wife. Hope to find an answer in that miserable place."

"And did you?"

"A back entrance."

She studied Miller's face to see if it revealed more than he said, but the shine dulled her observation powers and frustration filled her. She shouldn't have drunk so much. She needed something else in her stomach before she fell face-first onto the wooden floor. "Anything here to eat?"

"Rabbit in the fridge. We can fry 'em up." Miller started a fire in the stove while she sautéed the rabbit. They were already skinned. The meat wasn't white like that bought in a grocery store. This meat was dark in color and looked tasty, the same as she had eaten at one of Nashville's five-star restaurants—which served the same meat at exuberant prices.

"I figured," Miller said, "that anyone driving a fancy sports car would come calling in a dress and heels, not jeans and hiking boots."

The man was observant. Maybe he saw too much.

"I hiked to Ozone Falls this morning. The guidebook was right; the air at the bottom of the falls has more oxygen in it than normal, caused by the water separating into a fine mist. I felt refreshed."

Again, she watched Miller's reaction. She couldn't tell if he bought her story or not. "Did you find anything else in the cave?"

"Fat Bear did most of the exploring. If he did, he kept it to himself."

Her sixth sense told her that Fat Bear *did* find something, but what?

"And," Miller interrupted her thoughts, "someone took a shot at him. That was strange because there are no stills around the cave. Water isn't pure enough."

She unlaced her boots and kicked them off, then served their supper on tin plates. If Miller had real plates, he must have hidden them.

Rabbit and shine, they went together. She guessed everything went well with enough shine.

"Did God bless you with these steak knives?" She held one up. "Hell, there're hunting knives."

"No profanity, please."

"My apologies." She hefted the blade in her hand. Heavy and a nice balance, she wondered what the throwing distance was. She ran her thumb along the steel. Sharp enough to shave hair. "Is this what you used to skin the rabbit?"

"Making these keeps me connected to nature."

She cut the rabbit meat into thin slices.

Miller stayed silent for the rest of the meal. She could tell he wanted to say something but was sizing her up on the trustworthy scale. A couple of questions bounced around in her mind, and she wondered if they were the same as his. One, did they know who shot at Fat Bear? And two, what did they find in the cave, and would it clear Miller of murder? She needed answers.

Change of plans. This was going to take longer than she'd thought. Reggie would have to wait until tomorrow night. "You have any more shine?"

"I do."

"I cook a delicious breakfast."

Miller stood and left the cabin. She went to the door to ensure he'd gone to get the shine. When he lifted the secret door, she cleaned the table and tucked one of the knives into her boot.

She stripped, threw her clothes on top of her boots, climbed into his bed, and pulled the covers halfway up.

Twenty-seven

Coup set a pecan pie on the polished counter inside the 1838 Bar. The lights were turned low for the evening crowd, giving everything a yellowish tint.

"Frustrating day?" Paige asked. "You always bake when that happens."

"Interviewed a possible pedophile." She noticed Paige had changed tops from earlier. This one was pink with frilly sleeves and four large buttons down the front. Coup didn't think it matched the rest of her outfit.

"Shower time," Paige said.

"Twice, I lathered up, but I'm still not clean. I just want a quiet evening, to relax and have a good, stiff drink." She noted the patrons in the bar. Most of the town was here, shooting pool, gossiping, or drinking. The noise level was elevated to the point where she had to lean toward Paige to speak with her. Savannah-Jo wasn't here, which, at first, lightened her heart, but then made her squint. Where was the devious woman? And, to dampen her mood even more, in the back corner's shadow, Fat Bear sat scrawling in a small notebook.

"Do I get to eat all of this pie or sell it?" asked Paige.

The smell of beer was thick, and Coup wondered if it would taint the flavor. She turned back to Paige. "It's my father's recipe. Dad knew how to bake a pie. He added cinnamon to make it pop. Free samples. Let's see who likes it."

Paige cut the pie and placed the triangular slices on mismatched dessert plates. The filling oozed out with an enticing aroma. "You gonna bust this perv?"

"It would be a service to the community, but I need to keep tabs on him for a few more days."

"Speaking of keeping tabs on people, take a slice over to Fat Bear."

"Mind your own jiggers and bitters."

Paige wrote "Free Samples" and stuck it in a chrome card holder, then she cleaned tumblers and stacked them on the back counter between the rye whiskeys and bourbons.

A ruckus broke out by the pool table. Two elderly men with white beards to their chest and overalls with red handkerchiefs sticking out of the back pocket, started dueling with the cue sticks.

At first, Coup didn't care about their comical actions; they were both old enough to be someone's great-grandfather. Mountain slang spewed from the two of them. She guessed they'd soon tire themselves out and go back to their whiskies.

"Johnny-Ray, you butt-slapped my wife for the last time!" The man held his stick like a fencing foil.

"Chad, then tell her to stop wiggling her fine ass at me."

Chad lunged with the cue stick. Johnny-Ray tried to block it, but the force was strong and whacked him across the head. He fell, cutting his head on the edge of the pool table. Blood dripped down his face.

Chad stood poised to hammer down on the guy.

Coup slid off her stool and wrestled the stick from the guy's hands. "Get up," she said to Johnny-Ray. "And put some pressure on that cut. We don't need any blood stains on the pool table; they're in poor enough shape as it is."

"Sherriff, arrest him," Johnny-Ray said.

"Johnny-Ray, you and your brother take it outside," Coup said. "The two of you look ridiculous. You're both in your nineties. No heart attacks tonight, please. Now get."

Several patrons laughed as the two men helped each other limp out the door. Coup laughed also. They were fighting, again, over their cousin Lesley-Lee. She'd have to say something to the eighty-five-year-old woman about her mini-skirts egging on the men.

Coup walked back to the counter. A dark bourbon waited for her, its amber depths reflecting dreams of peacefulness. She raised the glass to her lips for a sip of the wet fire.

"Some women have no class," a voice a few stools down gravelly.

Coup knew who the woman was by the sound of her rough voice—the president of the Whispering Pines H.O.A., which bordered Fat Bear's property. It took a few seconds for her to recall his name for her. Fang. He'd dubbed the whole group *The Dobermans*.

Fang was joined by two other women. Coup only knew one—Sherry. They wore jeans and blouses. Their outfits were cute and so close to matching that they had to have bought them together, but their personalities were the complete opposite— sarcastic and condescending, with word choices that bit like a copperhead.

"Drinking whiskey and breaking up bar fights," Fang said. "Not ladylike at all. I wonder if she even owns a dress."

Coup ignored her. Hopefully, after a few minutes, their bitterness would be directed toward someone else. She wondered why they weren't chewing on Fat Bear.

"A lady simply does not become sheriff of a roughneck county," Fang said.

Paige walked over to Coup. "Want me to send their skinny asses out of here?"

"Give them some pie. Maybe they'll choke on it."

Paige grabbed three plates then scooted down to the ladies. "Pie? It's homemade."

After a few bites, Fang started again. "Best pie I've had in a long time. This would take the blue ribbon at our fundraiser. But, of course, you must be asked to be part of our event. We don't allow riffraff or unqualified contestants."

The other women nodded.

"Sheriff, you should try baking. It's what all properly raised southern women do. Maybe you could find you a good man and have babies."

"How much are you going to take?" Paige whispered, leaning over the counter.

"I'll finish my drink and leave. Don't want to gulp a good bourbon because of despicable people."

"Three," Fang said. "Yes, three babies are what us southern gals should have. We are, after all, more fertile and appealing than most women." She finished her pie. "But Coup is getting past her prime time for having children. Her eggs are probably close to hard-boiled by now. Maybe if she hurries, she can find someone to impregnate her at least once."

Coup could no longer hold her temper. She was not past any type of prime. Now she knew why Fat Bear had such a hatred toward them. Time to shove their words up into their fruitful lady parts.

She stood.

But before she took her first step, Fat Bear jumped between her and the Dobermans.

"Two slices of that pie, Paige," Fat Bear said.

"Here you go, sweetie. I saved the largest piece for you."

Fat Bear turned to Coup. "Please join me for some of this fine dessert."

"I have matters to attend to," Coup said.

"It concerns Miller," he said.

Coup stared at him. She should slap the pies out of his hands for his earlier actions.

Fat Bear smiled and held the plates shoulder high. "Please."

"Sure, why not? I'll take my frustration out on you."

At his table, they sat. She noticed Fat Bear tried to seat her, so her back was toward the Dobermans. But that would never fly.

With a shake of her head, she dropped into the seat beside him, which still allowed her to watch the room and him.

She studied his eyes. It was the first time she'd noticed how blue his irises were—like hot flames.

They ate in silence. Achy Breaky Heart poured out of the jukebox and muted all other sounds.

Fat Bear wore a stupid smirk.

"What?" she said.

"This pie is the best." He looked over to the counter. "And the Dobermans don't even know you baked it."

"How do you know it's mine?"

"I saw you bring it in."

"I did. Glad you enjoyed it."

"And the Dobermans enjoyed every mouthful." He grinned and held up two fingers to Paige. "That calls for the best bourbon."

"Yes, it does."

Twenty-eight

"The pack of dogs are leaving." Kole nodded to the door as the Dobermans stormed out. The sun had set behind the 1838 Bar and cast deep shadows over the parking lot. The three women melted into the darkness, though he thought they probably morphed into creatures of the night.

"They didn't look happy," Coup said. "I pity the next person they meet."

Kole swirled the bourbon in his glass. It was the second one he'd had with Coup. An hour of pleasantness had passed since he asked her to join him. It was nice they had a common foe, who was an irritant in both of their butts. He also liked the time of peacefulness with her, neither of them accusing the other of some problem. Could it last beyond the night? A part of him hoped so.

"You're right," he said. "They *are* up to no good. Those bitches usually attack during the day, but I think they have become red-eyed, demonic beasts. I expect they're plotting to do something disruptive tonight."

"Then there goes my evening."

The jukebox quit booming, and the noise level stayed muted. The clacking of pool balls continued, but the patrons talked in whispers. A hearty laugh or a high-pitched giggle from time to time carried through the thinning crowd. Maybe it would be an early night for the bar. One thing for sure, it would be for *him*. The day's events had settled on him as if an oak had fallen across his shoulders. He was ready to retire for the evening. Tomorrow would be another full day and he expected more surprises were coming.

"What did you want to tell me about Miller's case—or was that a ploy to get me to have a drink with you?" she asked.

He watched the smile form. What were his real intentions? He shook the thought out of his head. "I was Jim Dandy to the rescue."

She laughed. "I didn't need to be rescued. If I can't handle stray dogs, then what am I doing as sheriff?"

"Stray dogs." He had to laugh, too. "I like it."

Coup pushed back her chair.

"There is one item…" he said.

"Oh?" She straightened her spine.

"This." He fished a handkerchief out of his shirt pocket, laid it on the table, then gently unfolded the soiled cloth. The lipstick rolled onto the table and stopped in a crack in the boards. The subdued overhead light gave the silver tube a yellowish tint.

"Where did you get this?" Coup's voice was tense.

"In the cave. About nine-hundred feet from Aletha's skeleton."

"And you held it? No gloves, no baggie?" Anger was in her tone. "Hell, you ruined it as evidence."

"Miller filmed it in situ. We can forward the footage to you."

Coup pulled a pair of latex gloves and a clear plastic bag from her back pocket. She laid the bag on the table, then unfolded the protective gear and snapped them on.

"You always carry a pair?"

"I'm a cop." With her fingertip, she pushed the tube out of the fracture and onto a more even surface, then continued to roll it over a few times. Specks of mud and rust flaked off, speckling the table. "Interesting."

"Could it belong to the murderer?" he asked.

"I've never seen Miller wear lipstick."

"This proves another female was in the cave with Aletha."

"How far away from the body?"

"I counted almost four-hundred steps. My strides."

Coup lifted her chin and looked at him.

He hoped she was about to agree with him. That this find would cut Miller lose.

"If it was in Aletha's hand, then maybe." Coup looked down at the tube. "That far away, it's a stretch. It could have been dropped by other hikers who had nothing to do with this case. It was a popular place for kids and adults before the cave-in."

"Twist it open."

"You're unbelievable. Why didn't you take this over to the train depot and have everyone put their fingerprints on it."

"I used what I had." The peacefulness they'd shared earlier was gone. The lights seemed to have dimmed even more. Why did he try and be nice to her like intervening between her and the Dobermans? She kicks him in the ass every time.

As Coup worked the tube, the purple wax emerged.

Kole handed her his knife.

She scraped a few fragments onto the table, away from the other detritus. With the pointed steel, she scooted the pieces around. A faint lilac smell crept across the surface. She stabbed a piece as if it was an expansive cut of beef and held it up to the light.

"What do you think?" he asked.

"It's substandard quality. Something bought at a discount store. Probably used by a young girl who was learning and experimenting with cosmetic products."

"What I was thinking also."

"There's no blood on the tube. Also, no identifying marks."

"But you will test it for fingerprints?"

Coup opened the plastic bag, and, with the tip of the knife, rolled it inside. "Of course."

Kole didn't know if that was a win or not. It was as if the sheriff considered it trash and would treat it as a low priority item. His frustration continued to rise. "Not many girls wear purple lipstick," he said.

"And how would you know? Do you have any children?"

"No."

"Nieces?"

"No."

"Any friends who do?"

"Cherokee."

"And what color do they wear?"

"They don't."

He paused, hoping a miracle to drop into his lap. Or, as Miller would say, "Manna from Heaven."

Coup stood. "Most likely, this is nothing. But I'll have it fingerprinted since, you, as Miller's defense attorney, have requested I do so."

"You should have found this. I'm doing your job."

"What I have is a piece of crap. I suppose I could search the cave from one end to the other and fill up a garbage bag full of useless junk. Maybe find a soleless shoe and say, 'Hey, the killer wore a size eight.'"

"I saw no other debris."

"Good. I don't need my office looking like a landfill." She started to walk away, then stopped. Her voice turned soft. "Thanks for the bourbons."

"And I enjoyed the pie."

"Damn right you did," she said with a laugh.

He watched her walk through the dancing shadows and out the door into the darkness.

She had stomped on the only piece of evidence he had. It was time for him to leave. To prepare for his visit with the train courier. He hoped for the best.

This day was almost over and, thus, couldn't get any worse.

Twenty-nine

Kole turned the corner and headed down the gravel road leading to his house. The three bourbons he had downed at the 1838 Bar buzzed in his head. Above him, the stars looked like broken glass sprinkled around the waxing moon in the black sky. A feeling of wonderment and his place in the universe overcame him. What a great night to lie in the dry grass and gaze at the mystery of creation. A fine time to relax.

As he approached his home, he saw three cars had parked parallel to each other, with their headlights illuminating his front yard as if the noon sun shone down on this piece of earth. The whine of a chainsaw broke the evening's silence. Four rabbits ran across the road from under some pampas grass, into a patch of rhododendrons.

In the center of the harsh lights, Fang stood directing two other women toward a tree in his yard.

What the hell?

Kole parked his side-by-side in front of the sedans, blocking as much light as he could, then jumped out. "Get your ass off my property!" he yelled.

Fang pointed to the old hardwood. Its top was three times the height of his home. "This is a tree of heaven and is very invasive. We have the right to cut it down and protect the neighborhood ecology."

"You're wrong!" Kole shouted.

"I have taken several field classes," Fang said, "on plants ruining the environment. I have earned four certificates, making me an expert. Top person in each one."

"Then you should know that this is a black walnut. It's part of the native landscape and a primary food source and shelter for what few animals are left in our neighborhood."

"How dare you doubt me," she said. "I am an authority on the flora and fauna growing in Whispering Pines."

Kole pointed. "This is not the tree of heaven, also known as the stinking sumac. It has a distinctive odor." If only Fang would use her nose to smell instead of poking it into everyone's business.

"I know what I'm doing. This is a tree of heaven," she insisted. "It will destroy everything around it."

Similar to what this H.O.A. was doing with its expansion of homes. He didn't understand the woman's arrogance, or her proclaiming to be an expert. *She* was an invasive species like the tree she was talking about. Cherokee children learned which plants were edible and which ones had medicinal properties from the moment they could walk, and they certainly didn't brag about it.

Fang had no such knowledge.

"Come look." He motioned her to the two-foot-in-diameter trunk.

She, surprisingly, followed him. And without another incorrect lecture.

Kole picked a leaf off the ground. "Black walnut trees' leaves have serrations that are evenly spaced. See?" He held the leaf close to her face. "The heaven tree leaves are smooth." He placed his hand on the trunk. "Look at the bark. It's rugged and coarse, with deep vertical grooves, not smooth and thin like an invasive tree. Now get off my property before I call the cops."

"You mean your squeeze. Bet she'd do anything for you. Even arrest the innocent."

Kole wasn't sure if she was referring to themselves or Miller.

Fang ran her palm along the roughness. The car lights caught her face, and, to Kole, it looked like she had learned the difference between the two trees.

"When this land was granted to me, Grandfather and the elders held a special ceremony to bless this tree to prosper and restore what the ground has lost."

The light from one of the cars grew dim and started to yellow. The battery was losing its juice. The other headlights cast a shadow across Fang's face as she turned sideways. The corner of her eyes formed wrinkles, her jaw clenched, and her facial muscles tightened like thick vines, as her mouth turned downward, similar to a vulture picking at carrion.

"Cut it down!" she yelled.

Kole jumped back when the woman with the chainsaw revved it up and bullied her way between him and Fang.

She slammed the machine into the tree. The silver bar gleamed in the harsh light. Chips of wood flew in different directions. The sound of the saw dropped in tone as it bit deep into the wood.

Kole grabbed the saw from her and body-bumped her to the ground. He flipped the orange switch off, walked to the creek, then threw the device into the water. A trail of bubbles followed the steel as it sank to the rocky bottom.

A hush crept over his yard. He examined the tree's wound. The chain had cut deep in those few seconds. The gash showed the outer rings, dark brown circles against the white core. The gouge was three fingers into the heart of the tree. Even with Grandfather's healing ceremony, he didn't think it would survive the next winter.

"You've killed it," he said to the three women.

Fang up-turned her lips. "We plan to bulldoze every tree, plant, flower, and weed on this lot and turn it into a nice park for the decent people who live here, wiping out all evidence you were ever here, and plant creeping liriope. It's the prettiest grass there is."

"An invasive?" He looked at the hate in her eyes. "Which is it? Are you for getting rid of invasive plants or bringing more in?"

"I'm for getting rid of *you*. You're not wanted here."

One of the Dobermans started to beat on the hood of his

vehicle and chant, "Time for you to go. Time for you to go. Time for you to go."

The other two women joined her, all snarling at him.

Kole ran into his house and returned with his twelve-gauge. He fired once, high over their heads. The sound echoed through the trees.

The women pounded harder and yelled their chant. The peacefulness of the evening disappeared. He wondered if it would ever return.

Dents formed in the hood of his side-by-side as the Dobermans fed on the actions of each other. They screeched into the air like banshees. Their hands no longer open, but turned into fists, reaching high, then slamming into the metal.

He knew of only one way to stop the insanity.

A cool breeze swept across the yard. The hairs on his arm stood upright. It was as if nature knew what he planned to do and had given him the okay.

He aimed the cutdown and knew what carnage would happen when he squeezed the trigger.

Once, twice, three times he fired and pumped the slide between the booming. The ejected shells twirled in the air in celebration. Smoke trails and burnt gunpowder covered his face, and mixed with his sweat, and tasted nutty, vegetal, and smokey.

The quietness returned as did the night's blackness that settled on his shoulders. His emotions mixed—pleased but saddened with being forced to take such drastic actions. How would Grandfather react? Most likely disheartened and saying the Great Spirit would not condone.

He pulled a flashlight from the glovebox of his vehicle and pointed the beam at the aftermath.

Not one headlight on the Dobermans' cars had survived the deadly shots. A hiss came from one radiator. On another car, the hood had popped open.

He watched the three women run down the street.

Kole sighed. Time for bed, but he knew sleep would elude him.

Thirty

Kole woke to the sounds of bullfrogs croaking from the pond behind his home. Orange streaks colored the sky as the sun peaked over the tree tops and the first rays of day entered his darkened bedroom. It had been a restless night. His outrage with the Dobermans had played over and over in his dreams. Today, he expected the wrath from the husbands or, worse, the law. This would be a good day to leave the house early.

He vowed to remain calm from sunrise to sunset. To use logic to solve problems, not his darker emotions. But his head throbbed, and he needed caffeine.

He poured himself a cup of black coffee with a few drops of moonshine, then dialed Grandfather's number. "Grandfather, I need some information."

"About the train robbery?"

Grandfather had glimpses of the future, and, at times, knew what was about to unfold.

Kole didn't waste time asking him how he knew. "Yes. Who was the courier working the schedule?"

"Johnny Carlson. Lives on Desolate Bend near Tears of Departure. You will need to feed your spirit before you confront him."

Kole figured he would pour himself a second cup and hope for the best. "What should I know about him?"

"The man has no spirit animal, and he lives in darkness. Evil surrounds him. It is time for the heat inside of the earth to consume his body."

The click of the receiver being hung up echoed in Kole's mind for the drive to Carlson's place, a few miles from Cherokee sacred land. Did Grandfather's last statement imply he wanted Kole to act against the man and force Carlson to leave the area? And did that mean the state… or this earth? Had Grandfather instructed him to kill the courier Carlson and burn his bones?

He arrived at Carlson's home in less than forty minutes. The place was easy to spot, exactly as Grandfather had described it: a patch of land that had lost all its dignity, beauty, and light. In the shadows of the oaks, poplars, and sweetgums, it looked sinister.

Kole knocked on the front door. A young woman answered—actually, he was wrong. Her heavy makeup, pink mini-skirt, tube top, and fishnets and heels, helped the preteen girl to masquerade as a whore.

"Are you the guy?" she said.

Kole pushed past her. Inside the trailer, a black digital camera on a metal tripod pointed downward to a piece of fake fur shaped like a bear. Beside it on the floor was a computer, displaying the last photograph taken of the girl. The suggestive nude image roiled his stomach.

Carlson relaxed on a cushioned chair, working a keyboard.

Kole kicked over the tripod and smashed his foot into the screen.

Carlson stood, ready to swing a punch, but Kole had already started a one-two on the man.

Carlson yelled as he tumbled backward over the chair.

"Leave him alone, mister," the girl said.

"What's your name?" Kole asked.

"Candy Sweet."

He shook his head. The girl wasn't a newbie in the industry but seasoned and knew what she was doing.

"Your parents know you're here?"

"Daddy died in a coal mine. Mom and me live with Pops. He's got black lung disease and there's not much left of Mom. The doctors cut her so many times to get the cancer that she can't walk or speak. Quit eating, too. Pops set this up and Mr. Carlson pays me plenty of money."

"Find a new gig." Kole shoved her out the door.

He grabbed Carlson off the floor and tossed him into the only chair in the room.

"I'll have you arrested for breaking in and assault." Carlson rubbed his jaw.

"Here's how it's going to go," Kole said. "You'll answer all of my questions and destroy every one of your files. If you don't, then ask yourself if a eunuch is still a man."

"This is my living. I don't force the bitches."

"Tell me about the night of the train robbery."

"Someone hit me on the head that night. Don't remember anything."

Kole picked Carlson out of the chair, then punched him in the gut with enough force to drive Carlson back down. "I'm losing my patience."

Carlson sucked air. His eyes bulged.

Kole reached for him again. He figured one more blow would soften the man up.

But Carlson threw up his hands and yelled, "Wait!"

Carlson started to talk. For something that happened over a decade ago, Carlson described the night in great detail. He told how it'd been a secretive run, with mysterious men guarding the train, the two diamonds entrusted to him, and the teenage runaway.

"This girl," Kole said, "did you kidnap her?"

"No."

"Have sex with her?"

"I told you she hit me on the head."

"But you wanted to."

"She offered."

Kole grabbed Carlson.

"Don't hit me," the man said. "I'm cooperating with you."

"What happened to her?"

"How in the hell would I know? She talked about visiting some big cities."

Kole walked to the outside door. The top hinge hung by a single bent screw, and it was pulled out most of the way. The next windstorm and this door would be history.

He turned and scanned the trailer. Carlson was slumped, motionless. The inside reeked of unknown odors. No matter how many ceremonies Grandfather performed here—if Carlson would even think to ask—it would never be cleansed. The whole place should be burned to the ground so the wind could carry the ashes—and stink—away.

How could that pre-teen girl think this was a great place to sell her body? He guessed the cash was good.

He returned to Carlson.

"This girl on the train, how'd she get the diamonds?"

"I didn't say she did. She whacked me on the head. When I came to, she and the diamonds were gone."

"I doubt someone else jumped on a moving train."

"It happens all the time. Don't you watch westerns?"

Carlson's story had more holes in it than the Titanic. Grandfather always told him that the truth is never hidden— "Open your eyes and see. Don't the birds spot food from the clouds in the sky? Don't the deer hear the faintest footstep from the hollers? Be part of this earth."

So, what had he seen? Carlson was into porn. The man liked young girls. And, from what Kole saw on the computer screen, Carlson liked to bed them too.

Then a scenario came to him. "Listen closely," Kole said.

Carlson nodded.

"As the train disembarks, this runaway jumps on board. She knows the destination."

"The train only had one destination—the capital. Everyone knew that."

"But instead of detaining her until you arrive at the station to hand her over to the authorities, you see an opportunity."

Carlson smiled.

"But she's not into your type. And she's intelligent. She might even think she can outsmart whoever you turn her over to." Kole waited to see if there was a reaction from Carlson.

The man's eyes were glazed as if he was remembering that night.

"To entice her, you take the diamonds out of the safe and show them to her. Maybe you let her hold the sparkles and play with them."

"She wasn't that pretty. She was short and too skinny. Plus, no boobs."

"The kid reversed the tables and overpowered your ass."

"No way that bitch could beat me. When the train slowed to descend the mountains, she grabbed the diamonds, said something about her girlfriend would definitely go with her, and then jumped."

Kole walked to the doorway again. The fresh air felt good against his face. He inhaled the oxygen and let it clear his lungs of whatever toxins circulated in the trailer.

On his third deep breath, a crow flew and landed on a poplar tree branch beside a second crow. The first one offered a silver gum wrapper to the second.

Kole thanked the Great Spirit.

The runaway on the train knew Aletha. She must have gone to the cave to meet Miller's wife. Aletha would not want any part of the diamonds. But yet, the evidence suggested she'd swallowed one.

The crows cawed and flew off.

What happened next in the cave? This runaway was the key.

He turned back to Carlson. The courier had an ego. Probably didn't even realize he had described the girl and where and when she'd left the train. The fool. "You have one hour to destroy everything, including the camera and computer. If not, Coup will be back with pruning shears."

He left the premises proud of himself for not burning the place to the ground. He was learning self-control.

Thirty-one

Savannah-Jo woke up in a haze. The light felt like daggers when it hit her pupils. She closed them and, with both hands, squeezed her skull to keep it from cracking apart. Outside, a woodpecker hammered into a tree. The ricocheting sound throbbed her cranium. Yelling at it to stop would kill her. This hadn't been one of her better ideas. Damn moonshine.

Last night, Miller's brew had gone down smooth like refreshing spring water.

How much had she drunk? Had she guzzled a pint? Quart? Oh, hell. And where was the man?

She rolled to the side of the stiff bed, not wanting to sit up and cause a dizzy spell. Her clothes were stacked on her boots, undisturbed, just like she'd left them.

Savannah-Jo laid on the bed and closed her eyes for a few more minutes, and hoped a hawk would devour that devil woodpecker, before rising unhurriedly to a sitting position. Then she opened, first, one eye, then the other. The morning light streaming through the windows stung, but the pain was bearable.

She had a memory of Miller sliding under the covers to join her. He had rested his rough hand on her flat stomach, but that was where her recollection ended.

Straining her gray cells, she brought the room and her thoughts into focus. She flipped the sheet off. Shifting, she placed her feet on the floor and clarity returned like pieces of a mosaic.

Nothing had happened between her and Miller, not even with a condom—a woman knows. A missed opportunity for him.

Men treasured the memory of being with her. To her inner voice she responded, *of course they did.* Miller must be gay.

Had last night been worth it? Who was she kidding? She knew better. What did she know now that she hadn't twenty-four hours ago? Nothing.

She looked around his shack. He didn't seem to be home. Maybe now would be a good time to take a peek around this home.

Miller had said someone had shot at Fat Bear. They didn't know who, unless Fat Bear hadn't shared the information with Miller—which was highly likely. Her instinct told her that Fat Bear wasn't an open person. There was something about him that seemed off. His insight was deeply rooted in nature and Cherokee lore. He was the type not to be trusted.

Miller and Fat Bear had discovered the back entrance to the cave, however, neither of them had been able to pass through the exit. Since they weren't overweight, it must be partially blocked. An earthquake could do that.

The tap-tap-tap of that evil bird continued. Of all times not to have her gun. The woodpecker was more annoying than a young city councilman pawing at her during a charity fund raiser.

Miller hadn't mentioned finding the second diamond. It had to be somewhere in the cave. Had they found anything—any evidence that Miller didn't kill his wife? They must not have, or else he'd have danced with joy.

Nothing made sense.

The sunlight in the room became more intense. Why didn't the man have curtains? Her head felt like a pressure tank.

She turned away from the reflective walls. The rays of light casted a sliver of a shadow on the floor, revealing a crack between the boards of wood. She eased herself down to it. Everything else in this house was precision built; how did Miller screw up the floor? She noticed it wasn't a miscalculation in his carpentry.

After getting a butter knife from the kitchen, she slid it into the crack and raised a floorboard. Jackpot.

Stuffed inside where dusty letters wrapped in a rubber band. She read a few. Love letters from Miller to Aletha—how sweet. No mention of how Miller liked sex with her, must not have been any. The guy was definitely gay.

She laid the letters aside. Below them was a new single sheet of paper. She unfolded it.

At first, it looked like doodling. If her head hadn't been in a thick fog, it would have been easier to understand.

Then she saw the small print. Miller had the worst handwriting she had seen. He had labeled structures.

It came to her. This was a map of Devil's Cave.

A rush of adrenaline coursed through her. Lost memories from her childhood flooded her brain. "Of course, of course," she repeated as the images filled in gaps from a long time ago.

She returned everything as they'd been and refitted the board in place.

What should she do next? Follow Fat Bear or stick to Miller. Plus, she couldn't forget about Reggie.

Fat Bear had Grandfather and the Cherokee tribe helping him. Reggie knew Monterey's history and the local gossip. But everything revolved around Miller. If anything was discovered, or some event was going to occur, Miller had the right to know. And Miller and Fat Bear were client and attorney.

However, Coup was required by law to share with Fat Bear any evidence she uncovered. Not that Savannah-Jo could tell if Coup had discovered anything of significance. Even though Miller was the one on trial, everything kept coming back to Fat Bear's actions.

Fat Bear, it was.

She had to get back to her motel room, consume some aspirin, and rest for an hour or two.

Damn that moonshine. This was a setback in her investigation.

It took longer than she expected to dress. She had to stop and refocus her eyes a few times. After she had slipped her lime green panties on, she picked up a saucer from the table and threw it outside at the satanic bird. As she laced her boots, a realization came to her—Miller was a sneaky bastard.

He had taken the knife. But two could play this game of hide-and-seek.

Thirty-two

Coup stepped into Helen's hospital room. The drapes blocked the harsh morning light attempting to penetrate the room. The dim lighting filled the corners with shadows. Orange bulbs glowed from different monitors. A soft *beep, beep* broke the silence every few seconds. The place felt peaceful and secure.

But Coup knew better. Helen was in a coma. Not a damn thing peaceful or secure about that.

She planned to review Aletha's case file. The brown folder contained a few pages. The community, Mennonite and non-Mennonite, figured she had run away, and there was no evidence to suggest otherwise. She hoped the original detective had written down an observation that would be significant now.

She spoke out loud, "Maybe, just maybe, Helen would wake up. Wouldn't that be wonderful?"

Helen looked comfortable lying in the bed, with the sheet and blanket pulled up around her chest. Her arms, uncovered, lay straight, with tubes and wires attached.

Coup sank into an off-white, oversized, cushioned chair beside the bed, then opened the file she'd brought with her. "Let's see what this old file contains. Think we'll find something?"

The only answer was the machine's *beep, beep.*

"It says Aletha had a few friends outside the Mennonite community." Coup considered that statement. "What do you think about that, Helen? A Mennonite teen having non-Mennonite friends. I think it's strange because the Mennonites are a closed society. Well, mostly. They have their own school system to the eighth grade, and they're not encouraged to attend high school because it's too worldly."

No answer came from Helen.

Coup tried to stay positive. "I guess that, if she worked in their general store, she could meet girls her age. Yes, very likely." Coup stood up and walked over to the room's entrance, closed the door, then returned to her chair. She felt a little foolish talking out loud, but she had read a few articles that said people in a coma could hear others and that it helped them recover faster.

"The file says the detective questioned one friend, Terri-Mae, several times. States here that it was a dead end."

Someone said, "I bet Fat Bear thinks *you're* a dead end."

"Helen?"

"No." Paige walked into the room and smiled. She wore tight jeans and a snug yellow shirt. She ran her fingers through her windblown hair.

"You spooked me," Coup said. "Can we forget about last night?"

Paige nodded. "Any change in Helen's status?"

"The doctors said to be patient, and the patrolmen from Cookeville have volunteered to guard her door."

"I've met a few. All studs."

Paige always seemed to be on the prowl. She bounced around, never getting too serious. Coup wondered what it was like to be carefree.

"Did you get Fat Bear's number?"

Coup closed the file. "I'm a cop. I can get anyone's phone number. Plus, he is in constant trouble with the H.O.A. I often have to go to his place and settle disputes, so I know where he lives. Any more questions?"

"What's his bedroom like? Rugged, like him?"

"Never been inside and don't plan on entering his domicile."

"With a name like Fat Bear, and him being part Cherokee, I bet he likes making love under the stars."

"Paige," Coup used her stern sheriff's voice, "give it a rest."

"Yes, sir, officer." Paige saluted her and laughed.

Coup tried to stifle hers, then she let it come out.

Coup looked at Helen. Not even a smile formed on her pale face. The sight brought back the seriousness of Helen's injuries.

"I'll leave you be," Paige said. "I'll check on her after my shift."

Coup tapped the file. "Ever know anyone by the name of Terri-Mae?"

"Can't say I have."

"Okay. Thanks."

Paige closed the door behind her.

Coup let her mind wander. Last night had been nice, until Fat Bear had ruined it by giving her tainted evidence. He knew better. But he had found something that no one else had found— the tube of purple lipstick. Could it be the Cherokee in him that gave him extra talents? And was Paige right—did he like doing it outside versus inside?

What the hell was she thinking?

She ran her hands across her face, and then opened the file folder. "Where were we, Helen?"

Beep, beep. Had the monitor gotten louder? It was now getting on her nerves. Did it bother Helen, too?

"I have the Monterey yearbook for the year Aletha went missing. Go Wildcats." She flipped a few pages of the worn hardback. "Helen, their school colors are purple and black. Just great." She said the last word with as much sarcasm as she could muster. "Wouldn't be surprised if all the girls posed with purple lipstick and eye shadow."

After thumbing past the pages of sport photos and club group shots, she found the portraits.

For some reason, the original detective hadn't listed the girl's last name. Sloppy police work. He too, probably thought it was a runaway case.

Toward the end, she spotted Terri-Mae's headshot. Last name, Roberson. The teenager had long, black hair. And that was the only black in the color yearbook photo. The girl wore purple eye shadow, purple lipstick, and a purple V-neck top.

"This girl loves purple. What do you say I pay her a visit? Good idea, Helen?"

Beep, beep.

Thirty-three

Coup drove past the gnarly oak tree that gave the two-lane road its name, Hanging Limb Highway. Decades before it'd been no wider than two ruts pocketed with potholes. A few summers ago, the county had decided to pave it. They should have chain sawed the oak down at the same time. It didn't matter if someone was white, black, Indian, or somewhere in between, the locals served their own justice. Durning an execution, the community would read from the Bible, and yell, "Praise Jesus" as the rope were pulled taut.

This was another part of Tennessee where the residents didn't like meddlers. And if one showed up, they'd disappear, and the community knew nothing. Those lynchings were more of Coup's grandfather's times. She had never investigated a hanging at this rocky terrain, thank God.

She wondered what kind of reception she could expect from Terri-Mae.

The attitudes hadn't changed, but the method had—to double-barrels or nine millimeters.

For this visit, she changed the load in her auto to hollow points.

Coup pulled into the driveway of the modest vinyl house, then slid out of her car. She knocked rapidly on the front porch screen door of the basement house hard enough to make it rattle. The home design had once been unique to Tennessee. It was called this because the structural back of the dwelling was built into a sloping hill. A person could jump from the ground to the top of the tin roof, if the mood struck.

A woman in her late twenties appeared, wearing cutoff shorts and a tight-fitting, purple T-shirt. Her lips were painted purple. "I ain't broke no law, so take your business down the road."

"Terri-Mae, I have a few questions. May I come in?"

"No." Terri-Mae traipsed out of the house onto the porch. She crossed her arms across her chest.

The decking on the porch had long ago been painted purple, but it had scuffed off. The railings and wooden support posts clung to patches of the color.

Coup stepped back, but stayed in the shade provided by the overhang, partially glad she didn't have to enter the house. Even though all the windows were open, it had to be hot inside. The mugginess of the day rose to weather she could wear. And the breeze had died just like the grass in the front yard. If it weren't for the weeds, there would be no green.

"Ask your questions," Terri-Mae said, "and be quick about it."

"It's about Aletha Miller."

"That woman run away long ago."

"We found her body." Coup checked for a reaction.

Sadness crept into the woman's eyes.

Coup waited to see if Terri-Mae mentioned how Aletha was killed. The silence became awkward, so Coup said, "She was stabbed."

"Who would wanna go and do that?" Terri-Mae slumped into a rickety wooden rocker. "Nicest girl I ever met."

"You knew her well?"

"No. She worked in that Mennonite store. But when she got hitched, we'd meet in Devil's Cave to girl talk."

"Somebody killed her there."

"I guess that is as good place as any. She liked that cave."

"That's an odd thing to say."

"Aren't you past a few questions?"

"You seemed to have a fondness for Aletha. Just a few more. It could help to find who killed her."

Terri-Mae looked out across her yard, as if lost in days gone by.

It was quiet. No cars buzzed along the road. No birds chirped in the trees. Coup felt the loneliness of the place.

Terri-Mae rocked, the chair snapping more than it creaked. "She said God was there and she could feel His presence. Why the Almighty would go in Devil's Cave beats the hell out of me."

Coup removed an evidence bag from her shirt pocket and held up the sealed pouch containing the tube of lipstick. "Is this yours?"

Terri-Mae stood to get a closer look. "Yep, it's mine." She pointed to the casing. "Back in high school, I would scratch my initials into the metal. Don't do it anymore."

"We believe Aletha had it on her when she was murdered."

"That's nice to hear. I gave it to her as a gift of our friendship. Glad she didn't toss it."

Coup narrowed her eyes. "It could place you at the murder scene at the time of her death."

"Sherriff, you blowing more smoke than my stove." Terri-Mae raised her voice. "When she got killed, I can prove I wasn't there. I didn't do it. My story hasn't changed since that mean detective asked me questions years ago."

"What did he ask you?"

"I have a lunch date. You eating into my get-ready time."

Coup felt sure Terri-Mae wasn't cooking for this lunch date. With the windows wide open, the only odor in the thick air was a pine scent cleaner. "I'm sure if your companion sees me and my cruiser in your front yard, he'll have a lot more questions than I do."

Terri-Mae gave a harrumph.

"No one likes the police here, do they? What if he thinks we're buds?"

After a sigh, Terri-Mae spoke, "You want to know if I knew why she run off. She was a Mennonite and maybe wanted to break free."

"It's odd when a member of their community leaves. Did she tell you that was her desire?"

"No. She loved her husband."

Coup thought of Miller, a loner, who lived away from everyone, on top of a mountain with a difficult road. Did he live in isolation to be closer to God or because he felt rejected?

"In your girl-talk sessions, what topics came up?"

"Mostly God. She wanted me to become a Mennonite. But I would have to give up purple. Can't do that. It's my aura."

"It seems you have a lot of love for that color."

"So did Aletha. That's why I gave her the lipstick."

"She ever wear it?"

"No. It would make her a painted woman." Terri-Mae sat back into her rocker. "She said she had a lot of temptations, and she didn't want to add to them." Terri-Mae stood. "Are we done? I have stuff to do."

"Aletha have any other friends?"

"Tons. All Mennonites, except for me and Jennie-Lee."

That was a name that hadn't come up before. No mention of this girl in the original file. "You know her last name?"

"Simpson or Sandstone. Maybe Sampson. It was a long time ago."

"What was she like?"

"Never met her. But Aletha said Jennie-Lee always talked about traveling the world. I guess she wanted Aletha to go with her. Don't think either had any money. How does a high school girl get money in this town?" Terri-Mae entered the house and then said through the screen door, "You know your way back to town."

The train courier had stated that the woman who'd hit him had wanted to travel the world. Could that girl be Jennie-Lee?

I like it when my tea gets sweetened.

Thirty-four

Miller stood in the shade of the giant oak tree and ran his hand across the rough bark. The trunk had deep grooves and creases. A lone branch stretched out horizontally like a boney arm, and had a gouge worn into it from the countless times a rope had been tossed over it. The gray-brown color of the tree gave off a sense of sadness and sorrow. He said a prayer for both the innocent and the guilty whose lives ended here.

He walked down the path along Hanging Limb Highway to Terri-Mae's place. When he and Fat Bear had discovered the tube of purple lipstick, he'd known it had belonged to that worldly woman who had, no doubt, filled Aletha's head with impure thoughts.

The path consisted of broken limestone. The pieces were larger than dinner plates and didn't crunch underneath his feet. He preferred no one heard him, so he followed the trail off the road and down the steep embankment, low enough that he was hidden from the view of passing cars. That was what he liked best about this walkway.

As he marched, he thought about Savannah-Jo. What did she want with his knife? Was she so dumb that she didn't think he would notice it missing? City women… He didn't trust any of them. Nashville was full of strip joints and street hookers, a city of devious women. There was no room for the Divine.

Too many people lived in the cities. It was easy to lose one's direction. Rural living was better for every aspect of life. But he knew country life also had evil people. And he was on his way to confront one.

He didn't wait on Terri-Mae's porch. Nor did he knock on the screen door. He stepped inside and let the wooden frame door slam behind him to announce his presence.

She sat on a purple leather loveseat. When she turned and looked at him, Miller saw the change in her eyes go from "Who are you" to recognition.

"Get the hell out of my house."

"I'm giving you a chance to confess and repent."

"For what? Being a friend to your wife?"

"I know you killed her. You were in that cave that day."

"I'm not the one whose ass was thrown out of the church."

Miller paused. No matter how many times he was forced to remember what had happened to him, it still cut deep. He'd done whatever the church had asked of him. He'd helped build the annex, donated food to those who ran out, offered his home in the winter to those without heat. Then, with no evidence of any wrongdoing, he was excommunicated. Banned. Never to set his eyes on his community again.

It wasn't his fault. He had been abandoned, just like Job.

"You filled her head with leaving. That there was something better outside of our church."

"Miller, you've gone loony. If I believed that, then what am I still doing here?"

He glanced around the room. All of the furniture was top grade. And didn't look more than a year old.

"It must have cost a fortune to furnish your home. Where'd you get the funds?"

"None of your business."

"But no A/C?"

"I ain't wasting electricity to make you comfortable. I saw you walk up *and* that bitch cop. Shut the air off. So, leave. I'm getting warm."

"You didn't sell a diamond, did you? There's no way you can afford all of this stuff."

"I have a job. A good one. And I know how to manage my money. I'm smart."

Miller frowned. "Look how you paint yourself."

"Get out or I'm calling the police."

"Jeremiah, chapter 4, verse thirty, 'and when thou art spoiled, what will thou do? Though thou clothest thyself with crimson, though thou deckest thee with ornaments of gold, though thou rentest thy face with painting, in vain shalt thou make thyself fair, thy lovers will despise thee, they will seek thy life.'"

Terrie-Mae headed for the closet. "Forget the police." She pulled out a double-barreled shotgun, then cocked both triggers.

The sound didn't bother Miller. He was ready to join Aletha.

She pointed the black steel at him.

He grabbed the end of the weapon and pushed it against his chest. "Go ahead, blow a hole in me. Seal your fate in damnation."

She tugged the gun back.

Miller pulled it against his head. "Take my head off."

She let go of it, crossed the room, grabbed a purple landline phone, and dialed three digits.

He heard the muffled voice on the other end, "9 1 1, what's your emergency?"

"Hurry. I have an intruder in my house, and I fear for my life."

Miller kicked the screen door open, then stomped out into the heat. Passing clouds cast harsh shadows on her driveway as he walked on the gravel.

He reflected on the women who had crossed his path in the last few days. Coup wanted to convict him of murder. Savannah-Jo had tried to seduce him and steal from him. And Terri-Mae felt she had the right to end his life. But she didn't have the grit. Her eyes had told him she was bluffing. She liked money and what it could buy. Nashville was the place for her.

Were there any women left as pure as his Aletha?

Thirty-five

Coup slammed on her brakes when she pulled into Fat Bear's driveway. Her car fishtailed several feet, then skidded on the gravel. The complaint from Terrie-Mae justified locking Miller up until the trial. Why had Miller gone to Terri-Mae's house? Why had Fat Bear let him? If she had to, she'd lock Fat Bear up also to get answers.

And what were those wrecked cars along the road in front of Fat Bear's house doing here?

That man could turn a sunny day into tornado-blackened skies.

She stomped on the gravel when she slid out of the cruiser. The garage door was up. It looked like Fat Bear was checking his fishing gear. He had tackle spread out on the gray concrete beside a green plastic box, and a 3-in-1 oil can set beside a black fishing rod. Wooden matches, a banged-up steel frying pan, and some canned seasonings added to the pile.

"Get over here!" she yelled.

"You come over here."

She slammed the car door. A few birds flapped their wings and flew to a nearby persimmon tree. "I'm here on police business."

"Great. And I'm out of the sun. Why don't you join me? I have a few questions about the case."

The day's heat was building. The sun's rays burned her skin like Fat Bear was doing to her temperament. Plus, the brightness caused her vision to waver. God, she hoped an episode wasn't starting.

She closed her eyes and waited.

Nothing. So far, so good. She exhaled. "Do you know what that idiot Miller did this morning?"

"Cooked some corn in his still?"

"Harassed Terri-Mae."

"Did she deserve it?"

"Hell, no."

Coup wiped her forehead. Fat Bear angered her as much as Miller. This man flowed from one end of the spectrum to the other. Last night, he had seemed almost human but, today, he was back to his arrogant self. And he had that stupid grin on his face again, which added to her annoyance. Or did it irritate her because she liked it?

"I guess," Kole said, "that, at some point in this conversation, you'll tell me who Terri-Mae is."

She sucked in a breath, then let it out, hoping the anger and exasperation in her went with it. "The girl who owns the purple lipstick."

"Is Miller still with Terri-Mae?"

"No. He left."

Fat Bear opened a rusty, six-foot metal locker. It leaned to one side and looked like it'd been dragged home from the dump.

"You need to get him under control."

Fat Bear didn't respond. He was moving lumber to the side and reaching for something. Then he shifted and his back was to her, blocking her view.

"This gives me grounds for throwing his ass behind bars. The judge would agree."

Fat Bear continued to ignore her.

"Are you listening?"

He stopped, faced her, and held a blue, open reel fishing pole. "This should be a good one for you. I've caught a few fighters with it."

"I'm not going fishing. Especially with you."

"Don't think of it like we might actually do something

enjoyable today. Think of it as sheriff and defender meeting in an off-site location to discuss the latest developments in the Miller case."

"I'll admit, last night was pleasant for a few minutes, but the feeling has passed."

Fat Bear tossed a pair of tan, waist-high waders toward her. "You'll need those."

She left them lying on the apron to the garage. "You will be sharing some valuable intel?"

"To be divulged at the meeting."

"I'm not happy about being played."

Fat Bear walked to the opposite side of the garage, then opened an old, wooden, upright dresser. He pulled out a long-sleeve shirt and pants. "Best if you changed into these. Hate for your official uniform to get muddy."

"Where are we going?"

"See that creek alongside my property? We're going to follow it to a waterfall, then work our way down to its base. A deep pool is there, and with this warm weather, the largemouth bass will congregate in it."

Reluctantly, Coup notified dispatch that she'd be meeting with Fat Bear and most likely be in a radio dead zone. She then entered Fat Bear's house and walked into the guest bathroom to change clothes. The jeans and shirt fit loosely and smelled of the forest.

In the hallway were paintings depicting Cherokee life before the Europeans arrived, and, in the bathroom, frames of different styles of arrowheads were fastened to the wall beside the mirror. For a man who didn't want to accept his heritage, he had items contradicting that. He was a conflicted man, for sure.

After some thought, she resisted the urge to peek into his bedroom.

Once she was back outside, she saw Fat Bear had packed some basic cooking gear, a jug of moonshine—which she was sure had been distilled by Miller—and a sleeping bag rolled up.

"I don't have time to be gone all day," she said. "And I'm not spending the night with you."

"Let's catch some fish and fry them up."

"This isn't a date. It's an official meeting."

"Doesn't matter to me what you call it. I'm hungry for some bass."

Fat Bear slung the pack over his shoulders. He handed two poles to Coup, while he carried a tackle box and a cooler.

They passed two damaged cars as they headed toward the creek. Engine coolant had stained the road, and the sweet smell of the liquid still lingered.

"What happened to those cars?"

"Killer lightning bugs."

She laughed. Her gut told her that Fat Bear had something to do with it. Someone would raise hell, but not today.

This afternoon she wasn't on a date with Fat Bear; they were just going fishing together.

Thirty-six

Kole stood at the base of the waterfall and looked upward to its crest. The blueish water poured over a wide semi-circular cut in the limestone. But before the outpour plunged into the pool, it formed a spray that reflected the light into an array of colors. It was as if he stood inside a rainbow surrounded by a gurgling fog. Nature amazed him with Her different wonders. Here in this basin, he felt at peace with the mountain. It was a place where danger never lurked, and the fish wanted to be caught. He was ready to do so.

"Take a deep breath," he said.

Coup did so along with him.

The air was cool and energized. He hoped she felt it also.

"The ancient ones," Kole said, "say the water breaks apart, no longer a fluid, and cleanses the air and all is pure."

"It's magical." She held her head up to the mist and inhaled again.

Kole looked at Coup. The setting sun was dappled across her face. Moisture clung to her eyebrows and lashes. Her wet lips looked as if droplets of the morning dew had descended on them. It was as if the poplar, hemlocks, and hickory trees cast an illuminating shadow on her, showing a beauty, he had never seen before.

No longer the tough cop who separated people into criminals and future offenders, she had a smile that stretched across her face as if something had been unveiled to her.

He leaned in to taste her lips.

Coup moved toward him, then abruptly stepped back. "Did we come to fish and discuss Miller or not?"

The spell was broken. But something deep in him said it was only a pause.

A high-pitched note carried through the canyon. An indigo bunting with his metallic blue body looked down upon him. A few sharper, clearer notes from the bird came, as if hinting at a change was coming.

Grandfather would have said a transformation will occur upon hearing the bird. But he'd never explained what or how or when. For the better, Kole hoped—for mercy for Miller.

"We'll discuss Miller later," he said. "Let me show you how to cast."

Coup laughed. "My dad taught me to fish. He was the best. He always caught more than anyone else. The same goes for me."

"So was Grandfather. Only, he didn't need a hook, line, or bait. He summoned the fish, and, with his hands, tossed them on shore."

"He may have done it that way, but I bet you need a pole."

"I was taught well."

"The only way you can flip them out of the water is if you toss dynamite at them. And that's illegal."

Her responses were humorous and playful. This was a side of Coup he'd never seen.

"A challenge, then," he said. "Whoever catches the least number of fish must clean and cook them and tidy up the campsite."

"Knowing you, you'll fish all night." Coup checked her watch. "We'll fish for one hour, then it will be dinner time."

"You can work the basin. I'll attempt my luck around the rim."

"No farther than that. I want to keep an eye on you. Don't even think about cheating."

"Hope you know how to cook."

"You can have the first piece in case I burn it."

This was going to be fun. He didn't know which would bring the most pleasure—catching more than her or watching her cook. He turned to head to the bend in the run just beyond the basin. That place had always provided good results.

Coup whacked him across his butt with her rod. "One hour. A minute longer, and you forfeit."

He stopped where the outflow narrowed. The current ran strong and formed pockets in the stream bed. The white water swirled around black, polished rocks. He waded in. The ripples cooled his legs. Halfway across, he picked a spot and prepared to outwit the underwater world. His feet were shoulder-width apart. He arched forward so his chest hovered above the surface. He dipped his hands in elbow-deep and waited.

"Hey!" Coup yelled. "You should face the bank."

"I was checking the topography for the perfect spot." He adjusted his stance, so he was perpendicular to the stream.

Fingerlings swam around his legs and pecked at his waders as they ballooned in the current. Crawfish pulled at the rubber feet. A few small bass swam by. He didn't attempt to spoon those to the bank. Not only did he want to catch the most fish, but the biggest one as well.

One eased toward him, easily a foot-and-a-half long. The fish's gills opened and closed, revealing the red membranes inside.

Kole hunched in the shadows, a safe zone for the aquatic animals. Minnows nibbled on the hairs on his hands and arms.

Come closer big boy. His back twitched, wanting to straighten and stretch. But this catch would win the wager. A satisfaction filled him.

The fish came closer. The olive-green body contrasted against the white sandy river bottom, its mouth slanted upward in a predator look.

Kole could feel the slime of the fish's body scoot across his fingers and then into the cup of his hands.

The zing of Coup's line running jarred him.

"One for me!" Coup yelled.

He ignored her and set his feet again. He wiggled his little finger, teasing the fish back.

The big boy approached and stopped between his legs.

Another inch or two and he'd have him and victory.

The plop of an artificial fly hit the water beside him.

The fish grabbed it and darted away. The fishing line skittered against his leg. He felt the line tightened and then being reeled in.

"Two!" she said.

"What are you doing casting in my area?" he said and stood.

"No rule stating where I could or couldn't fish."

A crash sounded from above the falls. A semi-truck-long popular tree appeared on the precipice. Water built up behind it and flowed over the top. The trunk teetered back and forth.

Coup stood in the middle of the stream, mesmerized.

"Run to the shore!" he shouted.

The tree toppled over the falls, followed by more trunks and limbs. The backed-up water rolled in a wave of destruction.

He splashed to Coup and shook her.

She came out of the trance.

Kole pulled her after him.

The giant tree hit, top first, into the pool and then fell toward them.

They were out of the middle of the creek. Another few feet, and he and Coup would be on shore—a safe place—but debris churned the water, drowning everything in its path.

A branch swept by him, catching him at his knees, and he went under.

Coup clutched his arm.

The tree limb rolled them along the gravel. He was lost in a swirl of bubbles.

Coup rolled on top of him.

He grabbed her and crawled to shallower water. The branches raked his back and pulled him several feet. Finally, the snags let loose, and he was no longer being carried along the bottom.

He knelt in the water, Coup beside him.

"That's a first," he said.

"And I'm completely soaked." She stood, removed her

waders and poured the water out of them. She adjusted her watch on her wrist. "And your hour is up."

They pulled off their waders and walked back to their gear.

"I have two. You have a big goose egg."

Damn. The woman had out-fished him. "You start the fire, and I'll clean them," he said.

A boom of thunder brought his attention to the darkening sky. The weather had changed. The first drops of rain pelted the ground around him.

"Now what?" Coup asked.

He motioned for her to follow him and handed her the two poles to carry. He carried the rest of the gear. A narrow path led into a thicket of rhododendrons. It felt like the humidity doubled. Bees swarmed to one side, headed back to their hive.

After about a hundred yards, they broke into a clearing. Another few feet, and he led her behind the waterfall and into a cavern where a curtain of water separated them from the world. He helped her up onto a dry, limestone ledge. "We'll stay dry here."

A few minutes later, he had a wide fire burning. The heat took the chill out of the cavern. He threw a few cedar branches into the flames to season the fish, then he rummaged through his pack for cooking and eating utensils. Coup laid the filets on red coals between two aluminum mesh grids.

Kole opened a jar of Miller's moonshine and handed it to her. "Take it easy with this. It goes down like water."

She sipped it. Then she smiled and took a full gulp. "You're right."

As they ate, they watched the lighting brighten the sky in odd patterns. When the atmosphere burst into light, Kole could see the rain splashing the stream and pounding the rocks, but not hear it. The bellowing waterfall changed in color from blue to a chocolate brown.

Darkness seeped into the cave while the fire burned down to mostly white embers. The jar of shine lay empty between them.

"It's getting cold." Coup pulled her legs up to her chest and wrapped her arms around them. "The shine didn't warm me."

His head was foggy—too much of Miller's brew. He thought of pulling Coup close to him so they could snuggle together. This was a fool's plan, she'd toss him into the waterfall. In the back of his head was a warning from Grandfather, but he could not understand it. Images of a Cherokee tribe resting for the night entered his mind. They looked happy. A young couple disappeared into the back passages of the cave. They held each other tightly.

His stomach rumbled.

There was one large piece of fish left on the grill. He pointed to it and looked at Coup.

She waved him away.

Weaving some from the shine, he stumbled to the last bit of dinner and tossed it into his mouth.

He tripped.

Coup laughed at him.

The food lodged in his throat. He forced himself to swallow, but… nothing. It was still stuck.

A cough proved useless.

He tried inhaling, but no air passed to his lungs. A dizzy blackness overcame him. Coup was talking to him, but he couldn't understand her. He clutched his throat, then toppled over.

Someone lifted him, then pounded his back.

Coup squeezed his stomach inward with enough force it felt like a car had hit him. The piece of fish flew into the darkness.

Breaths returned.

"Being drunk and stuffing your mouth is not a good idea," Coup said.

"That sobered me up. Glad I brought you along."

Coup stayed close to him and ran her hand across his cheek and onto his chest, her breath warm on his face. She brushed dirt out of his hair, staying focused on his eyes.

After brushing some pebbles off the slab, he unrolled his sleeping bag. He removed his wet clothes, piled them at the foot and slid in. With one hand, he held the bag open. "Care to join me? If we cuddle, we'll stay warm."

She stared at him.

Unsure of the thoughts that went through her head, he was afraid she would stay by the dying fire and arrest him tomorrow.

"Hell, why not." She stripped and lay on her side alongside him. "Miller's brew is keeping me from thinking straight."

He wrapped his arm around her waist and felt the heat of her skin. Her body was smooth and firm. The smell of whiskey seeped from her pores, enticing him. Her hair fell across his face.

It wasn't long before his desires overcame him. To his surprise, he found she was an active participant… with her own ideas and positions.

Thirty-seven

Coup stood under the showerhead. The hot water sprayed out of the fixture directly above her like a hard rain. It felt wonderful. Of the three showers Fat Bear had at his home—in the master bedroom, the guest bath, and an outdoor, open-roof one—she chose the latter. She enjoyed the sense of liberation of standing naked outdoors as the warblers chirped from the tree branches. Although she did shoo off a crow who perched himself on top of the side and stared at her.

Fat Bear had put some thought into this stall. It had a cement floor six inches above the ground and sloped so the water ran off the foundation. A neck-high wooden fence with a single, roughhewn, hinged door surrounded the bathing area so she could see out into the forest. Plus, he had built the enclosure large enough that it had a dry area to hang a change of clothes, where hers hung, including her service weapon and portable police radio.

She was a fool for climbing into the sleeping bag with Fat Bear last night. She blamed the shine—although it hadn't affected her memories; those were hers to keep.

But now, how should she consider their relationship? Pretend it hadn't happened? Deny it, as in a he said/she said situation? Treat the two of them as cop and citizen? Or sheriff and defense attorney? Act the same as before last night?

No, none of that would be possible. There was a thin line she had crossed. If Miller found out, he could argue they were in collaboration against him, and the judge would rule in his favor, charges dropped. God, what had she done?

Her radio came to life. "Sheriff, are you there?"

She cranked the water valve off, then dried her arms and hands. "What is it, Dragging? Any problems filling in as the temporary dispatcher?"

"Been trying to reach you all morning."

"I was following up on a few leads."

Coup continued to towel herself. Not far from the house was a small meadow. The green field looked inviting compared to the surrounding forest where several trees had fallen and now rotted. The timbers were packed so close together, squirrels didn't have to jump from branch to branch. A fawn with its white spots munched on the tall grass. After satisfying its hunger, the animal hunkered down and disappeared from the world, still too young to know the dangers.

She, too, wanted to lie in the abandoned field and let the world pass her by.

After a long pause, Dragging spoke again, "Any success?"

She could tell by his voice that he didn't believe her and wanted to pursue what she really did. She wrapped the towel around her head. "Do you have something for me?"

"Fingerprint on the lipstick gave us a hit."

"It was Terri-Mae's."

"Correct."

Coup wondered if any of the Dobermans had seen her roaming around the woods with Fat Bear. Those bitches could spread rumors faster than a mountain wildfire in the heat of summer. Did Dragging know about the fishing trip?

If he asked her about it, how could she respond? Did she need to? She didn't want to blame it on the whiskey; that would make people think she couldn't control her actions. Not good for a sheriff. A law officer always had to have mastery over their conduct.

But what about her relationship with Fat Bear? Treat it as casual sex, no big deal? Maybe every couple of months when the urge rose, they'd get together. Could she keep that a secret? Did it *need* to be kept a secret? She needed to consult her doctor for some birth control.

The crow flew back and landed on the fence. After scrutinizing the enclosure, he cawed.

She swung her arm at him to get him to fly.

"Results on Miller's knife came back."

"It had Aletha's blood on it and Miller's fingerprints."

"True. But a match popped up on another set of the prints."

"Whose?"

"A Jennie Lee Sampson."

This was the girl Terri-Mae had tried to remember. "Terri-Mae said Aletha had a friend called Jennie. What's the address?"

"That's the strange part. Her prints came from the juvie file. Arrested twice for shop lifting. Minor stuff. Never served any time except for one night in the slammer."

"And?"

"That's it. She's never applied for a driver license, credit cards, or bought anything on time. No record of a death certificate either. She is not in any of our databases, the state's, or the fed's. The earth has consumed her."

"Say that again."

"She's a spirit."

Coup had to pause the conversation before Dragging dwelled on an ancient Cherokee belief that, when someone dies, their soul is manifested into the body of an animal. She counted to ten. "What about her parents?"

"Both dead."

"Any other relatives?"

"One—an aunt. She hadn't seen or heard from Jennie since she was a baby. And didn't want to. Guess the aunt didn't get along with Jennie or her parents."

"Keep digging," Coup said. "Check missing persons and any unclaimed Jane Doe."

"I've started that. Nothing so far."

"If she was a runaway, maybe she crossed the border

illegally and is in Mexico or Canada. Any way we can check that?"

"I'll see."

That last request was a long shot. Jennie could sneak into any country and buy a new identity. Maybe she did but had stayed in the States. "Run facial recognition on driver licenses for all fifty states."

"Okay. It will take days for the results to be completed."

"Better odds of finding a tick in the wintertime but do it."

Out in the meadow, the fawn's mother stood, glancing around at the surroundings. Protective.

Coup had another question for Dragging. She didn't really have to ask, because if the answer was good news, he would have already told her. But, still, she had to ask. She breathed deep and hoped. "Any word on Helen?"

Dragging sighed. "No change."

And that was bad news. The doctors had told her when Helen came out of surgery that they should know something in a few days.

A few days had passed.

Fat Bear peeked over the top of the wooden fence with a stupid grin. "New suspect?"

She wondered what he thought of last night. He'd enjoyed it; that had been evident. So, should she treat the event as if they were now lovers?

She thought about putting on some clothes.

That thought passed.

Thirty-eight

"Who is this mystery girl?" Kole asked Coup. He peered over the fence and watched her unwrap the towel from around her head and give her scalp a good rub. A thin stream of steam rose from the concrete pad. It reminded him of the early morning fog. Through the mist, he saw Coup had painted her toenails a sparkly, emerald green. He wondered if anyone else knew.

"I thought this wall was supposed to offer privacy. But you are peeking over the top, ogling a naked woman, acting like a pervert. Do you want to be arrested?"

He continued to stare, letting her curves, skin tone, and firmness, burn into his memory. He turned and leaned against the wooden structure. The rough-cut boards bit into his back and were the opposite of the softness he'd held last night. The woodsy scent of the soap and shampoo waffled through the slats. He smiled as he realized Coup hadn't covered herself, but had let him have his fun as a voyeur.

"How much of the conversation did you hear?"

"Enough to think Jennie Lee creates sufficient doubt to clear Miller."

"You'll need to do better than that, Counselor. Blaming a murder on someone who may or may not have been there is a long shot."

"Reasonable doubt is all I need." He felt like an adolescent boy wanting to look over the fence again. *Focus on the case*, he told himself. Yesterday, he hadn't had one thought about Miller's murder charge; today, he needed to concentrate on it fully. He'd find Jennie Lee.

"Have you come across this girl in your endeavors?" Coup asked.

"No. And never heard Grandfather talk about a runaway. But, then again, he wouldn't have. He never discussed white man's problems unless it involved the Cherokees."

"I don't think Dragging is going to find much more about her."

"Grandfather would say that she's smoke in the wind—here, then gone forever."

A damp towel hit him on the back of the head. Was Coup being flirtatious with him or was she throwing a wet blanket at his idea?

He walked to the clothesline, hung the cloth, then returned to the fence. A cool breeze ruffled the towel, signaling a false start to autumn. Grandfather had taught him to face the wind and embrace whatever changes that were about to occur.

Kole straightened, investigated the gust, and thought about possible transformations. Would they be positive or negative?

"I have a strong case for getting the charges dropped," he said, but not with conviction.

"No… what you have is a Mennonite girl killed with Miller's knife."

"Yes, but we know there were two diamonds, and one is missing. If that was the motive for the killing and Miller took the diamond, why would he still be living here? It's worth as much as the mega lottery. He could be living in a beach hut in the Caribbean, sipping umbrella drinks."

"He's a Mennonite. They store their treasures in heaven, and he doesn't drink," she said.

"He bootlegs whiskey."

"Miller thinks what he does is spiritual because Jesus turned water into wine."

"Let's not discuss what can happen with his shine."

Kole didn't blame last night on the whiskey. He wished he could, but Coup had acted differently yesterday—not like a cop. She'd been pure woman who'd exuded sexuality.

He'd never forget that waterfall. "What about the purple girl's fingerprints and the tube of lipstick?" he asked.

"Doesn't place her there at the time of the murder."

"It does put her there, though, and she knew Aletha."

"You're reaching again."

"I think I need to interview her."

"I already did. There are a few peculiarities about her, but nothing related to the case."

"She knows Jennie Lee."

"Doesn't *know* her. Just knew she hung out with Aletha."

"Did you ask her why she's fixated with purple?"

"No. It doesn't have anything to do with the murder. Maybe it's the same reason as you living in the middle of this H.O.A."

"This is tribal land." He hit his fist against the fence. The wind ceased, and the towel hung loose on the line. "And those white bitches aren't going to take it."

It surprised him how quickly the anger spewed out of him. His life was like a wounded hawk in turbulent wind, soaring, then spiraling down, and, before crashing, lifted by the Great Spirit— murder, Dobermans, and people disappearing, all swirled before him.

He hoped the upcoming change would give him clarity and direction. Both were needed to get Miller cleared of the charges.

"I'll tell you what," Coup said. "I have to go see Terri-Mae and follow up on the complaint she lodged against Miller. You can tag along."

He walked to the side of the shower enclosure and opened the door.

She stood before him naked. "I wondered how long I would have to stand here."

The breeze began again. He closed the door behind him.

Thirty-nine

Kole followed Coup, he in his side-by-side, she in her squad car. He pressed the accelerator hard to the floor to keep up with the woman who must have wanted to set a new speed record. It wasn't long before he slid sideways into Terri-Mae's front yard, digging ruts into the dewy grass.

Coup jumped out of her car but remained standing behind the open driver's side door and tapped her service weapon. "Wait here," she said.

Kole also felt something was wrong.

She strode to the front door. It amazed him how quickly she transformed from a sultry woman to a hardened cop.

He crept toward the house, staying out of the line-of-sight with the front door.

After knocking, Coup called out, "Monterey police!"

He stepped onto the porch. The wooden boards creaked.

"So much for you staying put."

"I'd go around back, but basement houses have no such door."

"Something isn't right."

"I agree," he said. "There are no birds in the trees. No animals along the tree line. It's too quiet."

She pulled her semi. "Then you know someone could still be inside. And, this time, you better listen to me. Stay put. I have to clear the house."

He rolled his eyes but did as she asked. He wouldn't put it past her to shoot him for being disobedient.

Coup called out a few more times, announcing her presence, then entered the dwelling. The groan of doors being opened filled the house.

Several minutes passed before Coup called out, "It's clear! I'm in the kitchen."

As soon as he walked inside, he heard the buzzing of flies. A few feet more, the odor of rotten cabbage hit him.

Coup pointed to the blood-stained floor.

Terri-Mae lay on the floor, face up. Her hands were bloodied and clutched her neck where a wide slit in her flesh extended from front to back. It looked like she had tried to stop the flow of blood.

The blood pooled around her, darker at the edges, and it colored her hair a deep red, looking like a morbid halo.

She had died while he and Coup had been at the waterfall. A gut-wrenching thought ripped through him. Had he kept Coup from doing her job? Would Terrie-Mae still be alive if he hadn't dragged her to the fishing hole? He studied the palms of his hands.

"First impressions?" Coup asked.

"No back door. When you cleared the house, did you see any broken windows?"

"All were shut and locked."

"Which means the killer came through the front door. I'd say Terri-Mae knew her killer."

"Or the person was a sweet talker. Maybe said his car broke down and asked to use the landline or some other kind of assistance."

Kole checked his phone; he had one bar. His gut told him the intruder was an acquaintance.

"She was killed in the kitchen. No drag marks." Kole continued to the pantry, the door ajar. "I'd say she was on her way to fix them some tea."

"Agreed."

"When she turned to fetch it, the person stepped behind her and slashed her throat." Kole knelt and studied the wound. No multiple cuts, just a single clean one. He straightened. "An extremely sharp knife."

"I know the owner of the knife."

"You've seen this before?"

"Look on the table, Mr. Observant."

He'd concentrated on the body and had missed the object in the center of the metal table. A knife coated in blood, except for the hilt. No stains covered it. He also recognized the weapon. Damn.

"Don't think your client is going to get off."

"It wasn't Miller. He's not that stupid to leave his knife in plain view."

"I think he subconsciously wants to be punished. He's making mistakes," Coup said.

"If that were true, he'd be sitting here, eating breakfast."

"He won't get bonded out this time."

"Someone could have stolen one of his knives," he said.

"Maybe Terri-Mae did." Coup paced the room. "Miller knew she did, he came here to get it back, and, in a rage, slit her throat."

"Not buying it." Miller had told him that Terri-Mae was a worldly woman, and he didn't like her. Kole decided not to share that tidbit with Coup. "I don't think you really believe that scenario."

"I don't. I think Terri-Mae was blackmailing Miller."

"For what?"

"She'd seen him kill Aletha."

"And she finally decided to tell someone after all these years? Sheriff, who's reaching for straws now?"

"Look at the furnishings in this house. They're all nice and pricey. Where'd she get the money?"

"The only thing Miller has of value is his moonshine. You think he paid her in shine, and she resold it?" Kole shook his head. "No. He is being set up."

"By whom?"

"The same person who killed Aletha."

"You better come up with a name, or Miller will get fried."

There were no names. The best guess he had was this

mystery girl Terri-Mae had mentioned. And she'd disappeared. Or the girl Carlson said had hit him on the head. She was gone, too.

"I'll give you until noon to bring him in. But as soon as I get in the car, I'm radioing Dragging to put out the alert."

Kole followed Coup out of the house, then sat in his side-by-side. He watched her speak into the mic, then drive off without looking at him.

He looked upward and it seemed the sky's deep blueness penetrated the heavens. No physical or spiritual sign of hope, clarity, or direction came to him. Loneliness seeped deep inside.

Miller, what the hell have you done?

Forty

Immediately after Coup arrived at the police station, she called the county sheriff. She didn't want to use the car radio because any scanner could pick up the conversation. She knew the man and worked with him a few times. His name was Harris. He'd been in service for thirty-four years. "I need backup for a manhunt."

"I have two cars within twelve minutes of you," Harris said with no emotion. "Need any additional fire power?"

"No. This is perfect." She hung up and checked her watch. She walked to the armory room and selected a twelve-gauge with two boxes of black shells. Both boxes contained twenty-five red soldiers, each of the same caliber used by tactical and SWAT teams. She could bring down an elephant or obliterate doors, if needed. She expected Miller to come peacefully, but she'd be ready for the unexpected.

Outside, she strode to her vehicle. Someone had tucked a blue sheet of paper under the driver's wiper blade. Before removing it, she secured the shotgun and ammo between the front seats. The sun reflected brightly off every piece of metal in the lot, like white lasers. She shielded her eyes, not wanting to set off an episode.

She opened the note and read the typed red words: *Kill Miller as he escapes or Helen won't see tomorrow.*

"Damn." She looked around. The front lot was empty, as was the two-lane road leading to the station. No one was wandering around the empty grass lots surrounding the police building. Whoever was leaving these threats was a ghost.

She folded the note and placed it in her front pants pocket. Who could be so stealthy? It had to be a Cherokee. They could stand in front of a person and be invisible. She didn't believe in their rituals, potions, medicines, or their mind tricks, but she had no other explanation. However, that didn't mean she couldn't track him down. And which Cherokee was it?

Dragging? No, she would have seen him leaving or entering the building. He'd have to walk past her office. If he'd left by the back door, the alarm would have sounded.

And Grandfather didn't concern himself with white man problems, as was true for most of the Cherokee population. They just wanted to be accepted and earn a living.

That left Fat Bear. Son of a bitch. She'd slept with the man. Could it be him? Was he playing her? *If so, it all ends now.*

She returned to the building. "Dragging, I want you in Helen's room starting immediately and until I tell you differently."

He walked to the front of the building where Coup stood. "We have a guard stationed there."

"He's not city. I don't know all the county boys."

"Yes, ma'am. Give me a couple of minutes, and I'll leave."

"Take whatever you want out of the armory."

Dragging had started to walk away, but stopped, turned, and faced Coup. His face hardened. "I'll take my knife."

She nodded. The nine-inch blade was as wide as the palm of her hand at its base. She'd seen Dragging practice with the weapon. The steel was a part of him. He wouldn't hesitate to end a life.

Two county cars entered the front lot. Both vehicles were white SUVs with "Sheriff Putnam County" in large green-and-white letters on the side. The second car brought a smile to her face. "K-9 unit" was written in red letters toward the back.

Deputy sheriffs exited both cars. The men stood over six feet, weighed north of two-hundred pounds, and were in their late thirties. One was bald—Masterson—and the other, Boyles, had black hair cut short. She had met both in the past. Friendly on the outside, bull dogs when called for.

"This is a manhunt," she said. "Follow me."

"Tif's in the passenger seat," Boyles said. "She likes to participate in a good chase and loves treeing dumbasses."

When Coup turned into the road that led to Miller's mountaintop cabin, she glanced into the rearview mirror. Neither police car had their *blues* flashing. They stayed on her ass like stock car drivers. If they were, then that meant their dads, or they ran moonshine. At that moment, she didn't care. What concerned her was that she saw Fat Bear in his side-by-side pull in behind the last car.

Fine, she'd let the K-9 drag him back to the station. She'd read reports on Tif. She was a female German Shepherd. Her name stood for Teeth in the Flesh. The brownish dog got excited on a takedown and gripped and shook hard. Sometimes, the vics' limbs lost their ability to function. One perp had sued the department. The judge had thrown out the case and said, "Next time, obey the police." That was Tennessee rural law.

She stopped in front of Miller's home. The two sheriff cars flanked her.

"We're looking for Memo Miller," she said to the two deputies. "You know him?"

"An excommunicated Mennonite," Matherson said.

"And sells shine," Boyles replied.

"I'll check the house. You two sweep the premises. His clunker is here. Careful, he's good with those homemade knives."

Tif pulled on her leash and sniffed the ground in front of her handler.

"Fat Bear," Coup said. "Over here."

Kole stomped toward Coup.

"I'm doing you a favor. Go in the house and surrender him."

Kole entered the dwelling, left the door open, turned, then walked out. "He's not home."

"Where is he?"

"Could be anywhere."

"Maybe knifing another innocent victim." If Fat Bear was

the man behind the threats, she wanted him to know she demanded Miller's blood. The pretense was the only way to protect Helen.

"He's here somewhere. Probably out hunting dinner."

"You're supposed to know where he is at all times. I can arrest you for not complying with the judge's order."

"I have, and I am."

"Call out. Tell him to turn himself in."

"A lot of terrain on this homestead. He could be exploring a cave. He'd never hear me."

"The sex we had gives you no special privileges," she whispered.

"I'd be a fool to think otherwise with you."

"If you know where he is, this is the time to tell me. No holding back or I'll cut your balls off the next time we're in bed."

"Next time?" Fat Bear grinned. "I'll wear a cast iron jock strap."

Coup turned to the dog handler, who was about to disappear into the tree line. Tif seemed interested in a narrow path that cut through a patch of beech trees and undergrowth. All Coup saw in the deep shade were two goldfinches. The birds' yellow bodies fluttered from branch to branch.

Clouds passed and no longer blocked the sun. A burst of light hit Coup in the face. She wasn't ready for the bright light. Her head spun. God, not now. She closed her eyes. The world continued to spin, and she was losing her balance. There was nothing for her to hold onto to keep her upright. Her legs weakened and she felt consciousness leaving her. Blackness entered her mind, and she knew she was falling backward.

Two strong arms gripped her and held her erect. She could hear Fat Bear talking, and his words were jumbled. She held onto him.

A few moments passed before equilibrium returned. She squinted and the world seemed stable. Taking a chance, she opened her eyes fully.

"Are you okay?" Kole asked.

He had his arms wrapped around her torso. She freed herself and stepped back. "Thank you. I'm good."

"Let's sit on the porch. You can relax and take a breath. Miller should return soon."

"I'm not wasting my time." She turned again to Boyles. "Release Tif. Let her run free."

Forty-one

Kole didn't understand Coup's behavior at all. Once again, she was hell-bent on finding Miller guilty. No, it was more than that. It was as if she wanted him dead.

Then she'd almost fallen over. If he hadn't caught her, she'd have been face-down in the dirt. Had any of the other officers seen her collapse? Would there be an inquiry into her health? And how had she responded to his help? Not even a *Thank you*. Instead, she'd wanted to let the dogs tear Miller apart.

What else would he not understand before the day was over?

The wind gusted up from the valley. Flocks of yellow and blue birds flew overhead. A buck, three does, and a fawn leaped across the clearing in front of Miller's cabin to disappeared through an opening into the forest.

Kole knew who was approaching. The intruder used warblers and buntings to announce his arrival. There were three white people on the mountaintop with him. The man who was about to emerge from the poplar and pine trees liked to make known his uniqueness, at times, and the close walk he had with the Great Spirit. The white man must not forget who he was.

Coup stood beside Kole. "What spooked the animals?"

"They're not spooked," he said. "They're publicizing Grandfather's arrival. He's paying us a visit."

"Why? He came to defend Miller?"

"Grandfather considers Miller a spiritual person and respects him. But I don't think that's the reason for his calling. I fear our lives are about to change. And not in a pleasant way."

Grandfather strolled into the glade. He paused and registered the activities before him, then he proceeded to where Kole and Coup conferenced.

"What are you doing here?" Coup asked. "This is not a good time to be in the woods. There are officers and dogs hunting for Miller."

"You will not find Miller," Grandfather said. "He is in the earth."

"Dead?" she asked.

"Meditating with his God. Wanting a closer walk."

His grandfather had worn his blue, long-sleeved shirt. Across the chest were bars of different shades of blue bordered by white stripes. Blue to the Cherokee meant disappointment. Kole knew Grandfather wore the shirt for him. Grandfather's hat, shaped like a fedora, had an eagle's feather tucked into the brim to help guide him with his visions. His chin was slightly raised, so Kole knew he had something important to convey.

"I have come to speak to my grandson—and, before you ask," he said to Coup, "spirit animals guided me to him."

"Grandfather, with respect," Coup said, "I'm not sure a bird led you here."

"You also need to hear what I must tell Fat Bear."

"Sure. I'd love to stop my search for Miller to listen to what you have to say."

Kole scowled at Coup's sarcastic answer.

"Uktena is coming for you," Grandfather said, pointing his crooked, bony finger at his grandson.

Kole felt an icy shiver run down the length of his body. It felt like freezing rain and left ice frozen to the hairs on his limbs and face. Grandfather had only said that name once before—and when he had, two protection ceremonies had been performed because a strong wall had needed to be built to defend themselves.

A wind blew across the clearing, full of dirt, leaves, and the smell of dead animals. Kole turned his back to it as he wiped the grime from his face. Then the wind died. Brittle sticks spiraled around his boots.

"Where'd that come from?" Coup asked.

"The snake's breath," Grandfather said.

"Uktena is a great snake," Kole said. "Its body is as thick as a hickory tree trunk."

Coup looked at Kole. "I don't know who scares me more, you or Grandfather."

"Know this, Sheriff," Grandfather said. "This spirit is alive."

Coup shook her head in disbelief. "Go on."

Kole continued, "There are two horns on its head, big and sharp enough to gore any animal. Scales cover the body like sparks of fire. Foolish men tried to cut the Ulun'suti—a blazing crest shaped like a diamond—from its forehead. It was born out of envy and anger. It is pure evil."

"Both of you believe this?"

Grandfather's eyes saddened. Kole knew that, too often, this great man had seen non-believers scoff at the legend and die horribly in Uktena's wrath.

"You can call it what you want," Kole said. "Rabid cougar, deranged bear, or evil spirits. If Grandfather says he's coming, you may as well put out the welcome mat."

"I came to warn Fat Bear. Only it is not a *he*. This time, it's a *she*. More powerful, more blackness, more deadly." Grandfather closed his eyes and sighed. "Fat Bear, she is coming for you. I told you not to get involved with the white man's problems, but you ignored my counsel. And now, it is too late. Stay in the light."

Gray clouds crashed into one another and created inky shadows dancing on the ground. The sky became gloomy. Ragged darkness worked across dirt patches in the gaps of grass toward Coup.

Kole pointed to the phenomenon.

Grandfather threw a handful of red beads in front of the darkness before it reached Coup.

The shadows dissipated.

"I'll be damned," Coup said.

"You are in danger also, Sheriff." Grandfather's words were tense and stern. "Best to stay away from Fat Bear."

"I'm not going to let the weather terrorize me from doing my job."

"A Cherokee woman would heed my words. You should learn from them."

"Fat Bear, maybe you should carry your twelve-gauge with you. I have some shells that will knock that spirit back to the beyond. And, Grandfather, I'm a cop, not a Cherokee, and my 9 mil will do the same."

"Man's weapons cannot kill the Uktena. Only the earth," Grandfather said.

Kole believed Grandfather was right; this was one Cherokee legend that was true. No white man's weapons could destroy it.

The sky darkened again, as if an eclipse occurred.

What had he done that had caused the Uktena to single him out? Kole wondered if he had twenty-four hours left on this earth.

Forty-two

Coup walked to the edge of the forest. Green fruit the size of apples hung from the pawpaw trees. Officers Boyles and Masterson waited for instructions under the leafy trees. Tif sat on her haunches while her handler snapped a transmitter to her pink collar.

"This is something new," Boyles said. "I have an app on my device, and I can track and store Tif's movements. Plus, I can overlay it on a terrain map. I no longer need to be with her all the time."

"Not much wi-fi up here." Coup fiddled with the transmitter.

It looked like a small black ring box. No antenna was visible. She assumed it was built in. The case was rectangular and smooth on all the edges.

"It has a secondary signal built into the collar when there are no satellites, and my electronic notebook can pick it up. So, line-of-sight, I can find Tif a mile away." Boyles grinned.

Coup looked around the landscape. Boyles' logic sounded good, but with all the hills, cliffs, and hollows, line-of-sight was a hundred feet at best.

"Does the collar save the information?" Coup asked.

"Five K-worth for about thirty minutes, but the app saves everything," Boyles said. "It's great. I love new technology."

Coup smiled. She'd have Miller cuffed quickly.

"Since there are three of us," Boyles said to Coup and Masterson, "we can have a point person. I'll go into the forest. Masterson, if you would, post yourself by the cliff. Sheriff, you stay here with the notebook. If Miller jumps from place to place, we might spot him before Tif does."

"Remember," Coup said, "Detain him and I'll cuff him."

"If Tif is no longer tracking, or you hear Miller screaming, start walking toward her. It means she has treed him or has him in her jaws. Matherson and I will meet you there." Boyles handed Coup the notebook.

The device was a little larger than a standard sheet of composition paper. The black frame enhanced the white screen. It had a black writing utensil attached to the right side. This device was much nicer than her clunky desktop computer. She wondered what this would set the department back.

Boyles kneeled in front of the dog and rubbed her chest. "Find."

Tif took off running.

Both officers scrambled to their respective posts.

Coup watched a red dot crisscross on the screen. The terrain map had incredible detail. A small yellow square indicated Miller's cabin. A green shade covered most of the screen to specify the forest. Caves, dry creeks, and bluffs were represented in brown. On top of all the colors were squiggly, black contour lines. She used her fingers to zoom in on the map. The dot tracked quickly over the screen, Tif must be at a full run.

Fat Bear walked over and stood at her side. "You won't find him."

Coup showed him the screen. She pointed to the dot. "This is Tif checking out the mouth of a small cave. Now, she's bouncing from side to side of this dry riverbed. We'll find him. He can't hide from modern technology or from a dog that wants blood."

"Miller has lived up here for over ten years. His scent is everywhere."

"It doesn't matter to this dog."

"Have you ever found Miller's still?"

"No."

"But, yet you think you can find him? The still is stationary.

Miller is on the move. He could climb inside a fallen black gum tree and roll himself down a hill. The dog would never find him."

"Never really looked for his still. But I've found every criminal I've searched for."

Fat Bear stepped away.

"Where're you going?"

"Back to the cabin to wait."

"No, you don't. You're staying by my side. I'm not letting you wander off so you can alert him."

A breeze puffed a cold wetness through the air, as if a winter fog was moving in.

Coup thought of Grandfather's warning. The breeze stopped after a few seconds as if someone had exhaled. She didn't believe the legend of Uktena, but strange occurrences were happening on the mountain top.

She shook as if a winter blast had hit her.

"Something bothering you?" Fat Bear asked.

"Yes, you. I said to stand over there."

She continued to watch Tif hunt in the woods, the clearings, streams, and limestone cracks, with no luck. At times, the movement would stop, making Coup's heart pound in anticipation that she would hear a scream for help, or one of pain.

But nothing.

When the wind gusted again, it smelled like it had swept across rotting carcasses.

"Fat Bear." She looked up from the screen. "What do you think of Grandfather's message?"

"All legends are based on fact. But as the stories are passed down generations, they could have been elaborated." He paused. "This one… not so much. It could be that Uktena, or someone impersonating him, is among us."

"Grandfather said *she*."

"That is troubling. I've never heard the legend crossing sexes. There is malevolence among us. Could be from the spiritual world or the physical."

Coup tried to make sense of it all. One thing for sure, she didn't believe in demons, ghouls, or the bogeyman, but something was spooky. She rubbed her arms.

She turned her attention back to the notebook. Some of the contour lines and the shapes of the different colors looked like ones she had seen before.

Again, using her fingers, she collapsed the map, then clicked on the menu icon and selected, "tracking history".

A blue line was painted on the map. It formed one giant circle. Tif had run it three times.

"Damn you, Miller."

"You found him?" Fat Bear moved to her side and looked over her shoulder.

She let him look at the screen. "Tif is running in circles. The bastard is gone."

Forty-three

"Miller is a loner. A hermit. He's been excommunicated by his church. Wife has been murdered. You have more fingers than he has friends. The only joy he has is exploring the woods. Coup, did you really think you were going to hunt him down?" Kole asked her.

"Wrap it up and go home," Coup said to Boyles and Matherson, twirling her raised hand.

"This mountain top is his territory. It has been his home for over a decade. If he doesn't want to be found, he won't." Kole had a good idea where Miller was hiding. He wrestled whether to reveal his thoughts. He decided not to in case he was wrong.

"You seemed calm all afternoon," she said. "Too calm."

"It's a pleasant day to relax."

"I think you know where he is. That's why you knew we wouldn't find him."

Boyles loaded Tif into the police SUV, then followed Matherson's vehicle down the narrow mountain road. Sounds of tires crunching rock and the car's undercarriage bouncing in the potholes lingered behind them.

The sun dipped below the top of the trees and cast long shadows across the clearing. An orange-colored sky burst between the branches.

"One thing Grandfather didn't tell you," Kole said, "is that, when he gives me a warning, I need to act within a day."

"Doesn't give you much time to prepare."

"I have not learned everything he tried to teach me. One

lesson, though, was to control my mind. Don't let fear enter it or it will control me."

"Hard concept to learn."

"He knows I'd spend time fretting instead of preparing. Thus, I get less than twenty-four hours."

"You think Uktena is coming?"

"Most certainly. And since Grandfather said *she*, Uktena will come in a physical form, but with spiritual powers. He didn't give me any blessing beads for protection, which is his way of telling me she is very powerful."

"What's your plan?"

"Meet me at the entrance of Devil's Cave at sunrise."

"If you're going to get us killed, could you wait until noon?"

"I want the rising sun to destroy the blackness of the night. Grandfather said to stay out of the darkness. The sunshine will be our ally."

"You're going into a cave that has never seen daylight."

"I'm hoping there will be shafts of light penetrating through the cracks in the limestone."

The sun dipped lower in the sky, the bottom edge now hidden by the mountain top. Darkness danced across the ground while the sky turned burned orange.

"I need to study the text of the ancients," he said.

"You have a library?"

"One book."

"Reading sounds like a waste of time. I'll be cleaning every weapon I own. I'll bring more fire power than this bitch as ever seen and light her up like a New Year's Eve party."

"You will be the one wasting your time. Grandfather said man's weapons can't destroy her."

"I'll be dammed if I'm going in naked."

Kole smiled. Her last statement reminded him of her climbing into his sleeping bag.

"I know what you're thinking," Coup said. "Reading and dreaming is going to get your ass wasted."

He had one more errand to run before the night covered the mountain, but Coup couldn't be part of it. He wanted her to leave quickly. He needed the twilight for his task.

"See you tomorrow," he said.

She didn't leave.

He had to move her along. The way she looked at him… It was as if she was trying to read his mind, and if that failed, crack his skull open to see what was inside.

Again, the wind blew—stronger than before—and curved the tops of the trees. The leaves fluttered against finger-like branches and sounded like rain had started to fall. On the ground, the hard clay dirt swirled in mini tornadoes.

"Weather is getting bad," he said. "I'm getting off this mountain while I can."

"Maybe we should have a drink at the 1838 and discuss your plan. I don't want any surprises."

"Then let me do what I need to do."

"How do I know you're not the Uktena?"

"First, Grandfather came to warn me—"

"He could be part of the deception."

"When has he deceived anyone or become involved in white men's problems?"

Coup remained silent. He could tell she was running different possibilities and scenarios in her head. She didn't trust him for some reason.

"And second, last night you saw for yourself that I'm no woman," he said.

"There is no absolute proof that the murders and the missing diamonds are tied together or done by the same person. The Uktena could be a deranged physco, Terri-Mae could have been killed by a jealous boyfriend, and Miller or someone else wanted all the diamonds. I'm still on square one."

"I think they are connected." He walked Coup to her squad car, then opened the driver's door. "When Uktena appears, the pieces will fit together."

Coup slid into her vehicle, then drove off.

The tip of the sun shone over the mountain. Darkness was gathering. He had time to complete the last chore before daylight faded.

In less than a half of a rotation of the earth, fate would force him to challenge Uktena, prepared or not.

Forty-four

Kole gave Coup a good fifteen minutes before he started his side-by-side. That amount of time gave him plenty of distance between the two of them. He guessed she was returning to the station to clean and reload her guns, and should be at the bottom of the hill, cruising the main road. But she was tricky and crafty, so he wouldn't assume anything about her actions.

He listened for sounds on the highway. The only noises he heard were squirrels jumping from branch to branch, deer trekking to their grass beds, and songbirds singing their last tunes of the day.

Kole drove down the mountain road until he spotted the ancient beech tree. He studied the ground to be sure this was the turn. There were no dirt ruts to be seen, but, in places, the waist-high grass was pushed flush to the ground. The trail bent around the old tree and dipped into a holler. He pushed the clutch to the floor and let the side-by-side coast downward into the high vegetation, the top of his vehicle no longer visible from the road.

Staying in first gear, he crept to a creek. The underbrush swished the sides of his vehicle.

The water cascaded over the black polished boulders, turning the stream white. The pounding noise created a sound barrier. He stepped out of his vehicle. Past the rapids, the clear watercolor turned azure with a ragged cavern overlooked the pool. He set out on foot.

The hair on his arms pricked up. Someone was thirty feet behind him. Possibly Coup. As much noise as he'd made plowing through the vegetation, Coup could have tailed him easily in her squad car.

The scent of rose water from Coup's shampoo was unmistakable.

"You may as well come out. A blind squirrel would know your location by now. Why did you lie and say you were going to the station?"

"I didn't lie. You assumed. Plus, would you have taken me with you?"

"Hell no."

"You're incorrigible. I can't stand you."

"That's the second time you've lied to me today."

He smelled the smoke of a hickory fire and baked yeast coming from the cave. He walked to the scent, Coup followed him. It looked like a light fog rolled out of the opening. If it was tomorrow, he could be convinced it was the breath of Uktena.

Miller stood inside the cave and faced copper tubing running from the boiler to the condenser and to the collector. His back was to Kole as he added split wood to the red-hot coals. Flames leaped upward when Miller added two crooked branches to the fire. Noise of the undergrowth being trampled caused him to turned.

Pointing to the water, Miller said, "Won't find any purer water than right here. That's why my brew is the best."

"Did you see what happed at your place?"

Miller turned to Coup. "Do you have chiggers in your panties? What was that all about?"

"Terri-Mae is dead," Coup said.

He watched Miller's body movements for a reaction if he knew the girl.

First, the Mennonite's eyes widened, then his body slumped slightly forward. Seconds later, he returned to his natural posture.

Miller knew the girl. But he still asked, "Did you know her?"

"No."

"Don't lie to me." Kole paused to give the words meaning. "You visited her, didn't you?"

"As soon as I saw the purple lipstick, I knew Terri-Mae had been in the cave with Aletha."

"You should have told me, and I should have been with you when you spoke to her. Anything she told you is inadmissible in court."

"I learned that she didn't kill Aletha. Terri-Mae conned old men out of their money to afford her home purchases. She had a soft heart—even killing an animal would be too much for her to handle."

"So, she was alive when you left?"

Miller wiped the wetness from his eyes.

Kole knew he shouldn't have questioned the Mennonite's moral character. Miller could no more have killed Terri-Mae than his own wife.

"That will be for the jury to decide," Coup said.

"I have to go." Miller nodded to two stacks of glass jars filled with his brew. "This batch will be ready in the morning. I have deliveries to make."

"Miller, you're clueless at times," Coup said. "I'm arresting you for the murder of Terri-Mae."

"On what evidence?" Kole asked.

"Both of you need to shut up. I am pissed to the point where I feel like locking the *two* of you up. Fat Bear, everything you do that concerns this case has to be shared with me. I'm not some afterthought."

"I wasn't sure he was here," Kole said. "After I confirm my suspicions, then I share."

"Turn around, Miller," Coup said. "Hands behind your back."

Coup walked over to Miller and cuffed him, then she led him out of the cave.

Kole followed. "You didn't need to do that. I would have brought him in."

"If I want your opinion, I'll cuff you, too, and you can whine from the back seat."

He didn't want to make matters worse for Miller, so he swallowed his words. But he wasn't sure what legal action he could proceed with. Plus, he felt Coup was beyond reason. Nevertheless, he had to do something. "The judge placed Miller into my custody."

"You violated that order by letting him roam around the countryside."

"The judge didn't say he had to be by my side all the time."

"Nor did the judge say Miller was free to harass the citizens of this county."

Kole stepped in front of Coup. "Grant this request and let me follow you to jail with Miller."

"I have him and he's staying with me." She pushed Kole to the side.

"We can't be adversaries. In the morning, we need to be solid to fight Uktena."

"Here's the deal. I'll process Miller and, in exchange, I'll be there… maybe. But we're never going fishing together again."

Coup led Miller out of the cave, down the path, then placed him in the back seat of her cruiser.

The red taillights of her squad car disappeared into the evening shadows.

Her help would be the turning point in tomorrow's battle. Had he screwed that up to where she wouldn't show? He should have been upfront with her about Miller and shared his hunch on the guy's whereabouts.

Kole found a bucket and with water from the creek dosed the fire. The coals under the still no longer glowed red but turned black. In the light of the waning gibbous moon, he saw a rattler move into a clearing.

Its tail sounded deadly.

He stood still. Was this a sign that things would not end well tomorrow?

Forty-five

Coup had turned off the potholed mountain road to Miller's place and onto the two-lane state highway that wound toward Monterey. All she planned to do was transport Miller to the jail, head home, clean her weapons, then sleep well.

She radioed the station. "Dispatch, this is Sheriff Coupland."

"Go ahead," Dragging responded.

"I was expecting our lender from Cookeville."

The static over the airwaves seemed to last too long. She was ready to punch the mike again to see if she was in a dead zone when Dragging spoke.

"He was here," the deputy said. "I sent him home."

"Why?" Coup scowled at the switch in personnel. All changes in shifts needed her approval first.

The road in front of her darkened. She hit her high beams. Crazy Tennessee weather. Five minutes ago, the bright moon had lit up the night like football stadium lights. Now, clouds had moved in and blocked the brightness. The unexpected change in the weather, which hadn't been forecasted, gave her the creeps.

She looked into the rear-view mirror. Miller's face was in shadows, but she noticed his glum expression.

Dragging came back on the radio. "My spirit animal told me to do so."

What is it with the Cherokee? Couldn't they say God or Great Spirit or Heavenly Father? Always bringing in the supernatural.

"You expecting trouble?" she spoke into the mike.

"It is best to go where you are led," he explained.

Coup sighed.

"Walk in obedience to all that the Lord your God has commanded you," Miller said. "Deuteronomy, chapter five, verse thirty-three."

"Stay out of it, Miller. You and Dragging can compare sayings after the steel door slams on your cell."

"Have you heard about putting on the whole armor of God? You'll need it for tomorrow."

She clicked the mike. "Dragging, I'm bringing Miller in. He's the prime suspect in the killing of Terri-Mae. Plan to stay the night or bring the temp back in."

"I think it best if I stay."

Dark clouds blackened the sky. Splatters of rain hit the windshield often enough that she turned the wipers to intermittent. The wind buffed her vehicle to the center line.

"What do you know about the Uktena?"

The radio static became thicker. "Do not speak of it."

"Fat Bear talked weird crap about it." She clicked the frequency of the intermitter up two notches.

"Was Grandfather present?"

"Yes. He gave a warning to me and Fat Bear."

"Heed it."

Coup's thoughts bounced back and forth between wondering if Uktena was truly a beast or a man acting as a wild animal. Either scenario had to be stopped.

"And behold, a pale horse," Miller said. "And its rider's name is Death. Revelations."

"That's enough from you, Miller."

"I don't know what Fat Bear, Grandfather, and you discussed, but I've been feeling all day like some sort of tribulation would come tomorrow. And these verses are in my thoughts."

The wind increased in strength. Forest debris blew across the road. She had to steer to the shoulder to stay in her lane.

She returned to the radio. "Dragging, I already told Fat Bear I'd meet him at Devil's Cave in the morning."

"Both of you should stay home."

"That's not an option."

The rain fell steadily. Water droplets formed spider shapes on the glass in front of her. She flipped the wipers higher.

"What is Fat Bear doing now?" Dragging asked.

"He said he had to go home and prepare."

"There is no preparing."

The static was thick with the last transmission. With that noise and the whoosh of the wipers, she barely heard him.

The way Miller and Dragging talked, tomorrow would be dismal.

She shook her head several times to get their nonsense out of her mind. There were lots of evil people in this world, and she had gone up against many of them. She may have gotten battered, but she'd been victorious. It didn't matter what kind of flesh and bones came at her, man or beast—spiraling lead punching through their torsos would end them.

The rain became as dense as the radio static. She wished there was another higher setting to the wipers. It didn't matter. Darkness gobbled her headlights. She cut her speed.

"Sheriff?"

"Go ahead, Dragging," Coup said. "Speak slow. This rain is causing some breakup."

"Adhere to what Fat Bear says."

Dragging didn't like Fat Bear because Fat Bear and Grandfather butted heads, so that was strange advice to give her. She didn't think it was the best recommendation because Fat Bear hid things from her. He never gave her the whole story. The only counsel she'd take would be her own.

"Sheriff." Dragging's voice was clear of static as if some benevolent spirit wanted to ensure she heard what he said next. "Even if you and Fat Bear defeat Uktena, the beast may have already unleashed evil into nature that could kill you. Do not assume you are victorious."

Her father had said something similar to her once: "Be on the lookout for others to harm you."

"Sheriff, I have one last thing to say. May I speak?" Miller asked.

"I don't think I could stop you."

"God destroyed evil with the great flood. If you are up against an evil spirit, expect another flood."

She didn't need a Bible verse for that one. With this downpour, she felt she was already in the middle of a flood. For her, there was too much hocus-pocus talk. She knew how to wipe bad guys off the table if she could keep Dragging and Miller's words out of her head.

She heard the crack of a branch being ripped from a tree trunk. It hit the road in front of her and bounced onto the hood of her car.

The screech of metal crumpling resonated through her.

The tips of the branch laid across the windshield and looked like a skeletal hand. Part of the tree looked like an index finger as it slid down the glass, swirling the rain drops.

She slammed the brakes to stop and expected the branch to slide off the hood. But the limb held firm. Stepping out of the car, she got soaked before she made it to the front of the car. She pulled the branch free, then the wind yanked it from her hand.

When it twirled to the other side of the road, she heard a howl. Goosebumps covered her body.

Damn wind.

She slid back into the driver's seat and wiped the water from her face.

Miller whispered, "Daniel chapter five, verse five and six. Suddenly the fingers of a man's hand emerged and began writing opposite the lampstand on the plaster of the wall of the king's palace, and the king saw the back of the hand that did the writing. Then the king's face grew pale, and his thoughts alarmed him, and his hip joints went slack, and his knees began knocking together."

"Miller, do you want me to duct tape your mouth?" Her body shook.

Both Dragging and Miller had given her some chilling cautions. Cherokee lore, biblical references… Did any of it apply to tomorrow's manhunt for the Uktena? She didn't believe in spirits, but she felt a sense of duty to find this person Grandfather had warned her and Fat Bear about. She could not let a crazed person run free. For her, there was a bigger question that would haunt her all night…

Could she rely on Fat Bear?

Forty-six

Kole awoke covered in sweat.

Naked, he stood in front of his open bedroom window. The moon peeked between ragged clouds and left silver streaks on the wet grass. The storm had cooled the night, and the weak breeze chilled his skin.

His dream had shaken him awake. All he remembered of it was bloody teeth biting his torso in a blackened forest. He ran his hands across his face. His palms trembled, but his body remained intact, no flesh missing.

He walked into his study and over to the table where the ancient manuscript lay, then clicked the desk lamp on. The yellowish glow did little to brighten the room. Earlier, in studying the passages, he had found nothing conclusive for battling the Uktena.

Was the beast too strong? Was there no way to subdue it? That couldn't be true. If it were, wouldn't the Utkena have wiped out the Cherokee nation long ago?

The lamp flickered. He assumed downed trees were causing the power outages. Loss of electricity didn't bother him; he had a generator.

He fingered a page of the manuscript. His home was protected from inclement weather, so, when it came to the house, he didn't have to battle the elements. Was that the answer, have your weapons in place before you need them?

When it came to the Uktena, maybe being on the offense was not the way to destroy it, but, instead, by going on the defensive. By protecting oneself, would that exterminate the beast?

How would that be possible?

Grandfather had taught him that evil roamed the earth. At times, it was not possible to avoid wickedness. And there would be periods when a Cherokee needed more than his teachings to prevent sinfulness. For protection, Grandfather had taught him the legend of the cedar tree.

Kole stepped out the back door and headed to the mature trees on his property. The moon knew of his intentions and sent its reflected light to illuminate a section of old growth. To the white man, the cedar was a symbol of greatness, of nobility, of strength, and of incorruptibility.

To the Cherokee it meant much more.

He must honor the tree and have discipline for requesting the powerful protective spirits for the Cherokee.

Grandfather taught him that he must first retell the legend in front of the tree. All of nature loved the story and would want to hear it again. He summarized it.

"When the Cherokee people were new upon the earth," he said, "they beseeched Ouga, the Creator, to change the day so there would be no night. This caused the heavy growth of crops, temperatures soared, and people could not sleep, so they became agitated."

Drops of rain rolled off the leaves and plopped to the ground. A great horned owl swept over him giving him a yellowed-eye stare. Kole's heart felt the deep hoot and he fanned his face as he embraced the sounds of the forest.

"The people said, we have made a mistake. Make it so it will always be night. But then, the crops did stop growing, and the world became cold. Many people died." He bowed his head. "Those who survived cried to the Creator to change it back as it was before. And it was done. The Creator felt sorry for all who had died and placed their spirits into a newly created tree. This conifer, an evergreen, was named a-tsi-na tlu-gv. The

magnificent cedar." He spoke in his native language, "Wado. U-we-hno," giving his thanks.

As he reached for the trunk, the branches started to shake. Leaves swirled around him. An aroma of camphor blanketed him. It felt cool, prickly, and the scent, minty. He knew the evergreen was blessing him.

He studied the trunk. It had a wide buttressed base and deep grooves running parallel to the growth. The cinnamon-red wood was fibrous and solid to the touch. He pulled a sliver of bark from the tree. It would be placed in a leather pouch and worn around his neck but concealed beneath his clothes. Uktena would not know the power he brought.

Then he thought of Coup and pulled a long, thick strand—a larger piece than his for additional protection for her.

Tomorrow would be a day of reckoning. He shuddered. Both he and Coup would need much help.

He hoped Grandfather would not have to observe the seven days of mourning.

Forty-seven

Kole stood in a deep shadow at the opening of Devil's Cave. The breeze coming from inside chilled his skin and the hairs on his arms stiffened. An orange glow backdropped the trees at the mountain's rim, giving a hint of the coming sunrise. Soon, the day would be hot. One of the last of the summer's dog days. That didn't matter because, in a few minutes, he would be in the cavernous gullet of the mountain.

Behind him, branches creaked against one another. He turned and looked at the opposite side of the ravine. A crow perched on a naked limb stared at him, cocking his head from time to time.

Was his spirit animal here to say goodbye or to bless him? He hoped for the latter. And that he'd have this mystery solved.

"Is it time?" Coup emerged from the narrow trail and stepped onto a large, flat rock. She had dressed in brown corduroys, a long-sleeved pink-and-white flannel shirt, and high-top hiking boots. She tossed her black backpack next to his, a nine-millimeter hung on her hip.

She had dressed similar to him—thick clothes to keep the coolness of the cave at bay and to protect from rock icicles and razor-edged limestone formations.

"What's in the pack?" he asked.

"What do you *think* is in there—cookies?" Coup inhaled. "A revolver with two quick loads, three clips for the auto, and a flashlight."

"Let me see." He opened the pack and pulled her light out.

Clicking it on and off a few times, he then threw it back in. He pulled a spare from his. The head was as wide as a cup saucer and a foot in length.

Handing the lamp to her, he said, "This one's better. It will light up the inside of the cave like a summer afternoon and is sturdy enough to crack skulls. I'll use one just like it."

"What else do you have?" she asked.

"Another light, three packs of batteries, and a short length of rope. And, to satisfy you, gloves and baggies."

"I think you'll have a better chance of dying of old age in there than of finding any new evidence."

"Then drag me out and bury me."

"Do I get to place you on top of a pyre and set fire to you?"

He zipped her pack, then his. "Let's hope it doesn't come to that."

"Of course. I'd feel bad arresting a dead body. You have a lot of explaining to do when this is done. You have pushed the boundaries of the law too far. I can't overlook it anymore."

"After today, I feel this will be all wrapped up. Miller will go free, and you and I can part ways."

"I'm looking forward to good times tomorrow. What's the plan?"

"In there," he pointed his light to the cave opening, "we find the second diamond."

She shook her head with an expression of disbelief. "You been smoking peyote this morning?"

He didn't understand the friction between the two of them. Pushing the boundaries of the law wasn't what he did. He reinterpreted them. In court, judges read an opinion of their findings; he had his own.

And didn't Coup push the law also. She was full of sarcasm this morning and he'd bet she wanted to pump a hole into someone. Maybe inside, she'd cool off.

"I think the Tarpon Diamonds promised an easy life. Instead, they bring destruction to the holder's life and death to others. Aletha and Terri-Mae both came into contact or knew about the diamonds, which caused them to be killed," he said.

"You think the killer left a confession note under the diamond?"

"Something better. A fingerprint."

"Why didn't the thief leave with the diamonds?"

"Follow me on this. Aletha swallowed one. She was stabbed the same time as the quake. The murderer was in complete darkness and the opening was blocked. Following the loose gravel and fresh air, he found the back door, but, while crawling, he dropped the second diamond. When he got out of the cave, an aftershock closed the back door, sealing the diamonds inside. Then, last week, another quake, and the cave is open again."

Coup rolled her eyes. "Too many ifs and coincidences."

"It's the only logical scenario."

"So, you think we'll shimmy into the cave, take a stroll, find the diamond, and yell Eureka?"

"Close enough, except for one thing."

"You brought us a picnic lunch to enjoy."

"We are going to have to battle Uktena. He won't let us leave with the diamond."

Coup stepped between him and the cave. She feathered the handle of her gun. "I knew you'd sweeten my tea."

He pulled the piece of cedar bark from his pack and, while her back was to him, slipped the protection into her rear pants pocket.

She turned and pushed him away.

He stumbled, lost his balance, and fell.

"What the hell, Fat Bear?" Her face reddened. "I didn't give you permission to play with my ass. Way too inappropriate. And not the proper time."

Rising, he brushed the rock dust off him and suppressed his smile. She didn't pat her fanny. He'd successfully placed the protection on Coup.

"I'll add sexual harassment to the charges against you."

Shadows disappeared around them.

"The sun has breached the treetops. It is time." Kole strapped on his pack, then laid belly-down, and entered the narrow sloping shaft. It looked like a giant wormhole to him. He spread his legs and used the side of his boots to control his descent.

Coup stuck her head into the shaft. "Truthfully, I think you're taking me on another fishing expedition."

He knew that this time, it wouldn't be as pleasant as the last one.

He relaxed his heels and flew into the darkness.

Forty-eight

Kole led Coup deeper into the cave. Their flashlights cast a wide beam, cutting into the darkness. It had as much effect on the blackness as pouring a glass of water into the ocean and expecting the salt water to rise, but he kept the illumination pointed at the pitted floor in hopes of seeing a colored reflection from the gem. The Tarpon Diamond had to be here. And he *had* to find it; Miller's life depended on it.

"Damn it!" Coup yelled, her voice resonating down the passage. "That's the third time I hit my head." She ran her hand across her scalp, then held her palm in front of her light.

"I told you to stoop low or hunch down." Kole focused his light to the ceiling, revealing jagged, brown limestone.

"How much farther before we can stand erect?"

"Soon."

That was a lie. The only other time he had been in this cave was with Miller, and he'd spent more time watching the Mennonite than their ingress into the mountain.

"We've been searching for over an hour," Coup said. "I think it's time to call it."

"We haven't made it to the back door yet."

"Based on your theory, that exit is not the one the murderer used because a second quake blocked it."

"If you'd shine your light on the floor as often you do at your hand, we'd cover more ground."

"Ten more minutes."

"Thirty."

"Fifteen and then you're on your own."

"That wasn't the deal. You have to be present when we find the diamond, so we do the chain of custody properly."

"Seventeen, then."

He guided her another twenty feet, then pointed his light upward. "The back door."

"Looks like only a skinny bastard could climb up through that," she said.

Continuing down the passageway, they were well past the exit in just a few minutes.

He started to doubt his own theory. The cave seemed damper than the last time. How far could a person travel in total darkness before insanity overtook him? The murderer had balls as big as boulders or was very determined to live.

Fresh air no longer blew in his face. The tunnel narrowed. He could extend his arms and touch both wet sides. The one positive was that the ceiling was higher. He stretched his back and was thankful. When he worked the kink out of his back, and continued, he walked on polished stones. A creek had run through here at one time. How many thousands of years ago had that been? He hoped it wasn't recently.

A muffled echo emitted out of the darkness. It could have come from in front of him or behind him; it was too faint for him to be sure of the direction. "Did you hear that?" he asked.

"Just us."

He forced his ears to detect the slightest sound, then counted to fifty. "Anything?"

"Bats maybe?" Coup asked.

"Not likely. I haven't seen any guano."

"Must be the wind."

He swung his light around them. "It could have been a footstep. Quiet." Turning, he faced Coup. The flashlights painted harsh shadows across her face and amplified the disgust on her mouth that they hadn't turned back. But there was something else in the glow of the flashlight. A beauty he hadn't seen before.

He stepped toward her, held her chin, and kissed her on the lips.

"Have you lost your mind?" She pushed him away. "This place stinks of mold and dampness, I've hit my head so many times I may have a concussion, and we haven't seen daylight for so long that, when we do, I may go blind from the brightness, and you think it was a great time to steal a kiss?"

"Yes."

She lurched at him, grabbed his neck, and pulled him close and kissed him back long enough to forget time.

"No one steals a kiss from me." She turned and slid her palm along the rock side. "Back to the topic at hand. Sounds like dripping water to me.

"Somewhere, stalagmites are growing." After a few minutes, he said, "Not the same tone I heard. I'm sure it was someone walking."

"Are you sure?"

"Turn off the lights."

The cave became black. He searched for the glow of a flashlight or lantern. Nothing.

Squinting his eyes, he focused on smaller areas and tried to see further into the darkness.

Again… nothing—well, except for the dripping water, which seemed to increase in frequency. Almost a steady stream.

Coup grabbed his arm and yelled, "Over there! Something's moving in front of us. Do you see it?"

Both clicked on their lights. They stared at the rock limestone side peppered with holes ranging in diameter of his finger to large enough that he could stick bowling balls in. He shined his light into several holes. Some ended abruptly, some continued beyond his beam of light.

"I swear it was in front of us," Coup said. "It looked like a horned serpent."

"Were your eyes opened or closed?"

"Open. Can't see anything if they're closed."

He laughed.

"What's with the joke?"

"In complete darkness, if you don't close your eyes, your brain expects to see something. If it doesn't, it will conjure up horrible images. In this case, the last monster we talked about was Uktena. It wasn't real."

"Sure, as hell looked real."

"I bet it did. People have gone insane from imagining things in caves."

"I'm seeing things, you're hearing things… It's time to retrace our steps and feel the sunshine."

"Except that I'm certain we are being followed." He swung his light behind them.

Coup focused hers in the direction they were headed.

He was breathing heavily, as if he had hiked to the top of this evil mountain. Holding his breath, he could sense his ear drums thumping. The place was getting to him.

Reaching for his chest, he placed his hand over the pouch underneath his shirt containing the piece of cedar bark. The noise of crunching stones under someone's feet reverberated again.

Coup's head snapped toward him. She'd heard it, too. "You tell anyone our plans?" She asked.

"No. Did you?"

She shook her head. Drawing her gun, she held it in front of the light and racked a round into the chamber. "Someone is going to learn a hard life lesson."

"Unless it's the Uktena." *Unless it's the Uktena*, he repeated to himself. *Great Spirit, if it is the beast, bless our pieces of protection.*

The beam from his flashlight mutated from a brilliant white to a jaundiced yellow.

He reflexively held the pouch again.

Forty-nine

Coup didn't see the point in traveling any further. They had hiked for over two hours into the depths of the cave. The limestone sides were pocked with numerous holes that, at times, made her think she was in a block of Swiss cheese—which reminded her she was hungry. And where the ancient, compressed shell fragments were solid, their lights caused disfigured shadows to walk across the sides. The background sound of dripping water had turned into a constant trickle. Plus, she couldn't get rid of the thought of the tons of rocks over their heads. Even the slightest tremble and they'd be buried. It was time for Fat Bear to admit defeat. She holstered her gun. How could she convince him of that? "I think it's time to turn around."

"The diamond is here somewhere."

"We could have walked right past it and not even know. After all these years, and as shaky as this mountain is, it could be buried under a layer of mud and gravel."

"Should have brought a rake."

"Just what I wanted to do. Have a metal comb tied to my ass, dragging it as I stumble around."

Kole shook his light, the beam pale. "Need to change the batteries."

She held her light at Fat Bear's pack as he retrieved fresh D-cells. After replacing them, he switched on his flashlight. The beam was still yellow.

Hers dimmed as well.

"I don't understand it. These batteries are new," he said.

"Our lights are failing. Another reason to head back."

"These caves are full of minerals—zinc, copper, manganese, even uranium. Uranium does release electromagnetic waves. That must be causing our problem."

"Then let's skedaddle and come back with a different power source."

"The pockets of minerals are never abundant. We should be pass it soon."

"Great. If this mountain doesn't fall on top of us, I'll end up with radiation poisoning and die slowly from some form of cancer. I'm so happy you convinced me to tag along."

Her light flickered a few times. It flashed white, then yellow as if she was in a disco club. When it stabilized, it shined gray. She was going to bring it to Fat Bear's attention, but he had continued to walk deeper into the mountain. She crunched rock bits under her boots, quick stepping to catch him.

"Heard any footsteps lately?" she asked.

"Not sure. At times, I sense a presence close to us; other times, nothing. I still think there's an intruder, and he knows we heard him."

"Could it be the Uktena?"

"Maybe. He could be hoping we hear his footsteps to instill fear into us. He's clever and is a master of terror."

"What if you stop, and I'll retrace our steps? With me staying in the dark, there's a good chance I can surprise him, cuff him, then we can leave."

"With no diamond?"

"There's a town about sixty miles west of here called Difficult. You ever think of moving there?"

"Sounds like a good place for you."

How could he think she was uncooperative, especially since the wetness of the cave caused her shirt to become damp. It clung to her body, giving her a chill. Of all the gear they'd packed, none of it had included Miller's shine. A good slug of that brew would warm her up.

She felt the odds of finding the diamond were against them and began to think Fat Bear had become obsessive and no longer had any logical thoughts. Being buried didn't concern him. He had lost his anxiety of the prowler following them. If they *did* find the diamond, and could extract a fingerprint, it could lead to a deceased person. Or someone living off the grid. But there was no guarantee they could even lift a print.

The Tarpon Diamond was most likely *not* the magic bullet Fat Bear hoped for.

The man had outpaced her again. He was almost out of reach of her beam which bothered her. His light had silhouetted his frame causing a white haze to form around his body, separating his dark stature from the never-ending blackness. The image hinted of a being from a spiritual world.

He stopped and flashed his light from one side of the cave to the other. Mineral chips reflected specks of silver like the Milky Way.

As she approached Fat Bear, the air seemed fresher, dryer, with a hint of pine trees. She stopped beside him.

The tunnel forked.

A faint wave of air came from the left. To the right, smelled of an old bog.

"As strong as the breeze is," he said, "I'd guess there's an opening down there. Most likely a shaft to the surface. We might be able to climb up it."

"You're assuming it's a big hole. I'm willing to bet it's a bunch of narrow chimneys."

"Listen," he said.

An imperceptible whistle came toward them, sounding like someone breathing through their teeth.

"You're right," he said. "It's not the way out."

Coup stepped several feet into the tunnel that branched off to the right. Shining her light upward, she saw that the ceiling looked blackened. "Look at this," she said.

"Soot."

"Was someone living in this rank place this far back?"

"Let's find out. It could be a good place for the diamond."
Fat Bear headed deep into the darkness.

Coup picked up a rock and threw it at him.

It hit his pack.

He kept going, not acknowledging her actions.
I'll never get out of this wretched cave.

Fifty

Coup took a dozen steps into the right chamber. The thick, stale air smelled of human stench.

"Uktena lived here," Fat Bear said.

Every time she suppressed the thought of the monster, this cave or Fat Bear reminded her of it. Chills ran throughout her body.

She panned her light around the cavern. The tunnel had ended, and an abandoned campfire lay in front of her. Blackened logs formed a boxy circle for a fire pit. Burnt wood chips piled a foot high remained inside it. Hammers, chisels, pic-axes, and other mining tools leaned against a pitted wall. Soiled clothes and cooking utensils hung from wooden hooks pounded into the ceiling. Bundles of hay, positioned like bunks for six people, had molded into what looked like dirt graves. This place looked as cheerful as her chances of Fat Bear calling it a day.

The hairs on her arms stood stiff. She had the feeling of someone hiding in the shadows watching them. She panned her light, turning around slowly. Who did this encampment belong to?

"Toward the end of the Civil War," Fat Bear said as if he'd read her mind, "the boys in butternut uniforms ran out of everything—food, munitions, but not spirit. They excavated saltpeter to make gun powder."

"Doesn't seem like they could provide much."

"Here in the Cumberland Mountains, hundreds, maybe thousands, of makeshift factories like this one existed. The boys would be in here for weeks."

Deep yellow crystals lay on the cave floor. Shadows from her light caused one ball to have eye sockets that were watching them. She used her boot heel and ground it.

The translucent ball crumbled like hard candy and the stench of rotten eggs rose.

She waved her hand through the air.

"That's sulfur in its raw form," Fat Bear said.

She reflected on life before and during the war. Some bad things had ended, along with a way of life. "Sometimes, it's hard to grasp what that era was really like. This, for instance—people living with the bare necessaries so others can fight for their right to live like they want."

At the edge of her beam, something flashed. She walked toward it.

"How long do you think it's been since someone camped here?" she asked.

"A hundred and sixty years."

"Come look at this." Her light focused on a sleeping bag, a green Coleman's stove, a Yeti cooler, and a red, inflatable mattress. "I'd say someone stayed here yesterday."

Fat Bear knelt and rummaged through the camp site. None of the belongings suggested more than one person had slept here. Cans of beer and packages of ground beef floating in water slush filled the cooler.

The sound of heavy breathing surrounded her.

Fat Bear continued to search the cooler. He hadn't heard it.

She inhaled and held it.

Stillness hung in the air.

The cave had to be playing tricks on her.

"What's that?" Coup pointed her light at the foot of the mattress.

Fat Bear picked it up, along with a white booklet, then stood by Coup. "Looks like a sci-fi ray gun," he said. "Maybe a laser tag team practiced in this place."

"In my day, we used paint balls. Stung like hell when someone hit you." She flipped through the dirt-smudged manual. "Guess the younger generation wants to play war without getting hurt."

He held the unit in her light so she could get a good look at it, then he pushed the "on" button.

Molded, hard, black plastic formed the base of the device, and it had a touch screen, color monitor. Adjustment icons below the readout consisted of up and down arrows, sound, and an oversized "OK" button. On the underside, was a hand grip, and, pointing out of the front, were two silver rods about a foot in length. One rod looked like a stainless-steel drill bit, and the other, similar, but twice as thick.

"Fat Bear," she said, "Your Great Spirit likes you."

"And why?"

"What you are holding is a Ger Detect Diamond Hunter."

Fat Bear's face changed from confused to a shy smile like a little boy on Christmas morning. "Look at this screen."

"This unit can probe a hundred feet into the ground."

"It found something," he said.

Coup checked the display. The monitor had three blue, curved bands pulsating outward. At the far tip, a red dot shone. She faced in the direction the unit pointed and stared into the hard substrate. "Is it set on the diamond setting or useless rocks?"

"We passed some rubble on the way in. I didn't pay it any attention then because of its proximity to the entrance."

"Maybe there were dual exits at that spot before the quake," she said.

"Let's take a closer look and see what this thing does."

Coup felt relieved as they headed toward fresh air, sunlight, and open spaces.

When she and Fat Bear walked into the main passageway, a wave of damp air swept past them. It didn't smell fresh to her as if it'd come from the outside. The gust reeked of old, wet dirt with a tint of something dead. The thought of Uktena returned to her.

No, she said to herself. *Stay positive. Can this device really find diamonds? Even the Tarpon Diamond?*

A thud of a footstep caused her to forget about the device.

Fifty-one

"Were the rocks this wet when we started?" Kole asked Coup.

"All I know is that my hair is soaked as if I've stood in an August downpour."

Kole stooped and studied the loose rocks. Water seeped in from somewhere. The fluid had crept to the ground level, no longer running off or seeping into the earth. And, to the touch, it felt cool, not cold as if it had been stored in the mountain for months. Last night's rain must have saturated the ground and now, the water had started to percolate through the limestone.

Standing, he swept the diamond finder in front of him.

The screen flashed black-and-white mosaic squares.

"Is it broken?" Coup shined her light on the device. "The seal must be bad, and the moisture has shorted it out."

"I'm hoping it's the minerals in this place screwing up the sensors."

"Looks broken to me."

"The owner would have thought the same. I'm guessing that's why they abandoned it back at the campsite without finding anything of value." Kole turned the device off.

Without the glow from the monitor, the tunnel became darker. They slowed their walk to the back door, and it seemed to take much longer than he would've expected. The soggy ground concerned him. At times, his feet splashed in clear puddles.

Would the water continue to rise, or would it flow into shafts? He did some mental calculations. The distance from the back door to the entrance had a walking time of about an hour.

Worse case, an hour and a half. If the water rose quickly, could they outrun it?

Hardly. And soon, they'd enter the portion where they had to stay in a stoop, not the ideal position for a speedy exit.

What scared him was that the water would not seep out of the limestone but come rushing down the tunnel in a wall of water, completely filling the space and engulfing them.

He could give up on finding the diamond and quick step it to safety, but that would mean sacrificing Miller's freedom. But to stay and hunt might cost his and Coup's lives. Should he tell Coup his thoughts?

He gazed into the darkness, unsure of what to do.

Standing still solved no problems and started walking. He counted each footstep. The distance to the back door stretched forever into a black gloom. Ideas and scenarios bounced around in his head. If he didn't share the truth with Coup and they died, the Great Spirit would condemn him. His soul wouldn't be allowed to live in an animal but would wander unseen and lonely. Deceiving people wasn't the way of Grandfather's teachings.

When the flood trapped them, would that be the time of Uktena's attack? He'd have to be of pure heart and strong mind when that battle started.

He stopped and listened to the water gurgling somewhere in the back of the cave. It was faint, not loud—a good sign. However, it was no longer a dripping noise, or a trickle. It sounded like a babbling stream.

At last, the narrow opening of the back door faced them. Sunlight filtered down the twisted crack and a spot of yellow danced on the floor.

"I need to tell you something," Kole said.

"Is it the change in the sound of water or the fact that you're scared we'll die in this wretched place?"

"Both." The water continued to rise and now covered the toe of his boot. "Best if you get out of here. I want to try this device."

"As much as I'd like to, how do I know you won't pull a

diamond out of your back pocket and say you found it? I could easily argue that in court."

"You're a fool, Sheriff, if you don't leave now."

"I came along to ensure that, if the diamond is found, the proper chain of custody is followed, and if that legendary creature of yours shows up, I'm going to give him a lesson in modern weaponry."

"Then let's find that piece of ice and get out of here." Kole switched on the diamond hunter and hoped there'd be no interference in this part of the cave.

The device emitted a soft hum; the monitor stayed black.

He thumped the side a few times with his flashlight. The unit felt moist. A droplet formed on top of the antennae and his heart sank. The damn thing was ruined.

They were out of options. What had he been thinking in the first place? That the diamond would stare them in the face? He had called Coup a fool, but *he* was the fool. He'd acted like a fool. It might be best to never leave this cave and save Grandfather the embarrassment.

Then the device beeped.

He pointed it to the left of the shaft where the wall had collapsed.

The boulders looked like a he-man had stacked them on top of one another. Dirt dribbled down the front.

Blue, semi-circle waves pushed outward on the monitor. A red dot shone at the base. He stared in disbelief, then closed his eyes.

After reopening them, the icon still glowed.

"Thank you, Great Spirit," he said.

Coup took the device and pointed it up and down and to both sides. "If this thing is right, the diamond is in front of us."

Kole knelt and ran his hand through the rubble. The pea-sized gravel were several inches deep around the base of the fallen rocks.

He held his flashlight close to the ground. Careful to touch only debris, he scooted the stones to the side. Then pushed more and more of the gravel aside. The discarded rocks formed a foot-high mound.

Then blues, greens, and reds were reflected in his beam. At first, he thought the moisture had formed rainbows, but the colors were sharper, denser, and they looked like fish scales.

He wanted to shout, laugh, and dance a jig. "Come look."

Coup knelt beside him. "Fat Bear, I guess your crazy theory was correct."

"Damn right." Pulling a baggie out of his pack, he pushed the gem inside with the blade of his knife. Then, he handed her the bag. "Chain of custody good?"

"Yes." She shoved the baggy into her backpack.

Kole stood and helped Coup to her feet and, before she stepped away, kissed her on the lips.

"Counselor!" she yelled. "What did I tell you about improprieties?"

"Wasn't listening. But that's for sticking with me in the search. I know you didn't believe we'd find it."

She smiled. "You found the diamond. We can head home, and I can have a hot shower."

"Me too."

Coup stepped to the side of the tunnel and adjusted her pack. "Let's go. My eyeballs need to see some daylight."

He held his light steady and watched her walk. Her hair was tousled, her clothes covered in patches of red clay and black soot, but she was the true diamond—

Then the earth swallowed her.

Gone.

No trace.

Then a faraway scream of pain came from underground.

In front of him, a crevice zigzagged across the floor.

"Coup!" he yelled. The word echoed throughout the tunnel.

Then silence.

Except for the rippling of water.

Fifty-two

Kole shone his light down into the crevice. Minerals in the limestone reflected their brilliance into the gloom.

There was no sign of Coup.

He yelled her name and waited.

No response.

Panning the wide, white beam across the top of the cave floor, along the ragged rock, he saw that the shaft had twisted and narrowed and had edges sharp enough to filet skin.

How far had she fallen?

Would the length of rope he brought reach?

"Coup!" he yelled again. "Can you hear me?"

Silence.

A black void stared back at him. Nothingness. An evil. A rottenness. A place not meant for human life.

He uncoiled his rope and tied one end around the base of a lumpy stalagmite. He ran his hand around the structure to ensure it would not cut the lifeline, then he tossed the other end into the crack in the earth.

No sound of the rope hitting bottom echoed up.

The line swayed from side to side.

Scenarios flashed through his mind. Was she unconscious? Or, worse, had she died upon impact? Then the unthinkable—had she fallen hundreds of feet, maybe thousands, and was barely alive, knowing she'd never be rescued, and her body never recovered?

After sticking the flashlight into his belt so that it pointed down, he eased his body over the lip and started his descent, feet first. The hole wasn't large enough for him to rappel. He used a slow process of hand-under-hand. The shaft's walls were slick as water seeped from the sides.

A primordial smell filled his nostrils.

Limestone mud fell each time he dug the toe of his boot into the rock. Sometimes, the foothold was enough to ease the strain in his arms, but, mostly, his boot slid away.

He continued to sink into the unknown, his face flat against the side, razor cuts digging into his skin. Foot by foot, he descended.

He glanced down. The beam wobbled, doing little to penetrate the blackness. He twisted, hoping he could see the bottom.

It didn't seem to have one.

He continued to drop. His feet didn't touch the sides. An openness surrounded him. His arm muscles burned, and a weakness entered his limbs.

Relaxing his grip on the rope, he plunged. His palms simmered while the rope sped past him.

Finally, he came into contact with rock, and he clenched the rope. He'd landed on a small outcropping. Steading himself, he noticed the rope's bitter end lay just beyond his feet.

Holding the light with both hands, he found Coup below him.

She had fallen into a hole that trapped her around her chest. Blood oozed from cuts covering her body and her head rested on her shoulder, motionless.

He dropped to the side of Coup. Here the chamber was damp and cold and smelled of decomposed animals. Water flowed from a crack in the wall and swirled around her before dropping into the depths.

Using two fingers on her neck, he found a carotid pulse, steady and thumping hard. Cupping the water with his hands he splashed some on Coup's face. "I'm here, Coup."

She didn't respond. Or moan.

Her lips had a blue tint.

The restriction had stopped her from falling deeper into the bowels of the earth, but had wrapped tight around her so her chest couldn't expand and contract.

He grabbed her armpits and pulled. She didn't budge.

She did, though, groan. "I'm dizzy, Fat Bear."

More pebbles rolled down the sides, creating a packing mud around her. Coup's head lobbed to the side.

He inhaled the mustiness.

What injuries had she incurred? Broken limbs, spine, a neck injury? Would he paralyze her if he jerked her body the wrong way? Would a broken rib pierce her heart?

He felt at a loss.

If he didn't act, she'd die. If he *did* act, he could kill her.

What would Grandfather do?

His flashlight slipped from his belt and rolled to Coup's chest. The flickering beam caused shadows to dance on the wall that looked like a raven hoping from one foot to the other, signaling him to hurry.

He tucked his light back into his belt, then brushed his hands through the mud, then grabbed her and pulled.

She was jammed tight.

Water sprinkled down on him as he tried again.

No movement. The force of her falling and tumbling down the shaft had wedged her in like a cork in a bottle.

If he heaved too hard, he might dislocate her shoulder or break ribs. He noticed her chest no longer moved in and out, she had stopped breathing.

Broken bones were better than being dead.

He planted his legs beside both shoulders, and against rock. Slipping his belt off, he wrapped it around her chest and under her arms. He dug his boots into the limestone to ensure they were solid, knees bent.

Bending over her, he laced his fingers around the belt and yanked upward. The leather bit into her flesh. He leaned back so her body would slide against his.

Water ran down his face. Pushing with his legs, his knees started to straighten, and his back throbbed in pain.

Her body shifted upward a few inches.

He didn't relax his hold but arched his back. Rocks dug into him as little whirlpools formed around Coup's torso, while gray water gurgled past her body then down into the depths.

Her body twitched, the earth's grasp on her lessening.

He planted his boots on slightly higher ground, then tugged again. The suction broke and he wrenched her body on top of his.

He scooted and pulled both of them to a flat rock, then opened her airway. Her pulse was steady. Kneeling beside her, he placed his ear over her mouth to listen for a breath.

Coup's body shook and he heard a gasp being sucked in.

The breath returned, warm and forceful. It gave him the first relaxed feeling since entering the cave.

"I hate this cave," she said.

He sat upright. "You think you can climb up this rope?"

"Not sure."

He removed his belt from around her and replaced it with the rope. "No problem." After he finished securing the rope and testing the knot so it wouldn't pinch her, he said, "I'll climb to the top and pull you up. Use your hands and feet to keep from banging into the sides."

He noticed the rope had turned red in places, then started to climb.

Reaching the lip of the cave floor, he dragged himself out of the hole. His arms ached and he gave them a quick rubdown. To pull Coup up, he tightened both hands on the rope and leaned backward, letting the weight of his body do the work.

Back and forth, he repeated the steps. Hold, lean back, new grip, again.

He swore the rope had stretched in length. His muscles were tired and cramping. *Rest*! was what his brain yelled, but he couldn't let Coup dangle below in the darkness.

He panted, his body burning more oxygen than he could

give it. The rope coiled beside him as he pulled and leaned. His strength waned and exhaustion started to overcome him. Lightheadedness swirled in his skull, and his fingers tingled. He feared his body would collapse. He had no more to give.

A raven appeared in his mind. Its blue eyes looked hard at him. The bird swung its beak back and forth in the same rhythm as him pulling the rope.

The bird cawed.

As the sound echoed in his skull, Coup's head appeared out of the hole. He dragged her the rest of the way, then undid the rope.

"Thanks," she said, then inhaled deeply.

He did a head-to-toe check, feeling for broken bones or paralysis, and, thankfully, found none. He grabbed the first aid kit out of his pack and administered to the more serious cuts.

Coup's clothes were ripped and muddy. Blood stains covered her limbs and torso.

He dabbed a cotton gauze on her cheek to wipe away dried blood and mud.

"I hurt all over." Coup used Kole as a brace to stand. "How bad is it?"

"I don't see anything broken." He stood and steadied Coup. "But lots of lacerations. You'll have scars in places. Plus, you'll be black-and-blue for weeks."

"Just like me." A voice came out of the darkness.

Then an intense light hit them.

"This wretched place almost killed me. I was one giant scar." The voice paused. "I can give you a name of a good plastic surgeon. He changed my whole body. I went from drab and broken, to sexy and fabulous."

Kole shielded his eyes. All he could see was a black muzzle of a semi-automatic pistol pointed at him.

"But, first," the voice said, "hand over the diamond."

Fifty-three

Kole pointed his light toward the voice. The face stunned him.

"Savannah-Jo," Kole said. "The water level is rising. We need to work together to get out of here." The height had risen to over his ankles. He had to shift his stance to keep from being knocked down and flashed his light at Coup. Her injuries and the running water made her wobbly. If the stream crept up to six inches, it'd wash her away. He needed a plan to deal with Savannah-Jo, or the bitch would kill them all.

"This isn't the first time I've had to fight my way out of this cave," Savannah-Jo said. "Sherrif, unload and toss your firearm."

"I don't think so," Coup said, her fingers touching the butt of her gun.

"What do you say I waste Fat Bear, then?" Savannah-Jo stepped toward him. The light strapped to her nine-millimeter captured both Coup and Kole in its beam. Her barrel focused on his chest. If Coup pulled her weapon, was he fast enough to jump to Savannah-Jo and knock her aim?

That was a dumb thought. The water would hinder his movements. The evil woman had them.

Coup pulled her weapon, ejected the clip, then ratcheted the round out of the chamber. She tossed it at Savannah-Jo's feet. The pieces of the gun made plopping noises. "You won't be able to fence this diamond; it's too hot."

"Honey, I know several private collectors who want it. Did you forget that I find precious artwork and sell it? With the abundance of cash they'll pay, I'll get another new identity and disappear again."

"To where?" Coup asked. "All law enforcement is linked together. The web has turned us into one community. Facial rec is everywhere."

"What you don't know is the number of nations that have warm, sandy beaches and don't care what the U S of A thinks, wants, or does. It's easy to get to one of them simply by traveling on freighters that have lonely captains. And when a gorgeous woman shows up on such an island, she'll have her pick of gentlemen who would love her company. Especially one with lots of cash."

The water swirled around the top of Kole's boots and started to dribble down the insides. His thick socks would soon be saturated and impede him from running. The idea of escaping became less and less of a valid option.

"Let's start walking out now," he said. "You can have the diamond once we're outside. Our time is running out."

"Dig the diamond out of your pack," Savannah-Jo said to Coup. "I'm getting impatient. Then we'll part ways. You can live, if you don't drown in here because, by the time you get out, I'll be history."

"Just like you let Aletha live?" Coup said, then, to Fat Bear, she said, "You realize this is Jennie Lee, the missing girl."

"Aletha turned into a bitch. I told her God wanted us to have the diamonds. Didn't He put me on that train?" Savannah-Jo directed the gun at Coup. "She and I could have travelled the world. Been anyone we wanted to be. But what did she do? She swallowed the damn diamond. She could have just given it back, but she'd wanted to teach me a lesson about God's forgiveness. I taught her a new lesson—don't mess with me."

From far down the passage, he could hear echoes of the torrential current smashing against the rock sides. The dip before the entrance was filling up. They needed to head out now or they'd be trapped.

"What about Terrie-Mae?" Kole asked. He needed time to think, to plan. He had to keep her talking. "Did she give you a Bible lesson also?"

"She acted worldly," Savannah-Jo said, "but that purple bimbo had too many screws loose for me. She'd figured out who I was and wanted to turn me in. Enough of this jabber. Gimme the diamond."

Kole noticed Coup could barely walk and it seemed her injuries caused great pain throughout her body. Odds were, he'd have to carry her out.

He stepped over to where she had dropped her pack and knelt.

Coup stooped beside him with her back to Savannah-Jo. "It's in here."

Kole unzipped her pack. The material was soaked. Water had seeped inside and wet everything. He heard Coup mumble something. The tone didn't sound good. When he saw her place her hand on her spare weapon, he whispered, "Is this a good idea?"

"Nope." Coup held a plastic bag above her head. She spun and fired two shots at Savannah-Jo.

Savannah-Jo stumbled backward and grunted. As she fell, she pulled the trigger on her auto. Echoes bombarded the cave walls.

Coup yelled and dropped her gun.

To Kole, things broke into slow motion. He saw the lead hit Coup's wrist and travel upward, ripping her skin from hand to bicep. The bullet left her arm and continued. Blood covered Coup's arm from the long slice.

Hot lead hit his shoulder. He spun and sprawled across the floor. Muddy water entered his mouth, and he gagged it out. His arm wouldn't move.

Water rushed over him, rising above him. If he laid there any longer, he'd start breathing water. Looking over toward Coup, he saw her face-down, the water streaming past her turning red. Pulling his legs up under him helped him to stand.

He limped over to Coup, rolled her over, then held her face above the water. "You have to stand." He felt the shivers course through her from the cold air.

Grabbing his arm, she climbed up his body. A surge of water passed them, pushing them forward. The water rose to their knees.

"No one pulls a gun on me and lives." Coup coughed out the words.

Savannah-Jo groaned, a bubble rising above her face. Then she stood.

Kole's light still lay in the water. It cast a blue glow at Savannah-Jo, and he watched as she reached down and retrieved her gun.

"She's the Uktena," he said.

The words reverberated in the darkness.

Fifty-four

Kole felt the deep bass rumble first in his chest as if the Cherokee nation was pounding on their dance drums. Before his mind registered what had caused it, his feet vibrated.

Shining the light down, he saw pebbles and gravel bounce upward out of the water around his boots then splash back down as if thousands of fish were hitting the surface. The tremor felt like it came from hundreds of miles below him and had been building for eons and was ready to spew its built-up energy. The sides of the caves crumbled into car-sized boulders and a fine, orange dust filled the air. The ceiling cracked and formed a fissure above him and ran toward the cave's entrance as far as the light beam reached.

Earthquake! his brain screamed.

"Time to go!" he yelled.

The ground shook. Coup wobbled and fell, then so did Savannah-Jo.

He lost his balance and landed on his bad shoulder. "Damn it!" he howled. His light popped out of his hand and lay underwater several feet in front of him.

The sound of gunfire blasted the cave walls. A bullet splattered in the water in front of him and the yellow beam of his light went out. Savannah-Jo still planned to kill them.

Wrapping his good arm around Coup, he pulled her to the back of a partial stalagmite with a base wide enough to hide her, then set her upright against the formation. The water lapped around her waist as fat drops dripped from the ceiling.

"Turn off your light," he said.

Coup complied.

Blackness covered them. He placed his fingers on Coup's lips to convey silence.

Slipping beneath the water so only his eyes protruded, he pulled with one arm from rock to rock to where they'd left their packs. Savannah-Jo flashed her light from side to side, looking for prey. The whiteness looked like a ghost flying in the fog.

"Fat Bear," Savannah-Jo laughed, "what kind of injun name is that? Guess your parents despised you."

He didn't take to the goading. Responding would give her the advantage. He would stay quiet and let his silence frustrate her.

"Did a pregnant bear run by your pathetic teepee when you were born?" Savannah-Jo waded a few steps, sending out a concentric circle of waves. "Must be embarrassing to be named after a female."

He pulled the straps of both packs up his arm. He could wiggle the fingers in his other limb only if he wanted the pain to shoot through his arm. A baggie floated on the water, and he stuffed it into his pants' pocket. His boots bumped against the contents that fell from the packs.

Savannah-Jo panned her light in his direction.

He didn't have time to search for the items; she'd find him if he did.

With a deep breath, he submerged and swam back to Coup, ensuring his feet didn't break the surface and give away his position.

Surfacing beside Coup, he handed her the pack. The water had worked its way up to her torso. Smeared across her shirt was a mixture of mud and blood.

Savannah-Jo worked her way back and forth from the sides. Each sweep brought her closer to Kole. The only good thing about that, he thought, was that her light reflected off the wall and increased his line of sight.

Coup dragged her pack onto her lap and rummaged through it. "I'm out of guns."

"She's Uktena. Bullets don't affect her." The roar of the rushing water allowed them to speak without fear of being heard.

"Savannah-Jo is wearing a vest. I didn't kill her, but she must be hurting like hell. Maybe in worse shape than me."

Kole pulled a nine-inch knife from his pack.

"Where did you get that frog-sticker?" Coup said.

"A blessing from Grandfather. He carved the handle from an elk's antler. The red coral and blue turquoise help with the grip. The blade is stainless steel, and he designed it to put down any beast. I just hope its power is strong enough to be used against Uktena."

"She's just a crazed woman, not a legend. She's flesh and blood." Coup held Kole's arm. "But you be damn careful. She's smart and quick. You have a plan?"

"I'm going to slip over to the opposite side."

"She'll see you."

"Not in this haze. Plus, I'll be low in the water. Count to fifty, then turn your light on."

"The hell I will. She'll know my location. I can't move fast enough to hide. Not sure I can even hobble."

"Don't keep the light. Toss it between you and me."

"She'll still know where I'm hiding."

"That she will."

He heard her sigh. Yes, his plan sucked.

"She'll shoot at the light a few times before she realizes you're not beside it. She'll walk over to it."

"I'm not liking this."

"When she reaches for the light, I'll come up behind her."

"I don't like being the bait."

He didn't like it either and tucked the knife behind his back. Nor did he like Coup's breath becoming labored.

"Show yourself," Savannah-Jo called out. "Give me the diamond and the two of you go free."

Kole slipped underwater. He'd noticed the level had risen to Coup's chest. Soon, wading out of the cave wouldn't be an option. The dip just inside the entrance would soon be flooded. He might be able to hold his breath and swim out if the cliff face didn't collapse, but how long could Coup hold her breath? He shook his head, knowing the answer.

Grabbing rocks with one hand and kicking his feet, he swam blindly. He was uncertain if his course was true or if he zig-zagged across the floor. The plan seemed unlikely to work the farther he went. When he surfaced, he hoped he didn't pop up beside Savannah-Jo.

His lungs burned. The water felt cold and squeezed his chest. He had to cover more distance. The key to this working was him sneaking up behind Savannah-Jo. She couldn't sense him near her, or she'd turn and fire.

He swallowed, forcing the air in his throat into his lungs, which allowed him maybe another minute. The burn returned to his lungs, hotter this time. He was spent, his good arm acted like a wet noddle, so he let his body float to the surface.

On his knees, he kept his face above the water and breathed through his mouth. First a deep breath, which he held, before letting it trickle out of his lungs, a trick Grandfather had taught him. No sound was emitted. That was the way to come upon wild prey. However, this time, it wasn't bear, elk, or deer, but human.

Coup tossed her light. It sailed through the air, not end-over-end, but stayed level as if someone carried it.

The quick-fire of a double tap exploded, the muzzle flash temporarily blinding him.

Savannah-Jo splashed through the water, unconcerned if she was heard or seen. Her light circled Coup's.

"Fat Bear." Savannah-Jo waded toward the submerged light. The water lapped against the sides, causing more rocks to tumble down. "I know where you're at. You can't hide."

He didn't stand, but eased toward Savannah-Jo, staying silent like a moccasin, the way Grandfather had taught him.

The woman stopped and turned away from him. "I was hoping to find Fat Bear," Savannah-Jo said to Coup, "but you'll do. You can be alive or dead when I take the diamond. You chose."

Kole stayed low in the water. Savannah-Jo was close, maybe twenty, twenty-five feet in front of him. He had to move slowly. He didn't want the water to betray him.

Savannah-Jo leveled her gun at Coup. "You look half-dead already. Pity to waste a bullet on you."

"You don't want to be a cop-killer," Coup said. "My colleagues won't quit until they find you."

A sinking thought went through Kole's mind. Even if he surprised Savannah-Jo and was able to knife her, she could still squeeze off several shots. And, as close as she was to Coup, those would find their mark.

"Oh, Sugar," Savannah-Jo said, "again, you're not thinking clearly. Your body will never be found, let alone be recovered."

He slipped beneath the surface. The glow from Coup's light outlined Savannah-Jo's boots. With his arm, he pulled himself along the cave's floor. No kicking, so he wouldn't boil the surface. The distance was closing.

Then Savannah-Jo's legs shifted. Was she planting her feet for a fatal shot?

Out of time.

He rose and launched himself at Savannah-Jo. His weight knocked her down and he fell on top of her. Pain exploded in his shoulder. The sound of her gun spitting out a bullet clenched his stomach. Was her aim dead on? What about Coup?

The only sound he heard was the water as it continued to rise, sealing them inside the cave.

Fifty-five

Savannah-Jo wrestled herself away from Kole. She stood when he did, now face-to-face. Her arm arced to bring the gun up.

He grabbed her forearm high, twisted his body then knelt, bringing her body over his shoulder. The water hindered his movements, but he reached inside himself for strength and flung her as far as he could.

He heard the splash. But it was more than that. The sound was like a falling tree hitting mud.

The cave echoed from the water cascading along the sides, but no longer gushing. Reaching down, he retrieved Coup's light and shone it in the direction of Savannah-Jo.

She lay on her back and appeared to be floating. Her hand twitched and trembled as it reached for her gun beneath her. Then the movement stopped. Her head rolled to one side and lifeless eyes stared at him, hate and surprise filling her face.

A stream of red water passed him.

He walked to her body. She was impaled on a rock icicle. The bulletproof vest she wore was tented upward. The razor-sharp calcium structure had gone completely through her. He felt no pulse in her throat.

Grandfather had been right. Only the earth could kill the Uktena.

He heard Coup moan.

Kole picked up Savannah-Jo's flashlight, dried it against his shirt, then did the same with Coup's. He noticed Savannah-Jo's still shined a bright white while Coup's had a dull yellow beam, and he wondered how long before both lights died. The pain in his shoulder had dulled, but it still seeped blood. Would he and Coup bleed out before or after the lights went black?

He waded over to Coup. She hadn't moved from the stalagmite where he'd set her.

The water swirled around her chest, and she shivered. The beam from Savannah-Jo's light created harsh shadows as if he was in a black-and-white movie.

"I want you to look at this." She pointed to the rock structure beside her head. The movement caused her to wince.

The flattened lead from Savannah-Jo's last shot protruded from the pillar.

It was too close to Coup's head. He was surprised her blonde hair wasn't scorched.

"Your plan almost killed me," she said, and he wasn't sure if the sternness in her face was from pain or anger.

She was right and he felt like the lowest creature on earth.

He sloshed over to Savannah-Jo's body and cut off the sleeves of her shirt.

Returning to Coup, he wrapped the material tight around her wounds, then lifted her by her armpits.

She tilted to one side and held her gunshot arm. The shirt sleeve was clotted with blood. If she didn't bang against anything, it shouldn't start to bleed again—but it was only a matter of time until she did it in this black tunnel.

"The dip right before the cave entrance is flooded. How long can you hold your breath?"

She sucked in a breath.

The way her body jerked, he knew the act was painful. She had to have a few cracked ribs.

Coup exhaled. "I counted to seventeen using the one-one-thousand method."

He handed Savannah-Jo's light to Coup.

"How much time will we be underwater?" she asked.

"Two, or three minutes."

"Can you drag me out and revive me?" She drooped her head. "This plan sucks, too."

He would have to hold one hand over her mouth and nose so her lungs wouldn't fill up with the muddy cave water. How much brain damage would occur?

He moved his limp arm and grimaced. The pain caused his eyes to shut. He wiggled his fingers. Clenching his teeth he raised his arm, but it wouldn't go higher than the water level. Was it his muscles working or was his arm buoyed up by the water?

They both needed medical attention, and if he tried to pull her to the opening, he'd drown them with that plan. But what choice did he have? Wait here for a slow death or die trying?

Then he heard a caw.

"Did you hear that?" he asked.

"What? My heart pounding in my ears or my brain screaming goodbye?"

"A caw?"

"Sure. Some bird wants his last breath with ours. You're hallucinating."

He didn't answer her. Possibly, he *was* going mad. The rising water masked most of the sounds. Except when they spoke, then, the echo bounced loudly around them. Was his brain inventing noises because there were few in this grave?

"Caw."

The sound came from the back of the cave. He looked at Coup. She didn't have the strength to walk far.

"Can you float?"

"Like a rock," she said.

He stood behind Coup and wrapped his arm around her waist. "Walk slow. I'll steady you."

"Where we going?"

"The back door."

"It's blocked."

"My spirit animal is there."

He nudged Coup forward. They stumbled the first few steps,

but the deep water helped them stay upright. The downside was that the current tried to push them toward the main entrance and the deep pool.

After a few more feet, he was able to splash their way forward, his legs in rhythm with hers.

"So," Coup said, "the plan is to trust the voices in your head?"

"No. To trust the Cherokee way."

"Grandfather would be proud."

He pictured Grandfather's face, hardened from the years, leathery from the sun, the jaw strong like the rest of his body, but a smile would form.

The narrow shaft of the back entrance formed in his mind. Neither he nor Coup could shimmy through it, even if they weren't injured. Another bad plan. Was he taking them to their final resting place?

With each step, they sent waves of water outward, some lapping against the cave walls. The other swells disappeared into the darkness. Kole felt his insanity had passed because he no longer heard encouragement from the crow.

Coup's head rested on his shoulder. He tightened his arm around her waist. She was losing strength. Every few feet, she'd grunt from a missed step or a gouge in the rock floor or from the time it took to make any measurable progress.

What could he do to lighten her mood?

"Looks bleak, doesn't it?" he said.

"Yeah." The word was more of a sigh.

"Nice that your head is resting on my shoulder. I remember the last time that happened. It was in a different cave and just as dark."

There was a pause in her step.

"If we're going to die," he said, "how about another kiss?"

She turned her head to him, her face in shadows. "I'll cook you dinner and *breakfast* if you get us out of here."

He saw her smile and caught her promise.

It seemed like hours to him—and maybe it was—before they came to the side tunnel that led to the miners' camp. He turned them in that direction. "We need to get the pickaxe," he said.

The axe lay in the water. How was he going to carry the tool and still hold Coup? He stood there, his light wavering through the water. The bouncing yellow beam looked like fish darting around the tool.

"Pick it up," she said. "I'll carry it."

It took him a few minutes of juggling to get the axe to Coup, tuck her light under her arm, position himself behind her, and start their trek.

After countless baby steps, he spotted a weak light trickle down the shaft of the back entrance.

"We made it." Coup walked to the light and leaned against the rock. She dropped the tool.

Kole studied the boulders and rocks wedged into the side of the vertical shaft. The bottom massive stones were lodged tight. He'd never budge them. About three levels up, was a single boulder, the size of a tractor's back tire. Everything above it looked small and loose. Prying the rocks loose seemed impossible. Even the axe looked weak. He picked it up.

After many attempts, he climbed up with Coup pushing his butt with her good arm.

He placed the broad, flat steel tool under the rock. It took him several attempts to wedge it in tight. The handle stuck out in the open. His weight on the end of the handle should be enough force to lodge the blockage free.

He scooted to the end of the tool then laid on it.

Nothing.

Coup stood to the side, her light giving proof to the long distance he'd fall if he slipped.

He bounced a few more times. It felt like the rock wanted to move. More weight was needed.

"Can you climb up a little and lock hands with me?"

"You've already dangled me once today."

"I need more weight."

"You should have eaten a larger dinner."

"Get up here."

"You want me to lay on top of you?"

"No. If we lock arms, your weight should be enough to break this rock out."

"You calling me fat?"

"You want to drown?"

"This is another bad plan. What makes you think this mountain won't tumble down on us?"

"I'm looking forward to you cooking breakfast." He scooted a bit more on the handle.

Coup rolled and humped more than climbed. She rested on the second rock up.

Kole reached down and locked onto Coup's wrist.

She hung in space.

"Hurry," she said.

He bounced on the handle. A crack sounded in the chamber. Was it the handle, the base of the axe, or the rock? He wasn't sure.

He thumped hard.

The axe moved until the handle was almost perpendicular to the floor.

It was working… or was the handle ready to break?

"Great Spirit," he said, "grant me one more try."

He raised himself up off the wooden handle, then pulled Coup upward until she was even with the axe. He shifted his weight and balanced on one knee. The force of his next action would either clear the boulder or send them both into the water.

Flinging himself toward the tip of the tool, he hit it hard. The weight of Coup plummeting downward felt like his shoulder was being ripped out of his body.

A whoosh of warm air filled with the scent of pine needles blew past him as he fell. Noise echoed everywhere. Coup no longer held onto his wrist. He splashed into the water, rocks pelleting his back.

Stones battered the water. He felt like a meteor shower was raining down on him as a wave pushed him forward.

He drifted with the current until calmness returned.

Standing, he tried to get his bearings. His light gone, but he saw the glow of Coup's light. She had climbed up on a ledge, inches above the water.

With one arm, he breast-stroked to her.

Reaching her, he grasped the ledge and looked upward. A wide ray of light shown down and it felt warm. The shaft was clear. They could climb out one at a time.

The water started to rise again. Coup sat on the highest ground. At the increase rate, the water would cover her soon.

"Not sure I can climb up through that. It's straight up," Coup said.

"It's not wide enough for you to cling to my back. We have to go one at a time."

The water gurgled around him. The tug of the current was ready to sweep him away.

"I think I can work my way to the top," he said. "It'd be slow. Then I could tie some vines together to make a rope and lower it down to you."

"How long to do that?"

"About five minutes more than you have."

He looked at her. Her muddy face tilted upward at the shaft. Her face was no longer ghastly like it'd been at the stalagmite, but her brown eyes looked like cinnamon in the afternoon light.

He turned his head toward the hole. He saw no hand or footholds. No roots clung down from the surface that they could hold onto.

"Do you have a plan that doesn't involve me dying?"

He wished he did.

Fifty-six

"The water is rising again," Coup said.

Kole noticed it also. Every couple of minutes, it crept up higher on his chest, causing each breath to be harder than the last one. They were trapped. Only one person at a time could climb up the shaft. Diving down into the icy depths to hunt for another exit wasn't an option. It wouldn't be long before the ledge they sat on would be several feet underwater. He needed to take action.

He and Coup had been in the cold water too long. His extremities felt numb. Coup shivered constantly. The sunlight which filtered down on them gave no warmth.

"I have another idea," he said.

"Hope this one is better than the other hairbrained ideas."

"I believe it is."

"Why don't you go ahead and climb out of here? No reason for both of us to drown."

"I won't let that happen to either of us."

"So we die of hypothermia. Great plan."

"I'm going to duck under, place your feet on my shoulders, and when I stand, you'll be part way up the shaft."

"Then what? My arm is useless. How will I continue to shimmy up that abominable hole?"

"I'll use my knife and stick it into the side. Little by little I can ease us up. Wedge the knife in, pull me up, use my legs to brace, then move the knife up, and repeat. As I work my way up, so will you."

Coup laughed. "I'd like to see you jam your knife in solid rock. Go ahead and try it."

She spoke the truth. No way would the blade dig deep enough into limestone and hold. Wishful thinking.

"Look at me," she said.

She moved close to him and leaned forward. Her lips met his. They were grimy from the mud, minerally tasting from the rock dust, but he enjoyed every second of it.

Wrapping his one arm around her, he held her in an awkward embrace while she quivered from the cold.

Coup backed away. "Now, get."

"As soon as I catch my breath." He lied, having no intention of leaving her. His animal spirit hadn't led him here to die. Was he supposed to climb out and leave her? Grandfather had never taught him to sacrifice someone's life to save one's own; it was always the other way around.

She nudged him.

He didn't move. Instead, he reflected on the events since entering this cave. It truly was the Devil's cave. A den of death.

A cloud passed overhead and blocked the last of the sunshine. Their small alcove turned black and Coup's face disappeared into the darkness.

Was this the Great Spirit's doing, turning everything dark, so they wouldn't see one another die?

The water continued thundering past them. The current pushed the air into a howl, and it sounded like a cry from Miller— the man he was supposed to represent and get the charges dropped. The Mennonite wouldn't survive in prison. The first time Miller quoted scripture, an inmate would shank him.

Kole shook his head. Another person would die because of Kole's failure.

The ledge they sat on trembled. The limestone was being eaten away by the rushing water. Soon it would crumble, and they would be sucked downward.

Would Coup's and his fate be the same as Savannah-Jo's, never to be found?

He felt abandoned by his spirit animal and the Great Spirit

because he was about to be wiped away, forgotten, no flesh to be burned in a ceremonial funeral, no ashes to be scattered in the wind.

Something knocked his hat off. He fumbled in the dark to find it, only to be slapped in the face. It felt like a vine had fallen down the shaft. The greater odds were that a rattlesnake had fallen into the hole.

He grabbed his knife and waited for the venomous strike to occur.

"When you're done being baptized, tie the rope to you and I'll pull you up."

The clouds passed and he looked up. Miller gazed down at him. How was it possible for the Mennonite to be here?

Kole didn't care.

Fifty-seven

"Would you believe a murder of crows forced me to this spot?" Miller asked.

Kole tied the rope in a manner so that it resembled a swing Coup could sit on, with the rope wrapped under her arms, so she didn't have to hold tight. He watched as Miller and Dragging pulled her up the shaft into daylight.

Then, it was his turn. The rope bounced with every hand-over-hand pull.

The sun struck his face. At first, the brilliance forced his eyes closed, but then they adjusted.

He knelt beside Coup. She lay on her back in the tall, green grass, Dragging attending to her wounds.

"She'll need to be transported to the hospital," Miller said.

"Who let you out of the cell?" Coup rolled her head and looked at Dragging.

"It cost me a lifetime supply of shine," Miller said. "Which you'll pay for."

"It wards off the evil spirits," Dragging said.

Miller reapplied the bandages to her arm and made a brace for her leg. Then he turned to Kole. "What happened to your shoulder? You'll need E.R. care, too."

"The same bullet that ripped Coup's arm bit into me."

"The two of you will forever be tied together." Miller chuckled. "Do I get time off for rescuing you two?"

"You're free to go," Coup said. "We ran into Savannah-Jo in that hell. We know the truth."

"Good to hear," Miller said.

"Except, we found and lost the second diamond," Coup said.

Kole reached into his pocket and pulled out the plastic bag. He wiped the mud from it, then tossed it onto Coup's belly.

She sat up, opened the bag, and pulled out the diamond. It sparkled with colors of light in blues and greens, like shimmering fish scales.

"What time's dinner?" Kole asked.

"Eight pm, the first day the hospital releases you and me."

"It's a date," Kole said.

"Yes, this time it is. Forget the wine, bring some of this man's brew." She nodded at Miller, then turned and smiled at Kole—the type of smile that made her eyes crinkle. "And bring something for breakfast."

Miller stood. "Psalm one-hundred-and-eighteen, verse twenty-four. 'This is the day that the Lord has made. Let us rejoice and be glad in it.'"

Kole smiled back at Coup and said in Cherokee, "Haw-dv."

Acknowledgments

A special *Thank you* to Karen Crisco for moderating the Royal Palm Beach Library ZOOM critique group. And to the special members who have encouraged, corrected, suggested, for my story, as well as for making each meeting an enjoyable time: Chuck Jackson, Kathleen Ghanem, Laura Fournier, Lori Flynn, Ruth Darrington, Sheila Hollihan-Elliot, and Vito Leonardi.

And to Claudia Richardson, who I met at the WilCo Pow Wow, for the great portrait of me.

More Books By
Jeffrey Hammerhead Philips

Azrael's Blade
Murder on Devil Ray Reef
Death at Obeah's Fire